THE FORGE

✦ ✦ ✦

OTHER NOVELS
BY CHRIS FABRY

Lifemark
(based on the motion picture
by Alex Kendrick and Stephen Kendrick)

Overcomer
(based on the motion picture
by Alex Kendrick and Stephen Kendrick)

War Room
(based on the screenplay
by Alex Kendrick and Stephen Kendrick)

Saving Grayson

A Piece of the Moon

Under a Cloudless Sky

The Promise of Jesse Woods

Every Waking Moment

Looking into You

Dogwood

June Bug

Almost Heaven

Not in the Heart

Borders of the Heart

A Marriage Carol (with Dr. Gary Chapman)

The Song (based on the screenplay by Richard L. Ramsay)

A NOVELIZATION BY

CHRIS FABRY

THE FORGE

BASED ON THE MOTION PICTURE BY
THE KENDRICK BROTHERS

CREATORS OF WAR ROOM, OVERCOMER & COURAGEOUS

TYNDALE HOUSE PUBLISHERS
CAROL STREAM, ILLINOIS

Visit Tyndale online at tyndale.com.

Visit Chris Fabry's website at chrisfabry.com.

For more information about *The Forge*, visit theforgemovie.com and kendrickbrothers.com.

Tyndale and Tyndale's quill logo are registered trademarks of Tyndale House Ministries.

The Forge

Published in association with the literary agency Legacy Three, LLC, Albany, GA.

Romans 12:17, Proverbs 20:22, and James 1:20 in chapter 36 are taken from The ESV®
Bible (The Holy Bible, English Standard Version®), copyright © 2001 by Crossway,
a publishing ministry of Good News Publishers. Used by permission. All rights reserved.

Romans 3:23, 5:8, 6:23, 10:9-10, and 10:13 in chapter 30; Hebrews 11:6 in chapter 33;
and Romans 12:20-21 in chapter 35 are taken from the Holy Bible, *New International
Version,*® NIV.® Copyright © 1973, 1978, 1984, 2011 by Biblica, Inc.® Used by
permission. All rights reserved worldwide.

All other Scripture quotations are taken from the *Holy Bible*, New Living Translation,
copyright © 1996, 2004, 2015 by Tyndale House Foundation. Used by permission of
Tyndale House Publishers, Carol Stream, Illinois 60188. All rights reserved.

The Forge is a work of fiction. Where real people, events, establishments, organizations,
or locales appear, they are used fictitiously. All other elements of the novel are drawn
from the authors' imaginations.

For information about special discounts for bulk purchases, please contact Tyndale House
Publishers at csresponse@tyndale.com, or call 1-855-277-9400.

Library of Congress Cataloging-in-Publication Data

A catalog record for this book is available from the Library of Congress.

ISBN 978-1-4964-8920-3 (HC)
ISBN 978-1-4964-8921-0 (SC)

Printed in the United States of America

30	29	28	27	26	25	24
7	6	5	4	3	2	1

To my son, Joshua. You've walked through discipleship from me and other men so well. I love watching you grow as a godly, capable man. I love you and am so proud of you!

—ALEX KENDRICK

To all moms praying hard for their sons.

—CHRIS FABRY

Part 1
THE WOUND

CHAPTER 1

✦ ✦ ✦

Cynthia

Trouble never travels alone and usually arrives when you're expecting somebody else. It's predictable, like bad weather. And if you find something good happening in your life, watch out for dark clouds.

Now, if you live like this, and I often do, seeing the worst coming around the corner instead of something good, you'll always be looking over your shoulder, waiting for the other shoe to drop.

When I was little, I overheard my grandmother say, "That Cynthia looks for weevils in her cotton candy."

All the struggle and worry and fretting and thinking the worst never seems to get me where I want to be, but I can't help going for the ride. I suppose it's how I cope with life. I'm constantly thinking bad things are just around the corner. No matter how good life might be, I drive with one foot on the brake.

Hope is a four-letter word I have a hard time spelling in my soul. And I suppose I'm living in a rut that began five years ago. It was a rut I began digging long before that.

Elizabeth, my twin sister, had gone through a rut of her own with her husband, Tony. I don't want to go into it, but Tony had gotten into trouble—well, I said I wasn't going to go into it. Things had turned around for them eventually, so I thought maybe that might happen to me.

Instead, the wheels came off the *I do* I said to my husband, Darren, because his *I do* had become *I don't care anymore.* I reached out to Elizabeth for help, which is not the easiest thing for me to do. I don't go running to others willy-nilly with my problems. I just need you to understand that.

Elizabeth tried to help, and she did to a point. But even if you have somebody who will walk through a dark valley with you, life can still hit you in the face with a brick.

Which brings me back to my husband.

The signs had been there all along, even when we were dating. I kick myself now for not seeing it (which is a double wound—a brick to the face and I kick myself years later— what's up with that? I've got bruises on my bruises).

I won't go into all I didn't see about Darren. That would take way too long. When I met Darren (I will not say that his middle name was Trouble, but I've often wondered), he was sweet as talcum and smooth as cow butter. He gave me compliments. He told me how pretty I was, seemed amazed at my intelligence and vocabulary, and he would look at me with a twinkle in his eye, like he saw something deep inside me. And that smile of his? It could melt an iceberg. There didn't seem to be anything he wouldn't do to win my heart.

I should have seen what others saw (I'm talking about Elizabeth), but there are things you can't hear or see when you're under the spell of what you think is love. It's like that blind man by the side of the road in the Bible. When he finally made it to Jesus, the Lord asked what he wanted and the man said, "Rabbi, I want to see." I wish I had prayed that. But I didn't want to see. I wanted to stay blind because it felt too good keeping my eyes closed to the signs on the dashboard of my heart. I just slapped some duct tape over the flashing lights on the spaceship headed for planet Darren.

I can still see him, down on one knee in the middle of a crowded restaurant. He put a sparkling ring on my finger and my first thought was, what did he pawn? He didn't have a job, which was another truth I pushed aside.

When I said yes, the people around us applauded and Darren beamed. The waiter brought complimentary desserts, which was nice. It would have been nicer if Darren had offered to pay for dinner, but as I said he was out of work and I was flying high and couldn't wait to tell everybody. I didn't, of course, because the people who cared about me could see the road ahead and that the bridge was out.

Elizabeth's husband, Tony, called Darren a bum. I heard that secondhand from my niece, Danielle. I had to drag it out of her by telling her over and over it was okay for her to tell me. But I wasn't surprised. By then I knew Tony was upset that Elizabeth was lending me money to help with rent and a car payment, so he had a right to be upset. But calling somebody a bum sounded too harsh. It was like saying Darren was never going to change.

Tony was right. Darren drank and played games all day and I'd come home dog-tired to a messy house. I'd get on his case and the next day I'd come home and there he'd be. I complained and nagged and told him if he liked games so much he could sleep on that couch. Then we'd start the cycle. He'd get an interview, get the job, talk about how he was going to one day own the company. A few days later he'd be on the couch telling me his boss was a jerk. It was always somebody else's fault.

Which brings me to a bright spot in our marriage: Isaiah. That child was a shining light, wind in my sails, silver lining in the clouds. I could be having the worst day of my life and I'd see that smile and it changed everything.

I honestly thought becoming a father would kickstart Darren's sense of responsibility. He'd land a job and stay employed and would take Isaiah fishing and play ball in the park. But as Isaiah grew, that dream died and it tore my heart out for my son. Isaiah longed for a father who would take an interest in him. I saw it in his eyes.

Isaiah was fourteen when the world as we knew it came to an end. And the world as we knew it was me burning the candle at each end and in the middle all at the same time. I was working at a salon and had some faithful customers who always asked for me, which caused some friction with my coworkers. I was also doing a little side work for friends and family at my house.

I had thought about starting my own salon for years, but I was scared. What if I failed? What if I spent a lot of money on equipment and rent and nobody showed up? How do I make payroll and pay the right taxes? The questions and the "what abouts" paralyzed me.

I was meeting with my sister about every week by then and she was sharing more about the changes she and Tony had been through. She had been studying the Bible and found a deeper relationship with God and thought that might be something I would be interested in. I told her I was worried that it would be like when we were kids—even though we were twins, I always got the feeling that she knew all the answers. I felt stupid compared to her. But there was something different about her reaction this time. She said she was learning some hard things about herself and that studying together would be a help to her as well.

Elizabeth, Tony, and Danielle came over one Saturday afternoon. Darren heard about it and said he had something to do, but I knew he just didn't want to see Tony.

I did Danielle's hair and then Elizabeth sat down and we started talking. I hadn't shared much with her about my salon idea, but that day I just opened up. And to my surprise, given our history of competing and arguing, Elizabeth didn't shoot me down or tell me ten reasons why I ought to forget it. She told me she believed in me and that my business would fly if I took the chance.

Then, Tony sat down. He had been tossing the football with Isaiah in the front yard. I cut his hair close the way he likes it and I held up a mirror and he turned his head this way and that and looked straight at me with those piercing eyes.

"Cynthia, you have a gift," he said. "This is exactly what I wanted. If you want to open your own salon, we're behind you."

You could have knocked me over with a hairnet.

Then he put some money in my hand. I put it in a drawer but he told me to look at it. What I saw made my jaw drop. It was way more than I would ever charge for a dozen haircuts. I tried to give it back. He said that was a start to my salon fund.

When they left, I went to my room and had myself a good cry. It had been so long since I'd felt encouragement, especially from a man. It was exactly what I needed.

Elizabeth is a real estate agent, and even though she sells homes, I asked her to look into the business market. A friend of hers told her what had happened at a salon on Heartwood Street, about a mile from my house. It was a small shop but they had a good list of clients. The owner had dreamed of doing hair on the set of a movie. She finally got her chance and on the first day of filming, she didn't show up on the set. She had passed away in her sleep of a heart condition no one knew she had.

I won't go into everything that happened, but the day I signed the lease was the most exhilarating, scary day of my life. Within two weeks, I had to hire two more stylists just to keep up. Tammy and Keisha have been with me ever since.

I was so busy with the salon, I didn't have time to focus on Darren. We limped along in our marriage and I'll be honest, I was jealous of what Elizabeth and Tony had. He had turned things around in his life, or maybe I should say he turned his life over to God and let God turn things around. I couldn't understand why God would answer my sister's prayers and work in her life and not lift a finger in mine. Sometimes it feels like God wears earplugs when I pour out my heart.

Then, Isaiah had a freshman basketball game and Darren offered to drive him. I thought that was a good sign. I had no idea the trouble ahead.

CHAPTER 2

✦ ✦ ✦

Isaiah Wright found his white Montclaire High jersey at the bottom of his laundry basket, wrinkled. His coach would have a fit if he showed up wearing it that way. He tossed it in the dryer, hoping that would smooth it a little. His jersey was the least of his worries. The bigger problem was the game against Central High, a powerhouse. Coach Bascom had been preparing them for this one for weeks.

He stood by the dryer, as if that would speed the process, like constantly pushing an elevator button. He had hoped his mother would be at the game, but his dad offered to drive him. After that she suddenly had something to do.

"This is a big game, Mom," Isaiah said.

"I know," she said, lowering her voice. "I want to hear all about it after."

His father's offer sent a jolt of anxiety through Isaiah. His dad was often late or didn't show up when he said he would. But this time he was waiting in the driveway. Isaiah breathed a sigh of relief.

The high school was a ten-minute drive. But five minutes into it, his father took a turn.

"The school's not this way."

"I need to run a little errand."

"I can't be late. I'll get benched."

He gave Isaiah a look, rolling his eyes as he pulled into the bank parking lot. He got out without a word and walked through the glass doors. Isaiah watched the clock and thought about jogging to the high school, but he would probably be late. If his dad hurried, he could still make it.

Isaiah's life was out of his control. Again. And he thought that his mother would never do this to him. She'd drop him off, then run an errand.

His father finally returned, putting a fat envelope in the glove compartment before he drove to the gym entrance. Isaiah jumped out.

"Right on time," his father yelled, then chuckled as Isaiah sprinted inside.

Isaiah hit the door to the locker room as JV Coach Lonnie Bascom exited. He glanced at Isaiah, then at his watch.

"You'll sit for the tip-off," the man growled.

"Yes, sir."

The game was back and forth from the opening tip. Central was bigger and more physical under the boards. But Montclaire had Kenny Donaldson. Kenny was lightning fast and Central had a hard time guarding him.

Isaiah sat on the bench, scanning the stands for his father. He finally spotted him near the top sitting next to a woman Isaiah had never seen, talking as if he knew her.

"Wright!" Coach Bascom yelled. "Check in."

Isaiah tried to get in the flow of the game, bringing the ball up court and setting the offense, but something felt off. What was it?

At halftime, Central was up by three, but all Isaiah could think about was his dad in the stands. As he came out of the locker room after halftime, he looked for his father but couldn't find him.

With thirteen seconds left in the game and a two-point deficit, Coach Bascom called their final time-out. He yelled over the noise of the band and the sparse crowd, "Nobody shoots but Kenny. Get the ball to Kenny and collapse under the basket for the rebound, just in case."

Isaiah's heart pounded as he inbounded the ball to Kenny who dribbled to the top of the key, then put a crossover move on the defender and drove down the lane for a layup. Another Central defender stepped between Kenny and the basket and swatted the ball. It bounced straight to Isaiah behind the three-point line.

He glanced at the clock.

Four seconds.

Everything in him wanted to rise up and take the shot, muscle memory overwhelming him. But Coach Bascom had been clear. A defender lunged at Isaiah and he rifled a perfect, one-handed pass to Kenny under the basket.

The ball bounced off Kenny's hands and went out of bounds just as the horn sounded.

Every Central player celebrated, hopping and slapping high-fives. Isaiah sank to his knees.

Kenny walked slowly past him, frowning and shaking his head. "You should have taken the shot, man."

No "sorry" or "my bad" or anything like that. Isaiah got up, put his head down, and followed Kenny toward the locker room.

The Montclaire players sat in front of their lockers, heads down, shoulders slumping, as if they knew what was coming. Coach Bascom entered, fuming and pacing. He was a tall, heavyset man who looked more like a former linebacker than a former basketball player. His head was shaved and reflected the flickering fluorescent lights. Some coaches present such a calm demeanor you never know if they've won or lost. Not Bascom. When his team won, he smiled and patted players on the back and even if he had corrections, he smiled as he gave them. But losses made him throw things. Clipboards. Towels. Gym bags. Even his shoes. He had gone through three whistles he'd smashed that season.

Bascom paced empty-handed, as if looking for something to throw. When he came to Isaiah, he stood with his hands on his hips and leaned down, the veins in his neck bulging.

"What were you thinking, Wright? Tell me! What was going through that puny little mind of yours?"

"Sorry, Coach."

"Sorry? That's what you were thinking?"

"No, I was trying to get the ball to—"

"The ball came straight to you. There was time for one shot. But you didn't take it."

He said it like Isaiah had burned the school flag at center court. Isaiah stared at the floor. He knew it wouldn't do any good to defend himself.

Kenny Donaldson spoke up. "I told him he should have shot it, Coach."

"I don't want to hear it, Butterfingers. You catch that ball and we're in overtime right now."

It was Kenny's turn to look at the floor. But Bascom wasn't finished with Isaiah.

"You don't think when you get in a situation like that, Wright, you react. You knew how much time there was. I saw you glance up. How much time was left?"

"Four seconds."

"Four seconds! You don't pass with four seconds left. Especially a risky pass under the basket. Why didn't you shoot it?"

Isaiah wanted to say, *Because you made it clear Kenny was the only one who was supposed to take the shot.* But he didn't say that. And he also didn't say, *And if I had missed it, you would have been upset that I didn't pass it.*

Instead, Isaiah said, "Sorry, Coach."

Silence in the locker room.

Coach Bascom took a breath and headed for the door. "Practice right after school tomorrow. Be ready to run." He turned. "Especially you, Wright."

Bascom reached for the door, then stopped, grabbed a jacket hanging on a hook, and threw it into the showers. Kenny grabbed a towel and muttered something.

"What was that?" Jamal said.

"Wasn't talking to you. I was talking to Wright." He glared at Isaiah. "Next time, take the shot, man."

"Next time, catch the pass," Jamal said. "It was right to you."

"What did you say?" Kenny said.

Jamal stared at Kenny. "We win as a team and lose as a team. Right? That's what I've heard all year. So get off his case. He was just doing what coach told him."

Isaiah sat a little taller, but the truth was he couldn't stand losing or the tension in the locker room. He didn't need Coach Bascom telling him he'd let the team down, he knew it in his gut. He headed toward the gym, still soaking in his jersey, and did a three-sixty, scanning the stands.

Jamal's mother waved at him and he ran to her. "Mrs. Rae, have you seen my dad?"

"I saw him earlier," she said, looking toward an exit. When she turned around, the look on her face didn't seem right. "He asked if we could give you a ride home."

"What for? Why can't he take me?"

She shrugged. "He said he had something to do. Where's Cynthia? She at the shop?"

"I think so."

She nodded and tried to smile, but that didn't look right to him either. What was going on?

"Nice game tonight," she said. "Too bad about the end."

"Yes, ma'am." He thought a moment. "I don't need a ride. But thank you."

"Are you sure? It's no trouble."

"Yeah, I'm good."

He hit the exit door and ran along the sidewalk to the main parking lot thinking about the last time both his parents were at his game. They sat on either end of the bleachers. There was a lot of tension in the house these days, more than usual. Angry words or just silence that felt as heavy as a medicine ball. Isaiah tried to stay out of their way, going to his room to listen to music or playing a game. Sometimes he even did homework.

Isaiah wasn't afraid of hard work. Every practice he went all out, leaving everything on the court. But he had to see a reason to work hard, a purpose behind it. There had to be some end result, and he didn't have that kind of vision for school and grades. That wasn't his thing, or as he often said when some opportunity was put in front of him, "That's not me."

Despite what he'd heard from Mrs. Rae, Isaiah scanned the parking lot for his dad's rusted Buick. Riding in that car felt like standing on a raft at the water park. The shocks were shot and the thing swayed down the road. And he couldn't help thinking that Buick was like his father's life, the uneven wear on the tires, the alignment way off, and the engine needing a tune-up.

He walked all the way to the last row of cars. It would be like his dad to back into the last spot, as if he wanted to make a fast getaway. But his dad wasn't there. Where would he have gone?

Isaiah felt a pang in his chest. He and his dad didn't talk much. His father had made promises about stopping his drinking. He was going to fix up the Mustang with Isaiah, the car that sat in the garage in the same condition it was in when it was towed there. His dad was going to take him to an NBA game. And a hundred other things that never happened.

Still, Isaiah wanted to talk about the shot he didn't take and the guilt from Coach Bascom. He wanted his dad to encourage him. In his head, he knew his father couldn't give that. He only thought about himself. But Isaiah still wanted to have that conversation, which only made him mad at himself.

He couldn't go back to the gymnasium, couldn't face the stares of his teammates or the parents who had seen his gaffe. Instead, he slung his gym bag over one shoulder and started the long walk home.

CHAPTER 3

✦ ✦ ✦

Cynthia

I got a text from Sarah Rae about Isaiah. **Didn't see you at the game. Tough ending. Darren asked me to give Isaiah a ride home but Isaiah left.**

I had a bunch of questions but texted back **What happened with the game?**

I'll let Isaiah tell you. They lost by two points. Had a chance at the end and it didn't pan out.

I stared at her words and promised myself I would never again miss one of Isaiah's games.

Why did Darren ask you to give Isaiah a ride?

He said he had something to do. I'm sorry, Cynthia.

I called Isaiah's phone and it went to voicemail. Same with Darren. I texted Isaiah. No response.

I hurried home wondering if Darren would be there, but his car wasn't in the driveway or on the street. Isaiah's room was empty. I texted Isaiah to call me. Maybe he had stayed for the Varsity game.

I grabbed my keys and headed for the door to drive to the high school just as Darren walked in. Alone. I hadn't heard the car pull up.

"Why didn't you bring Isaiah?"

He walked toward the hall without looking at me. "He's at the game."

"I know he's at the game. What was so important that you asked Sarah to bring him home?"

Darren raised a hand, dismissing my question as he disappeared into our room.

My heart raced. "Come back here and tell me what happened!"

No answer. I followed him down the hall to the bedroom. He was throwing clothes into our biggest suitcase.

"What are you doing?"

On the dresser was our wedding picture. The sight of it turned my stomach. I leaned against the door, every muscle in my body as tight as my clenched teeth.

"For once in your life, don't run away. For once in your life, be a man."

That stopped him. I could tell I had stepped over a line as soon as the words were out of my mouth. Darren straightened and looked at me, his eyes dead pools.

"Be a man? Is that what you want, Cynthia? You're finally going to give me permission after all you've done to take my manhood?"

"Take your manhood? What are you talking about?"

"Everybody knows you wear the pants around here. You call the shots. You're the businesswoman who brings home the bacon."

"I can't help it if I'm the only one who can hold down a job. I've worked myself to death trying to provide for us while you sat and played. Somebody had to put on the pants."

He grabbed some shirts from the closet and stuffed them, hangers and all, into the suitcase. Where was he going?

"Did you even go to the game?"

Darren gave a chuckle and shook his head. "Ask Mama's boy when he gets here. He'll tell you all about it." He zipped the suitcase. "I'm done."

"No, you're not. You owe me an explanation."

"I don't owe you anything, Cynthia. You've been trying to control my life ever since we got married."

Not even a punch in the stomach could have taken more air from me. None of what I saw was computing. I took a shallow breath. "Don't blame me for whatever you're planning to do."

He rolled his eyes. "No, you're not to blame, Cynthia. You never are. That's because you're always right. Always responsible. Always have a plan. Always looking out for yourself."

"How dare you say that! I have sacrificed for you and our family. I've given you space to get your life together. I've done everything I can, and you accuse me—"

"Yeah, I knew you'd say something like that," he said, interrupting. Darren picked up the suitcase and turned to the dresser. He held up our wedding photo.

"The fellow in this picture. Look at him. See how alive he is? Filled with hope? I lost that a long time ago. But I've found somebody who makes me feel that way again."

Those words cut to the bone. I couldn't take them in. I finally looked at his face. As much as I wanted to run from the room, I had to stay. Darren was doing something he had never done with me. He was being honest. He was taking off the mask. And what was underneath was as scary as anything I'd ever seen.

"So you're throwing us away? Walking out on me? What about your son?"

"He'll figure it out." He tossed the picture frame onto the dresser. "And so will you. You always figure things out."

"This is crazy. Darren, you're not thinking straight."

Darren walked past me into the hall. "I'm finally doing what I needed to do a long time ago." Footsteps through the front room. The front door opened and slammed shut. Everything in me wanted to look out that window to see if the woman was waiting in the car, but my legs wouldn't move. My knees gave way and I sat on the bed. Then his muffler sounded from the street and the car zoomed away from the curb and from our lives.

I sat there thinking about my heart. It had been wilting like a flower needing water for a long time. I had wanted Darren to be strong, to be the man we needed, to take responsibility, to love Isaiah and me with his words and actions. But I couldn't make him be a man. I couldn't make him love me.

I've found somebody who makes me feel that way again.

I don't know how long I sat there, but when I looked up, Isaiah was standing in the doorway in his jersey. I wanted to be strong and not fall to pieces, but I couldn't hold myself together.

"What's wrong, Mama?"

Tears were all I had right then. That and a low moaning sound that came from the basement of all my hurt. Isaiah just stood there, as if he knew I needed something but wasn't sure what to do.

"I'm okay," I managed. I wanted to protect him from this pain, but I couldn't. "It's just that your father . . . ."

He took a step into the room, then another. I had my eyes closed when I felt his hand on my shoulder. That sent me further over the edge. Finally, I gathered myself.

"What happened with your father tonight?"

He sat on the edge of the bed and the story came out slowly, like he wanted to keep me from the pain but couldn't hold it in longer.

"When he took me to the game, he went to the bank. He came out with a thick envelope."

My mind spun. Darren had planned all of this. He'd accessed our joint account. I added rage to my broken heart.

"What happened, Mama?"

"Your father is leaving us."

Isaiah's face was a mix of questions and disbelief. Then he turned his head and his hands balled into fists.

"I should have said something," he shouted. "I should have done something."

"No, don't do that. This is not your fault, Isaiah. Your father is making his own choices. You are not responsible. You hear me?"

"Yeah," he said, but I could tell he didn't mean it.

He walked into his bedroom and closed the door. It was the loneliest sound I've ever heard. Alone in my room, I wondered if I could believe my own words for myself? Could I live not taking the blame for Darren walking away?

The anger welled inside. Anger at Darren for being stupid and selfish. Anger at myself for loving him in the first place. Anger at God for letting it all happen.

I mustered the strength to stand. What to do? Then it came to me.

CHAPTER 4

✦ ✦ ✦

Isaiah sat in his room, numb, like he was in a dream or watching a movie about somebody else's life. Deep inside, he knew this was a turning point.

Isaiah had always known his family was messed up. There was a lot of conflict, and when his dad was home, he wasn't really there. Still, they were together. It was their "normal." And there was hope things might get better. His dad would laugh at something on TV or say something that made Isaiah's mother smile. That gave him the feeling that their family wouldn't wind up in the dumpster.

But his father had the chance to tell him what was happening when he drove him to the game and he didn't say a word. He felt like he meant nothing to his dad, less than nothing. How do you deal with a dad who doesn't care you exist?

He could have said any number of things in the car. *You're the man of the house now. Take care of your mother.* It would have been cruel, but at least it would have been something.

Isaiah played that scenario in his head like a video game and each time, the game ended with no resolution. There was no winning with his father, especially since he had run off with another woman. Why would he throw their family away for her? It was like trading them in on a different model.

Those thoughts ran laps in his head—like the suicide runs Coach Bascom gave them up and down the court until they collapsed. Isaiah needed to be more careful with what he said to his mom because he could tell she was hurting. He could hear her through the wall and he didn't want to add to the weight she carried. But what could he do with the weight he was carrying?

He got online and tried to play a game with some friends. But he felt distracted until the faces of the enemy became his father's face. That helped him focus and eliminate them one by one.

The online game was a respite, but he couldn't shake the rejection from his father. He hadn't punched or kicked him like other dads he'd heard about, but part of him wished he had. He would have at least felt noticed. Instead, Isaiah felt like a carpet stain. Something you stepped over or around.

Then Isaiah allowed a sliver of hope to enter. What if his dad changed? What if he remembered how good he had it? What if the other woman kicked him out? Maybe he would come to his senses and knock on the door and beg his mother to forgive him. And with that thought, Isaiah went down the trail of his dad tearfully begging Isaiah's forgiveness and promising to change.

Isaiah wasn't much for praying. His mother was and she was always trying to get him to go to church or read some book she thought he would like. The truth was, Isaiah didn't feel like God cared any more for him than his dad did. Too busy running the world.

But that night, with the way things had worked out, he prayed. He asked God to change his dad and help his mom not get too depressed. He prayed God would make everything come out okay and would make them a family again.

Then came the silence. Like God had walked out the door.

Breaking the silence was a sound from the living room. Banging and knocking and clattering. Isaiah thought maybe his dad had returned for something. Instead, he found his mom with a trash bag unhooking the game console and cords to the TV. She tossed every one of his dad's games in there.

"Hey, don't throw all that away," he said. And then he wished he hadn't.

She looked at him like he had spoken forbidden words.

He softened his voice. "I could probably sell that stuff. You know, to help out."

She gave him the mom stare. "I don't want any of this around here. I don't want you to sell it and I don't want you to use it." She tossed the rest of the games and controllers into the bag and tied the top.

Isaiah nodded like he understood, which he did and didn't at the same time. Why would anybody toss perfectly good equipment and games? And then he looked at her face and the pain there was the answer. She wanted to get rid of any reminder of the man. *Would she toss out the couch, too?*

"You want me to take it out?" he said.

She shook her head. "I need to do this myself. The truck comes in the morning."

So, he let her. And he watched out the back window as she placed the bag in the garbage and closed the lid.

✦ ✦ ✦

At breakfast the next morning, he heard his mom in the kitchen. She had made breakfast for them both and from the look in her eyes he could tell she hadn't slept at all and hadn't stopped crying.

"You okay?" he said.

"No. I don't even know what okay is supposed to feel like."

She spooned eggs onto a plate and added three pieces of bacon and a buttermilk biscuit. He figured this was her way of handling the hurt. Get busy doing something.

"I didn't get to hear about the end of the game," she said. "What happened?"

Isaiah shrugged. "Doesn't seem as big as it did last night."

She poured a cup of coffee and sat.

"Coach yelled at me."

"What for?"

He told her about Coach Bascom, Kenny, the shot he didn't take and the pass that went out of bounds, then what happened in the locker room. The more he talked, the tighter her grip on the coffee mug.

"That sounds confusing," she said. "You do what he says and you get in trouble."

"Exactly."

"Must feel lonely to get ganged up on that way."

"Coach was just upset we lost, I guess."

"Yeah, he's human. But he missed a good opportunity."

"For what?"

"To give you confidence. He could have said something like . . ." She put on her best Coach Bascom voice, sitting straight and holding her head back. "'Isaiah, next time you get the ball like that, you take that shot. Your first instinct was to

24

shoot it. Trust that.' If he had said that, it would have given you confidence the next time."

Isaiah nodded. His mom had gotten outside of her pain to enter his. But all he could think about was the empty spot at the table.

For Isaiah, the next month was like living on a boat that was leaning to one side. His whole life felt off-kilter. Growing up with a phantom for a father, someone who was always there and wasn't at the same time, he got used to that kind of life. When his dad left, he felt off-balance, like the person on the other end of the teeter-totter got up and walked out of the park.

He didn't tell his friends what had happened and he thought maybe he should have. For many of his friends, fathers were men to be avoided. A lot of guys in the neighborhood had parents who had split, so it wasn't weird, he just didn't want to talk about it. And he promised himself he would not let it bother him.

Until he went to Andre's house. Andre and his dad had put up a goal and backboard in their backyard. And they had a concrete pad poured that was green and red with white lines just like a real court. Even a three-point line and a net that made a *swish* sound if you hit it just right. The backboard was thick plexiglass, the same kind they used in college or the pros. Playing on that half-court was a dream.

But when he walked home after shooting around that night, he felt tight inside, like he had eaten bad guacamole that made his stomach swirl. But he hadn't eaten anything. Isaiah couldn't figure it out until Andre called again. Isaiah saw the name on his phone and the feeling returned. He let the call go to voice-mail. No doubt, Andre wanted Isaiah to play hoops, but Isaiah couldn't. Why?

And then it hit him. Andre's dad had invested all kinds of time and money on something he knew his son would enjoy. Andre said they designed the backyard together—there was a sandbox for his little sister and posts in the ground for a volleyball net. They planned a space for an above-ground pool. They'd worked together and made an idea become a reality.

Part of Isaiah was happy for Andre. But playing on that court showed him what he didn't have, what his own father hadn't given. Someone who cared. Someone who saw him. Someone who wouldn't walk out the door. So every time Isaiah went there, he couldn't see a nice court. He saw what he didn't have and what he would never have. It was a knife to the heart.

He knew it wasn't fair to Andre, but every time he called, Isaiah made an excuse.

CHAPTER 5

✦ ✦ ✦

Cynthia

Darren had been gone several weeks and Isaiah and I had settled into a routine. In one sense, not having my husband around made life easier. Less conflict. In other ways, I felt more confused.

I couldn't think about the future because the present and the past were so heavy. I guess in one way, the weight of each day helped me just put one foot in front of the other. It was all I could do.

Elizabeth and Tony said they were praying for me. I couldn't help feel that Tony was thinking, *I told you he was a bum.* But to his credit, he never came out and said it.

Add to my struggles the fact that Darren's father was in bad health. And instead of contacting Darren, he reached out to me. He didn't know Darren had left us, and when I told him, I could tell it hurt. He asked if Isaiah and I could come see him. He sounded so sad. I promised we'd get there as soon as we could.

I worked all day at the salon, trying to keep my customers happy as well as my employees and the government. I had no idea all the rules and regulations and taxes that go into a small business. I looked forward to the cutting and styling because when I had a customer in front of me, I could lose myself in the work. My job was to focus on the person in the chair and make her look and feel pretty. There's a sense of accomplishment I get when a customer walks in and sits down and all the worries and the struggles inside settle a bit, like rain settles a dusty road. The work kept my mind occupied.

Inevitably, my friends and coworkers found out about Darren. Some looked at me with eyes that said, *I know what you're going through.* Others had to throw in their two cents.

"When are you going to divorce that loser?" Tammy said. She was one of the first stylists I hired. Always opinionated. Always ready to tell you what she thinks without a filter.

"I haven't talked with any lawyers, but I did speak with my pastor."

"And what did he say?" Tammy said.

"That I have biblical grounds. Adultery and desertion. But he also said a person who can get a divorce doesn't have to get one."

Keisha was listening, of course. Another stylist who has an opinion but is a little more measured in her responses. "Why wouldn't you move on if you have grounds?"

"He says sometimes people change. They think the grass is greener somewhere else but with time they understand what they've given up was what they wanted all along."

Tammy cocked her head and looked at me with eyeballs rolled to the ceiling. "So, you're supposed to sit around and wait till Darren sees how good he had it? While he's run off with another woman? Something is not right with this picture."

I was coming up with an answer when Keisha said, "I don't know if that's healthy for you, girl. I don't pretend to be a pastor, but it doesn't take a rocket scientist to see what's ahead."

"And what is that?"

"Darren's going to wait until you get real successful, then he's going to come after you. You said he made you the bad guy before he left, right?"

"He blamed me for our troubles."

"He's going to do the same thing in front of a judge. And you'll be the one paying for it. You need to prepare for that."

I chewed and stewed on those words. I told God I wasn't going to worry, that I was going to give everything to Him and let Him work things out, but the more I thought about it, the less I slept at night, all the "what-ifs" looming ahead.

I shared some of this with Elizabeth and she suggested a counselor who could help me think through my issues. I barely had time to do everything on my plate. How was I supposed to fit in an appointment and pay for a counselor?

There was also the question of Randall. I hate to reduce a person to a question mark, but that's what he was in my life, a complicated question mark.

I used social media mainly for my business, reaching out to customers and inviting new ones. Specials and whatnot. Randall sent a message one day and that took me down the rabbit trail of my past.

I had gone to Middle and High School with Randall Bentley. He was on the quiet side, reserved, respectful. He wasn't an athlete and didn't make a big splash in school. He was just kind of there in the background. A good guy, not wild and rowdy. Someone you could trust.

I looked up his profile on social media and Randall had done well for himself. Randall in a cap and gown. Randall in a suit at some business expo. Randall and his parents at what looked like their anniversary party. He messaged me to ask if I'd like to get together for dinner.

I stared at that message for a long time and finally decided to tell the truth. "I'm married. At least for a little while longer." I hit send and then regretted it. Would he read more into my response than I meant?

Of course he did. "I'll wait a little while, then." He put a smiley face emoji after it. Then, every couple of weeks I'd get a message from him. It turned out to be a bright spot in my day because I'd get a notification and feel something inside. Of course I didn't tell anyone about this. Who would I tell? So it was my little secret, which made it more exciting.

I imagined what it would be like to have someone steady, loving, and kind instead of what I experienced with Darren. And every time I thought of Randall, I remembered the good. How respectful he was to teachers. He was kind to younger kids. I made him into the person I remembered instead of asking who he had become. No matter how close you come to the truth about a person you used to know, what's in your head is always part fantasy. So I tried to put Randall on a shelf and keep moving forward, but every so often he would creep into my mind.

One afternoon I grabbed a turkey and muenster bagel sandwich at my favorite shop, and Tammy met me at the door when I returned. She lowered her voice and got up in my grill and nodded toward my station.

"She wants you," Tammy said.

I double-checked my calendar. "She doesn't have an appointment."

"You think I don't know that? She wouldn't take no for an answer so I told her to sit. She's all yours."

The woman had long, highlighted curls. Probably from a box and done in her kitchen by a friend, from the looks of it, but not

CHRIS FABRY

a bad job for an amateur. She didn't look like she needed much of anything done. She was just over five feet tall and wore a tight skirt and high heels that barely reached the floor when she sat in the chair. She glanced in the mirror as I came around the corner.

"Cynthia," she said all bright and bubbly. "I know I'm not on your schedule, but I'm hoping you can give me a little trim. Can you work me in? It won't take a minute."

I stopped behind her and tried to recall where I had seen her. Was it a post online? Maybe a friend of Randall's? He wouldn't send someone on a scouting expedition, would he? Maybe this was Randall's wife?

"Do I know you?" I said as gently as I could.

She smiled and shook her head. "No, but I heard through the grapevine that you do a really good job. Just an inch or so off the length would be great."

I wondered what grapevine she was talking about. And where did that saying come from? Through the grapevine? I tried to put that out of my head and focused on the length of her hair. Again, it didn't look like she needed a trim.

"Just an inch?"

"That would be perfect." She turned and held out a hand with immaculate nails. "My name's Sandra, but everybody calls me Cricket."

I glanced around the shop. Three customers were in various stages of cuts or perms. "I have a few minutes before my next appointment. Let's see what I can do."

I put a cape over her and snapped it in the back, then spritzed the end of her hair and began snipping about an inch.

"Why do they call you Cricket?"

"My daddy called me that when I was little. I guess because I jumped around a lot. Couldn't sit still. It stuck."

I kept snipping and smiled in the mirror at her.

31

"Looks like your shop is doing well."

"Mm-hmm. We're busy."

"Must be hard to keep all the plates spinning. The business. Taking care of your son. I hear he's something on the basketball court."

I let go of her hair and stepped back. "You know my son?"

"I saw him at one of his games. He seems like a nice young man." There was a lilt to her voice now. It almost felt like a taunt. She stared at me in the mirror. "Looks a lot like his father."

I looked down at my hands and the hair that stuck to my fingers. Something in my stomach churned.

"You know Darren?"

She smiled in a way that let me know who Cricket was.

"Did he put you up to this?" I said softly so only Cricket heard me.

The room got quiet. Other conversations stilled and all I heard was my beating heart and Gladys Knight on the oldies station singing about a midnight train.

Cricket pulled back her head in mock surprise. "Why Cynthia, I don't know what you're talking about."

I dropped my scissors by the mirror and walked toward the office. I wanted to smash Cricket under my shoe. I wanted to grab her by the hair and drag her out the door. I clenched my teeth and said over my shoulder, "You need to leave."

She was up from the chair in a flash. "You can't leave my hair like this! Come back here and finish."

I knew everyone in the room was staring at me. I gathered myself and turned, pointing a finger at the door. "I'm finished with you. Get out."

She ripped the cape off and threw it on the floor. Then she gave one final smirk. "I wanted to see for myself. Now I understand why he left you."

I closed the office door behind me and leaned against it. Her high heels clicked on the tile and the little bell rang as she left. A minute later came a soft knock on the door.

"You okay?" Tammy said.

"Give me a minute."

"Take all the time you need."

I tried to still my heart and took a deep breath. Was there enough time in the world to recover from what had just happened?

CHAPTER 6

✦ ✦ ✦

On the drive to his grandfather's house, Isaiah noticed his mother was quiet. He offered to play DJ but she said she needed to think. Then, a minute later, she was begging him to plug in his player.

"I always learn a lot when I hear what kind of music you like."

"This is not my music, it's yours." Whitney Houston came through the speakers. "I hear you playing oldies every time I walk into the shop."

"I don't pick the station, Tammy does. You can blame her."

His mother couldn't help moving to the beat, then when she saw him watching her and smiling she stopped. "Okay, I like the oldies, but you can introduce me to new music, too."

Isaiah knew he had to be careful with his music around his mother. He didn't want her hearing everything he played, but there were some things he knew she'd like. The beat, the lyrics, the feeling the songs gave him.

"Why do you like that song?" she asked after he played something new.

"I don't know how to answer that. It's like trying to dissect a natural jump shot. You just go up and snap your wrist and let it go."

As the song faded, she hit the power button on the radio. "I need to tell you something about your Pop."

"Sounds serious."

"You know he hasn't been feeling well."

"Yeah, but he always snaps back, doesn't he?"

She smiled. "He does. I'm worried about him this time."

Isaiah thought the worst, wondering what life would be like without Pop. Isaiah had spent time at his house in the summers. The tire swing out back. The spot on the lake where they would catch bass. And if they didn't catch anything, they sat in the boat and ate sandwiches his grandmother had made.

"Does Dad know he's not well?"

"I don't have any idea what your dad knows and doesn't know. I hadn't told Pop about us splitting up until about a month ago. I could tell it just about broke his heart. He told me he was sorry."

"Why should he be sorry? He didn't leave us."

"Right. But I think he carries the weight of your dad's choices."

"Just like you do," Isaiah said.

She glanced at him. "Just like we both do."

"Does seeing Pop . . . Is it hard for you because of what's happened?"

"Things get stirred up inside for all kinds of reasons. But I can separate Pop from Darren because his heart is toward us. He's a good man."

✦ ✦ ✦

Pop was sitting on the front porch when Isaiah and his mother arrived. He had a tube in his nose and a bottle of oxygen nearby

CHRIS FABRY

that hissed every time he breathed. He tried to stand when they got out of the car.

"Stay where you are, Dell!" his mother called.

"I always stand when a pretty lady parks in my driveway," he said, laughing, then coughing.

He shook Isaiah's hand and then brought him in for a hug. His clothes had a musty smell Isaiah associated with his house and all the rooms he used to explore as a child.

Isaiah and his mother sat on either side of the man, and she asked him questions about what the doctors had said and what medications he was taking. Isaiah excused himself and walked into the backyard and found the tire swing. It wasn't as far off the ground as it used to be, or so it seemed, and the rope that was so thick in his memory was much thinner.

Behind the house was a barn and Isaiah wandered into it, inspecting the scattered tools and boxes that come with a long-lived life. He gravitated to an empty spot in the corner and stood there. When he was little, he would run to this spot and pull the cover off Pop's '66 Mustang and sit behind the wheel. In his mind, Isaiah could feel the wind in his hair and the looks of his friends as he drove past them. That car was an impossible dream Isaiah didn't dare hang onto, a cherished item passed from one generation to the next and then to him, that he would never possess. The empty spot in the corner brought back the ache. Something lost he'd never really owned.

Footsteps shuffled behind him and he heard hissing. Pop rolled the oxygen tank on the uneven ground. Isaiah wondered how he had made it off the porch.

"You shouldn't be out here, Pop. You need to rest."

"Don't tell me what I need. I got people giving me orders left and right." He gave a cackle, then put a hand on Isaiah's shoulder. He took as deep a breath as he could and said, "I remember

you would come out here every time you visited. You'd have slept
in that Mustang if we'd have let you."

"I wish you had kept it here."

"Mm-hmm. Your father never worked on it with you?"

He gave his grandfather a sullen look and the old man nodded.

"I bought it from a friend. It was running, barely. The day
I drove it here, your father's jaw dropped. I told him we would
fix it up together. He said it was a good idea. But every time I
would try to get him to help me, he had something more important to do. So it sat here collecting dust."

"Why did you give it to him?"

"I gave it to him so he would give it to you. I thought it
would move the needle on his heart. Encourage him to spend
time with you. A boy needs a father to show him how to change
the oil and fix a fuel pump. I always tried to figure a way to
nudge him toward something better for his life. But there are
things you can't control, I guess. And one of them is other
people you love. That's not an easy lesson to learn."

Isaiah faced his grandfather. "He told me we were going to fix
it up together. Turned out to be just another broken promise."

"I'm sorry, Isaiah."

"Not your fault."

"I know. What I mean is, I'm sorry for the pain he caused
you. And your mother. I hope you know it's not your fault."

"Yeah."

"You don't sound like you mean it."

"Knowing it's not my fault and believing it's not my fault are
different things. I've even thought . . ."

"Go ahead."

He had to turn away to say it. "I keep thinking it would have
been easier if he died in a war or an accident or something like that.
I'd be sad, but it would make more sense. Him not being there."

Isaiah thought his grandfather might be upset. Instead, he reached out a hand and touched his shoulder. "I know exactly what you mean. I don't fault you for thinking that. My son has been prideful and lazy and stubborn. He wanted what he wanted out of life. And it's like he's thrown everything valuable away. I can't understand it."

The man turned and walked toward the house. Isaiah grabbed the oxygen tank and pulled it, the wheels squeaking over the dandelion-filled yard.

"As far as I'm concerned, that car is yours now. You talk with your mother about it. If you want to sell it for what you can get, go ahead. If you want to hang onto it, that's fine."

"Why do you think my dad turned out this way, Pop?"

The man stopped and looked toward the sky, his eyes glistening. He had white stubble on his brown face.

"I don't know, son. Your grandmother and I blamed ourselves. She went to her grave praying for him every day. In the end, it's one of life's unanswered questions." He looked down at Isaiah. "What do you think?"

"I don't know either. All I know is, I don't want to be like him."

The man nodded. "That's good. But just being different from somebody like that is only half the battle. Avoiding his mistakes will only get you so far. The question is, what do you want to do with your life?"

"I'm pretty good at basketball."

"I know you are. You've got real talent. But talent's not enough. Hard work makes the difference."

"You sound like my coach."

The man laughed. Then he stopped walking because of the coughing and wheezing. When he caught his breath, Isaiah said, "I'm hoping to get a scholarship and play for a Division 1 school."

"Good, you keep working hard and something good will happen."

His mother helped Pop up to the front porch. He was out of breath again and when he'd settled, he crossed his legs and sat back.

"I want to say something to the both of you. Cynthia, I told Isaiah that he can do what he wants with that car. It's his now."

"Okay," she said.

There was a long silence, just the hiss of the oxygen into his nostrils. His eyes locked on something in the trees and Isaiah glanced at his mom. She reached out a hand to touch the old man, but before she could, he spoke again.

"Cynthia, I wouldn't fault you if you got a divorce. I would understand if you said you couldn't forgive him. But I will go to my grave believing that as long as a man has breath in his lungs, there's a chance to change. A chance he'll wake up and smell the coffee. I don't know if it will happen. I've prayed for it and I'm going to keep praying.

"When he first met you, Cynthia, I was hopeful that you would be the one who could help straighten him out. But I was also scared that he would drag you down. He'd let you do all the work."

"I made my own decision to love him. In spite of the red flags."

"I know that. I just keep thinking . . . Maybe I pushed him too hard. Maybe if we'd raised him differently, things would have turned out better for you and Isaiah."

A slight breeze blew across the porch and a wind chime rang. Isaiah thought of his grandmother who loved to hear those chimes ring.

"That Mustang was supposed bring Darren and me together. I had the plan all laid out in my mind. We would restore it, get it looking like new, and our relationship would be the same. Standing side by side working on something can change your heart toward another person. That's what I believed would happen. But Darren didn't have the same vision. So that car was like our relationship. It's just . . ."

The man stopped, his shoulders shaking. Isaiah's mother put a hand on Pop's shoulder and kept it there. Then he turned and focused on his grandson.

"Isaiah, I'm praying one day your father will show up unexpected in your life. You'll see him standing there. And when that happens, I'm praying you will find a way to forgive him."

Isaiah nodded, but inside a storm brewed. If his dad ever walked in, he had a few words memorized for him. He had a whole speech ready. And knowing his dad, he wouldn't stick around to hear it.

And on the front porch of his grandfather's house, Isaiah made a promise that he would be different. He would never make the same mistakes as his father.

CHAPTER 7

✦ ✦ ✦

Cynthia

I like to keep things simple. No loose or split ends. Make my bed every morning, open the shop on time, and at the end of the day fall into bed knowing I've at least tried to finish my duties.

I like everything wrapped and tied up in a reasonable amount of time. If a hair dryer breaks, I buy a new one. Leaky faucet? Schedule a repair. Fuse blows? Call an electrician that day. I go down my list and cross things off and move on.

But there was no crossing off and moving on from Darren. He wasn't there, but he was, just like when he'd been there and wasn't. Darren was the ghost of heartbreak past, present, and future, a specter that haunted every moment.

Every thought of him brought a physical reaction. I'd shake my head, ball my fists, and grit my teeth. I was hurt, of course, but the pain had turned into the kind of anger that leaks from the pores of your soul. And I knew deep down that it was poison, but I couldn't let go of the bubbling rage inside.

I had parented Isaiah pretty much alone for most of his life. But with Darren physically out of the picture, a new kind of fear arose. I had to be both mother *and* father, good cop and bad cop, the nurturer and the discipliner. That was too big of a load to carry, but I did not know it at the time.

I'd wake up and stare at Darren's side of the bed. I'd make coffee and see his mug in the cupboard. I'd pass the trash can and remember the video games I'd tossed. Everything in that house brought a memory, and most of the memories brought shame and guilt as a package deal. And the guilt and shame brought unwanted thoughts.

Why in the world did I say yes to him? Why did it take so long to figure out he was no good? Maybe I deserved Darren.

It was like a boxing match, only I was connecting every punch with my own heart. And the longer I stayed awake, the more punches I took from myself. The thoughts were harder to control when I was alone and exhausted. I finally threw in the towel one night and went to my closet where I keep a few notebooks and journals. Elizabeth and I had done a Bible study together and I had written thoughts and quotes. Unfortunately I couldn't find it, so I dialed Elizabeth and immediately regretted it because of how late it was. I ended the call and felt like she would never speak to me again if I woke her and Tony up.

My phone rang almost immediately.

"Liz," I said, "I'm sorry to call so late. I didn't realize the time. It can wait until morning."

A yawn. I could see her stretching. "I'm up now, Sugarplum. What's going on?"

I told her about the thoughts swirling inside. Before I could ask about the study we'd done, she interrupted.

"This is classic. God will convict you of things to help you see the truth. To get you on the right path. His kindness leads to repentance. But there's no condemnation for those who are in Christ Jesus. The enemy accuses. The enemy wants you paralyzed and feeling all that shame and guilt."

"Okay, so what do I do?"

"First, be encouraged."

"What? How could this be encouraging?"

"The accuser doesn't bother people who don't matter. And you matter. He's afraid of you. He's afraid of the power at work in you."

"Afraid of me?"

"If he can keep you down and discouraged, feeling guilty all the time, making you think that Darren's choices are your fault, he's won the fight. He wants to paralyze you and keep you from believing who you really are."

I hadn't thought of it that way.

"Here's another thing he'll say," she continued. "You deserve the bad things that are happening. You brought them on yourself. And God is punishing you."

The air went out of the room. It was like my thoughts had left a voicemail on Elizabeth's home phone line. "I have felt like that. And I've also thought about how I'm messing up Isaiah's life and he'll never recover from this. And it's all because of me."

"Exactly. All your problems are your fault. Everything bad is because of you, and at the same time, you have no control over your situation. There's nothing you can do. Those are lies."

"So what do I do?"

We prayed together, which was the most helpful thing. When the thoughts swirl you just feel so alone, and when shame and guilt rise up, you isolate and hide, which is the worst thing I could do. So calling Elizabeth was the best step I could have taken at the time.

She gave me some verses and I wrote them down. Of course, as soon as I put my head on the pillow, the thoughts swirled again like a tornado.

"This is going to take some time, Lord," I prayed. "I need You to still my heart and quiet the storm. Help me see the truth about You and how You see me. And give me peace that You really are in control. I trust You."

My heart calmed that night. And every time I talked with Elizabeth, she encouraged me. But the storm known as Darren, which I termed a "Himicane," still raged inside and outside.

Elizabeth encouraged me to pray for Darren, so I became intimately acquainted with the imprecatory Psalms. I pulled some verses out of context so I could entreat God to "break his teeth" and "pour out wrath on him" and those types of things. The more I read, the more I realized those verses weren't about getting revenge on an enemy, they were asking God for justice. So I started looking for the Psalms that talked about tears and I found a bucketful.

"Day and night I have only tears for food . . ."

"Those who plant in tears will harvest with shouts of joy."

"You keep track of all my sorrows. You have collected all my tears in your bottle. You have recorded each one in your book."

So instead of God frowning at all the emotions I felt, I started looking at my tears as something God treasured. And in faith, I gave Him each one and asked Him to use them as He saw fit. I think that was my first act of surrender of everything about Darren. When I let the tears flow, it was almost like I was allowing God access to part of my heart I wanted to keep to myself.

In the process, I began to pray differently about Darren. Now, I had prayed for him through the years, but mostly I asked God to move him off the couch and help him get a job. I also prayed he would become the husband and father God wanted him to be. And from my perch, there was a big gulf there. Where he was and where I wanted to be were like two sides of the Grand Canyon.

That often led back to the swirl of thoughts. If he was so lazy, how did he get the power to pursue me? And why did he stop after we were married? It felt like some switch turned off inside.

"That's an easy one," Elizabeth said when I brought it up. "Darren set his sights on you and when you said, 'I do,' his job was over. He got what he wanted, so why should he do more work wooing your heart?"

I had thought something like that, but Elizabeth had a way of boiling things down. I talked with her, Miss Clara, my pastor, and others I trusted, and after reaching out to Darren and hearing nothing back, I made the decision to go ahead with the divorce.

And this is humbling to say, but I used to make fun of Hollywood marriages that sputtered and ended with a press release that put a positive spin on a marital train wreck. "The relationship ran its course," or "We're different people than we were when we married," and "We will love each other from a distance now." I don't make fun anymore. You have no idea what people go through and how they cope with the pain in a public breakup like that.

Going through that process myself gave me a different perspective, and now when I hear of a Hollywood divorce or a friend around the corner going through trouble, I just beg God for mercy on the people walking through that calamity.

And that's what it is, a calamity that sets you on a hard road. The lawyers, the legal fees, the court filings, trying to find out where Darren was living and not wanting to know but having to know. Contacting the Sheriff to serve him papers. Then seeing his name pop up on my phone. I had the presence of mind that day to let him leave a message, which I let my lawyer hear later.

I won't go into everything that happened and how it felt like my heart was being dragged through the gravel and then broken glass and then stepped on by Cricket's high-heeled shoes. At one of the meetings where we negotiated terms, Darren asked for his video games and system. After all we'd been through, that was what he wanted. In measured, careful tones, I informed him that the night he left, I disposed of all of that.

"Disposed? You mean you sold them?"

"No, I put them in a trash bag and took the garbage to the curb."

He scrunched up his face like I had told him I'd burned down the house. "What did you do that for?"

His lawyer glanced at him and shook his head a little, which I interpreted as, *Don't go there, Darren.* Smart lawyer.

We dealt with the money he took from our account. My lawyer made sure my business would not be part of the settlement, but Darren wanted half of the sale of our home. We'd only been in that house a few years and the housing market had tanked—if we sold it, we would lose money. There was a long back and forth, but in the end, he wanted out. But his lawyer made it clear that Darren would not pay child support for Isaiah.

"You can't get blood from a turnip," Darren said.

I wanted to say, *I thought I was marrying a man, not a turnip!* But I didn't say that or a hundred other things going through my mind. I kept wanting to bring up the word *cricket* in a sentence, but I decided against that, too.

So, a year and a half after Darren left the house and ripped my heart in two and left Isaiah without a dad in the house, the divorce was final. Walking out of the law office after everything had been signed, I should have felt like I'd put the pain behind me. But there was no party. Divorce is a death without a tombstone. It's a life sentence without parole because it's always part of you.

I knew I had to move on and let the anger toward Darren go. But how? At least Isaiah and I wouldn't ever have to see him again.

Or so I thought.

Pop, Darren's father, passed away a month later. Isaiah and I went to his funeral knowing Darren might be there. What kind of son wouldn't attend his father's service? Of course he'd be there.

So, instead of sitting with the family in the front, we slipped in the back of the church. Just before the service, Darren's sister, two aunts I had met briefly at a summer picnic, and some cousins and other extended family were seated and the service began.

Where was Darren? With every movement at the door I kept waiting for him to stagger in with Cricket. Toward the end of the service, which was hard to concentrate on with all my fear and dread, the pastor invited anyone who wanted to pay tribute to come forward. To my surprise, Isaiah stood and walked to the front too quick for me to grab his arm to stop him.

I was so proud, but also petrified. (I didn't know you could be both at the same time.) Proud that he wanted to speak about his grandfather, but petrified of all the questions that would come. Why didn't we sit with the family? Where's Darren? You got divorced? I didn't want any of that, but here was my only son standing in front of God and everybody.

Isaiah swallowed hard and looked at the congregation. My heart was beating at hummingbird speed.

"I'm Isaiah. I want to say something about Pop. I've been thinking about his laugh. How easy it was. And his hand on my shoulder. I can still feel it. The way he'd look at me when we talked. The way he'd show me how to bait my hook when I didn't like picking up a worm. The jokes he'd tell. None of them were funny, but you couldn't help but laugh. And once he started laughing, he'd snort. I'm going to miss his laugh."

The audience chuckled in places and responded to Isaiah's warm memories. I kept looking at the back door.

"Most of all," Isaiah said, "I'm going to miss the way Pop listened. He was All-Pro at hearing what you were saying even if you had a hard time saying it. My Pop was the best. He gave me things that . . . I didn't get from other people. I love you, Pop."

I noticed a few glares my way when Isaiah returned. I honestly expected more conflict. Those who were upset avoided us after the service but most who came up to us were kind and told Isaiah his words meant a lot. Instead of feeling ostracized, we felt embraced. Funny how a family you've been removed from can surprise you.

My plan was to slip out the back as soon as the service was over, but Isaiah's message changed that. We headed to the Fellowship Hall for a meal that would have made Pop smile from ear to ear. Whoever organized the buffet knew all of his favorite foods. Corn on the cob. Potato and macaroni salad. Baked beans. Barbecued pork sandwiches. Deviled eggs. You name it, it was on the table. I wish he could have been there.

Isaiah was in line getting food when someone touched my shoulder. I turned to see Randall Bentley smiling at me—THE Randall from my high school days. I had only seen his picture online, so to see him standing inches from me, that blindingly white smile and his tall frame, took my breath away. Some people from our class had changed a lot since high school. Weight gain. Gray hair. But Randall had become better looking. How did that happen?

"How did you know?" I said to him.

"I keep track of the obituaries in the local paper and I saw Darren's father had passed. I thought you might be here."

I had the same feeling as when he messaged me. Except it was tingly on steroids. How thoughtful of him to come.

"Can I get you some food?" he said.

"No, don't bother. I'm not that hungry."

He looked at me sideways. "I'm going to take that as being polite when you're really starving. The long drive from your place. You probably had coffee this morning, but that was it, right?"

I demurred. "Maybe a little salad?"

"Stay here. I'll be right back."

I don't know how he did it—he must have cut in line—because he was back before Isaiah with a plate of food that had my mouth watering. Then he got me some sweet tea and sat by me as Isaiah returned.

I introduced Randall and he and Isaiah shook hands.

"You've had some impressive games this year," Randall said. "Especially the one against Central."

Isaiah was surprised. "You came to my games?"

"No, but I've seen some of the highlights parents post on social media. Plus, the stats on the school's website."

Randall talked about the Central game and asked questions that showed he knew basketball. Isaiah was polite and spoke with him, but something felt strained. After a half hour I told Randall we needed to go and he walked us to my car.

"Very nice to meet you, Isaiah. And what you said about your grandfather, we could all tell it was from the heart. Again, I'm sorry for your loss."

On the ride home I asked Isaiah about Randall and what I'd picked up between them.

"I don't know, Mom. I mean, I'm glad you have a friend who's interested in my games, but it felt kind of weird."

"How so?"

"A guy shows up at your ex-husband's father's funeral and talks about basketball?"

"Well, he was there to see me. He reached out online a while ago."

"While you were still married? That feels weird, too."

The more we talked, the more uncomfortable the conversation became. I wanted to defend Randall. He was being nice. But the more Isaiah talked, the more I began to wonder if I was missing something. Or was my teenage son becoming territorial?

I changed the subject. "Did you know you were going to stand up and speak today?"

He shook his head. "Didn't occur to me. But when the pastor gave the chance, I felt like I needed to do it for Pop. His son wasn't there to say anything. I needed to."

"I wonder where your dad was?"

"Probably playing a video game. Or drinking. Or both."

I wondered if Darren had even heard about his father's death. I was still hurt and angry at him, but what if he was sick or in the hospital? I tried to put those thoughts out of my head, along with the thoughts about Randall.

Before I went to bed that night, I saw a notification on social media. I clicked and saw a message.

"Cynthia, it was great seeing you and Isaiah today. I'm sorry about the loss of Dell. Hope you made it home okay. Let's talk again soon!"

If Isaiah was right, I needed to nip this in the bud. But was he right? What was so bad about feeling the tingles again? Didn't I deserve to feel the tingles? It had been so long since I had felt noticed or cared for. No, I had to come to my own conclusion about Randall. And I pushed him and Darren and all the other conflict to the back of my mind and tried to close the door on it.

CHAPTER 8

✦ ✦ ✦

Isaiah waited on the front porch for Courtney. They had been going out six months. He had been interested since he first saw her on the cheerleading squad. She was gorgeous, tall, athletic, had a great figure and an easy smile. She laughed at his jokes and smiled brightly when he passed her going to the locker room.

He'd had two girlfriends in Middle School and those relationships had ended badly. That made him tentative to ask Courtney out at first. But one day she passed a note to him in English after he had compared their short story assignment to a movie he had seen.

The note said, "Since you like movies so much, why don't you take me to one?"

He glanced at her and she raised her eyebrows. That was all he needed. The feeling put him over the moon and they met at the mall theater that weekend.

Though he was past sixteen now, he didn't have his driver's license. In his mind, until he had a car to drive, there was no hurry. The guys on the team made fun of him for having a girl-friend who drove him everywhere, but he shook off the jab. He'd get the license when the time was right.

Courtney pulled up to his house and Isaiah hopped in and leaned over for a kiss. She turned her head slightly and he gave her a peck on the cheek. She was a little slower with the physical stuff, which frustrated him, but it was Courtney. That was her preference. He just had to wait until she was ready.

Courtney was a little taller than Isaiah with perfect hair and eyebrows, dark brown eyes, and chocolaty skin. She'd had her hair done once at his mom's salon and he'd asked her about Courtney and what they talked about.

His mother gave him a look. "Son, what happens in the chair stays in the chair."

Courtney pulled out and Isaiah reached for the radio. "Man, I've been looking forward to this movie for so long. It's going to be great."

"I've heard it's pretty good. Lots of car chases and explosions."

Isaiah laughed. "Yeah, but there's a love story, too. So we'll both like it."

Courtney drove to the back of the parking lot and as they walked toward the entrance, Isaiah reached for her hand. She adjusted her purse on her shoulder and kept walking. Something was up and he couldn't figure out what it was.

He bought popcorn and a soda thinking they would share, but Courtney politely declined. "I'm okay."

As the trailers began he leaned close. "Is anything wrong? Did I do something?"

She shook her head. "Let's just enjoy the movie."

He tried to push his feelings down, but the more he thought about it, the more agitated he became. During the romantic parts when the music swelled and the couple on-screen kissed, he glanced at her hoping she would look at him. Maybe give him a smile. Raised eyebrows. Anything. She didn't look at him.

The sun was down by the time they made it to the car. Inside, he put his hand over the ignition to block the key. "Can we talk?"

She sat back. "What about?"

"Courtney, what's going on? You've hardly said two words to me the whole night."

"I wanted you to enjoy the movie. I know you've been looking forward to it and I didn't want—"

"Courtney," he said, interrupting. He spoke with as deep a voice as he could muster and tried not to whine, but he couldn't help thinking he sounded like a two-year-old who wanted an ice cream cone.

She gave a deep sigh. "I'm just processing everything."

"What does that mean? Processing?"

"What I'm thinking and feeling."

"Okay, about what?"

"Us."

He stared at her and when she didn't look him in the eyes he felt queasy. "You want to elaborate?"

"Isaiah, I like you. You're a great guy. Talented at basketball. You're fun. You're a good friend."

"Friend?" The kiss of death. Queasy turned to swirling. "I thought we were serious."

"Yeah, it's just that . . ." She stopped and put her hands on the steering wheel.

"I hate it when you don't finish your sentences."

"Give me a minute," she said. She stared out the side window and it was more than Isaiah could take.

"Does this have something to do with your parents? Your dad? He not think I'm good enough for you?"

She stiffened. "Don't bring my parents into this."

"I'm trying to figure it out. How could things be going along so good and then all of a sudden—"

"It's not all of a sudden," she said. "This has been building."

"What has?"

Another big sigh. "Let me ask you straight up. What are you gonna do after you graduate? No, wait. Are you planning to graduate?"

"What kind of question is that? Of course I'm going to graduate. Give me a little credit."

"And what about after?"

"You mean college? Is that what this is about?"

"I mean what plans have you made for after graduation?"

He shook his head. "I don't know. That's down the road. I don't live in the future. I try to live in the present."

"You want to play college ball?"

"Of course."

"What are you doing to make that happen?"

Isaiah bit his cheek and tried to stay calm. There was a wound here she didn't understand. Something he hadn't told her or anyone else for that matter.

"Zay, what is it?"

"Remember I told you about a scout who might come to our game?"

"Three weeks ago, wasn't it?"

Isaiah nodded. "Do you remember how many points I scored?"

"No."

"Kenny heard about the scout. He told the guys to get him the ball and he shut me out."

"How do you know?"

"Jamal told me. Kenny didn't say anything to him, but another player said the plan was to keep the ball away from me."

"That's dirty. Coach Bascom would have yelled all day—"

"Coach Bascom knew about it. He had to. When we huddled up he never said anything about me not getting the ball. That scout never said a word to me. And no schools are knocking at my door."

"You could walk on at the community college."

"You don't think I know that? Courtney, where's this coming from? If I go to college you'll be my girlfriend? What's up with that?"

A long sigh. "Okay, here's what I'm seeing, Zay. You like having fun. You love gaming with your guys online. But life is more than that."

"You sound like my mother."

"Maybe you should listen to her."

"Okay, so I need to stop gaming. I need to go to college. Which means I need to get straight A's between now and graduation. What else is on your list to make you interested in me?"

"Your GPA isn't the point."

"Then what is the point?"

She finally looked at him. "I think we're in different places, Zay. We're looking for different things in life, you know?"

"No, I don't. I thought I found who I was looking for when I found you."

"I'm sorry."

"That's it? You're sorry?"

"I just want to be friends."

The air went out of the car. He couldn't breathe. He wanted to say something to change her mind, to get her to see she was making a mistake, but she had a look of resolve. She'd set him up by going to the movie and then dumping him in the parking lot. He wanted to punch the windshield. He wanted to do something, anything to relieve the pain building inside.

"Isaiah, tell me what you're thinking."

He set his jaw and shrugged. "Fine. From now on, we're just friends. Thanks for the ride."

He opened the door and jumped out, slamming it. Courtney yelled something, then rolled down the window.

"Isaiah, don't do this. Get in and let me take you home."

He waved at her and walked across the landscaped grass and through the carefully manicured shrubbery, crossed four lanes, and ran down the sidewalk until he reached a housing development. He heard Courtney pull out, but she had to drive a few hundred yards to get onto the street. Just enough time for him to slip between two houses and let her pass. She went by twice before she gave up and drove away.

No tears came. No moans from deep inside. He was just angry and hurt. Girls wanted him to be who they wanted him to be. Courtney didn't really care. She wanted somebody who fit in the picture she envisioned. Some college-bound success story.

"Forget that," he whispered.

In fact, forget all girls, all women. He never wanted to let anybody hurt him like this again. Love somebody and you get hurt. Girls were trouble and heartache and expectations. The only way to please them was to follow their rules, goalposts that moved without notice. It had happened before Courtney. But he wouldn't let it happen again.

When he was in Courtney's car, Isaiah felt like he was dying. He didn't know how to respond to her words and he hated that out-of-control feeling. But as soon as he walked away, he was back in control and he could breathe and walk or run at his own pace. Make his own choices.

He thought of his friends. How would he explain it? No reason to tell them.

What about his mom? He would just say they had grown

apart, which was true. No hard feelings. Instead of getting all childish, they were being grown-up about it, moving on. Blah, blah, blah.

Then Isaiah thought about the movie—he'd looked forward to it for months. Now, he couldn't imagine watching it again because there were too many bad memories. It was like getting food poisoning at a restaurant. Every time you saw it, you remembered what it had done to you.

He walked through the neighborhood, then started home. He thought about calling his mother or one of his friends for a ride. Then he thought better of it.

And as he walked, one idea rose inside. He was alone with his problems. He was alone in the world to figure out how to deal with the hurts and disappointments and a girl who said she just wanted to be friends.

Isaiah set his jaw and kept walking.

CHAPTER 9

✦ ✦ ✦

Cynthia

I always say never judge a person until you've walked a mile in their flip-flops. But I'll admit I'm guilty of judging people for the smallest things. And when your life has fallen apart in ways you never saw coming, it's humbling. Stepping off your high horse is hard. Getting knocked off is harder. I like to think that experience has changed me and made me more kind, but you'll have to ask my employees and family members. The proof is in the pudding, as they say.

When my marriage fell apart, I took all my anger and rage and the energy bottled up inside and popped the cork and poured it into providing for Isaiah and me. All my waking hours were spent trying to scratch and claw and provide.

Every day I woke up with these thoughts: I am not going to let the past rule me. I'm not going to let my fear about the future overwhelm me. And I will not let the title of "single parent" hold me back.

Mind you, I never wanted to be in that group, to be defined

by what I had lost. When it happened, like everything else, I threw myself into it and expected results.

This is how I cope with all the disappointments and failures. I got in my mind what I wanted to happen and figured out how to get from where I was to where I wanted to be.

After providing for us, my biggest goal was to help Isaiah avoid becoming his father. Don't judge me for that unless you've been there. I set down rules and regulations out of that fear. And when you live by fear and not faith, that will leak out on the people you care for the most.

My expectations were for Isaiah to get with my program. He would follow my rules because he would see that I loved him and wanted the best for him. I communicated in a language he understood, the language of sports. I couched everything in terms of us being a team and working together and moving downcourt to the goal. We were going to score on every possession by communicating well and playing in sync.

I had heard stories of frazzled single mothers who were upended by life's challenges. I was determined to be "the single parent who could," chugging up the hill like the little engine in that children's book I used to read to Isaiah.

I think I can. I think I can. For me, that became *I know we can. I know we can.*

So, when Isaiah graduated high school, I should have been over the moon. We had reached that goal—and I had the picture of him in his cap and gown to prove it. But I couldn't focus on his achievement that day because he didn't have a scholarship. And to be honest, that was a blow to my ego. I felt I had failed because he wasn't getting a free ride to higher education, and I knew he had the athletic talent to get it. Was this about Isaiah's future or my own ego?

I can see now that Isaiah was his own person, making his own decisions. But we had been through so much trauma and

I felt so much guilt that I had made life harder for him, and I couldn't separate him and me. The truth was, I had built my life around him. If he achieved something good, I had done a good job. If he didn't, I was bad. So, I began to nudge him to apply to the community college that's less than a half hour away. I left an application on the breakfast table. I printed a flyer about their basketball program. I suggested he walk on and get a tryout. I did everything but dribble a basketball all the way over there myself.

This college idea meant some financial sacrifice. He would need a loan and a car. The Mustang in the garage was not an option. But I told him we were a team and we'd meet the challenge together.

I could see it in my dreams. He'd be one of those stories they presented on the Final Four weekend. Kid from a single-parent home walks on at a community college and then transfers with a full scholarship to some ACC team, maybe Duke or North Carolina. And on the Monday when they play the championship, I would be there in the stands watching Isaiah hit the winning free throw, and the confetti would fall and he would cut down the net. And then, in my dream, he would run into the stands, leaping over people to give me a hug.

Oh, I could taste it. I had it all mapped out.

But I learned the hard way that your dreams for your son are your dreams. I'm sure Isaiah would have said yes to the scholarship and the championship and all of that, but there was something holding him back. And I never asked him what it was. I never said, "Tell me why this is such a hard step for you?"

Oh, I talked *to* him a lot. I said, "Baby, if you walk on and don't make it on the team, that's okay. But you'll never play for a team if you don't try." Made perfect sense to me. But it didn't move Isaiah from his room. He had no interest in being a walk-on. I couldn't believe it. What had I done wrong? Or was this something I had no control over?

Those thoughts sent me to my knees more than once. And it helped me understand that prayer is coming to the end of yourself and realizing that you were at the end of yourself all along. That's not original with me. It came from a woman named Miss Clara. She was instrumental in helping my sister and her husband through a rough time in their marriage. Of course, I still wonder why God couldn't help me through my rough time like He did Elizabeth and Tony.

One Sunday afternoon I drove across town to see her. I usually listened to music that helped calm my spirits, but I just let my thoughts roam to the sound of the tires on pavement as I drove toward Charlotte.

Elizabeth had helped Miss Clara sell her house—which is how they met. But to hear my sister tell it, she got a lot more than a commission on that sale. She got a baptism in the power of prayer.

After the house sold, Miss Clara moved in with her son and his family, who were gone the afternoon I drove there. She met me at the door and showed me to her room, which was like her own little apartment.

"My son is a worrywart," she said. "He thought I was going to fall down the stairs or slip on the tile in my kitchen. But I realized he just loved me and wanted to care for me. And now I have a granddaughter I am praying for who is in close proximity to my prayer closet."

"Elizabeth told me about your war room."

"Come on, you need to see it." She opened the closet door and what I thought was peeling wallpaper was really all the requests that lined the walls. There was a small rug on the floor where she could kneel, a wooden chair, and a bookshelf that held her Bible and journal and some books on prayer.

"This is where I go to war for the hearts of people who come on my radar. The Lord and I do business together here every day.

I fight my battles on my knees in here, and sometimes when my knees hurt I lay flat on the rug."

"Is there something special about the room itself?"

Miss Clara chuckled. "The place is not the point. God will hear me whether I'm here or in a cardboard box. No, linking my heart with the Lord is the point. And I've seen some amazing things happen."

We moved to the kitchen and Miss Clara offered me some herbal tea. While she heated the water I asked, "Why do you think one marriage holds together while another one breaks apart? I mean, Elizabeth and I both prayed hard, but it feels like I got the short end of the prayer stick."

She smiled. "Honey, you and me both wonder about such things. Why does God heal some and not heal others the way we want? Why does He do the miraculous in one place and seem like He doesn't hear our prayers in another?"

"You've had those thoughts too?"

Miss Clara drew close. "Absolutely. But I remind myself that I don't see the whole picture. I don't know everything going on in people's lives. But I can join my heart with Someone who does. And I trust Him. I believe that God can do miracles. I've seen them. But my trust is not in the miracle, it's in Jesus."

"I think I understand."

"See, a lot of people think prayer is getting God to do what you want Him to do on your timetable. The longer I live, the more I think it's like stepping off the platform onto a train that's starting to move. It takes faith to take a step, but once you're on and you submit to His control, you're headed in the direction He wants you to go."

This was exactly what I wanted to hear, a Prayer 101 conversation. The water began to boil and Miss Clara spoke with her back to me. "And prayer is not supposed to be all neat and tidy.

Sometimes it's just a long cry to your heavenly Father where you can't find the words. Read the Psalms. David cries out to God and just pours out what's inside. David's secret was that no matter what trouble he was in, Philistines coming after him, his son betraying him, he acknowledges God is there and cares for him. He trusts God no matter his situation. That's a hard lesson to learn.

"So you talk to God about your feelings regarding your husband and what happened to Elizabeth and Tony and you ask Him to help you. You tell Him you didn't want to be a single parent. Tell Him all that's going on and He'll comfort you with His word and His presence in the middle of the pain."

"So you're saying I don't have to be somebody else when I pray."

"I've never known anyone who could give somebody else's heart to God. The greatest gift you give Him is yourself. All of you. And that becomes the greatest gift you give the world, the way you allow God access to every nook and cranny of your life. And here's the best thing. Doing that will lead to a gift you'll give to your son."

I felt the emotion when she mentioned Isaiah and I told her the details about Darren walking away and abandoning both of us. I could see the pain on her face as I described the night he left and what he said. She sat with the mugs of tea and leaned closer.

"Tell me this. Has your husband had any contact with Isaiah since he left?"

"No. Isaiah hasn't mentioned anything and I think he would have told me."

Miss Clara shook her head. "Losing a parent to death will change a child. It's a wound that's with them every hour of every day. But having a parent walk away, a parent who could reach out but doesn't, is a double wound. They wonder what's wrong with them. What did they do to deserve dad leaving like that?"

Miss Clara rubbed her hands, then covered her face and shook her head, as if she was taking on some of our pain.

"Mm, mm, mm," she said, finally taking her hands away. "I feel like the Spirit has touched on something deep here. Tell me why you wanted to see me today, Cynthia."

I thought about what she had said about the Psalms. I poured out my heart about my son. What I was seeing in him. How he didn't seem to be able to take responsibility. How he frittered it away with gaming and pickup basketball. And his lack of desire to go to college or even get a job.

"I feel sorry for him for having to go through this pain with his father. And I feel guilty because I was part of it. I want to say the things he needs to hear, but I can't be his father. But if I don't say them, who will?"

"Does he think he has to go to college in order for you to love him?"

I sat back. "I hope not. That's never been in my heart. He doesn't have to accomplish big things to make me happy. I just don't want to see him squander his life and . . ."

"Go down the same road your husband did," she said, finishing my sentence.

"Exactly."

"Let me ask you an important question, Cynthia. Do you trust God?"

What kind of question was that? I squinted a little, as if I might not have heard her correctly.

"Do you trust God?" she said again.

"I think so. I mean, I want to."

"You trust Him to save you. You don't add anything to the holiness of His Son."

"Right. I have trusted Him for that and continue to."

"Do you trust Him enough to let him work on your son?"

That question hit me below the belt. I stared at the mug of tea. "I tried that with my husband."

"Mm-hmm," she said. She went to her room and returned with a blank card, the kind that lined her closet wall. She wrote Isaiah's name in bold letters. "Now I'm going to pray for the both of you when I bring you to the Lord. But from what you've said, here's what I'm sensing about Isaiah. It sounds like his biggest need is not college or employment, but to surrender his life to Jesus."

"Yes."

"I'm going to pray that God would enlighten him, open the eyes of his heart to his need of a Savior. And how God does that is up to God, of course. Does he have any Christian men in his life?"

"His grandfather had a big influence on him, but he passed away."

"I'm sorry to hear that." Miss Clara stared at the card. "What really needs to happen is for Isaiah to let God be his Father. To let God nurture him and validate him and give him strength."

"But isn't it hard to believe in a good Father when your earthly father has let you down?"

"Absolutely. That's why I'm going to pray for a man who can stand in the gap."

My heart beat faster. I almost reached for my phone. "What about Tony? He'd be perfect because he already knows Isaiah. Isaiah likes him."

She held up a hand. "I think Tony would be good, but this is not something you can manufacture or manipulate, Cynthia. Isaiah is going to see right through it if you parade Tony in front of him. And it might be Tony who comes alongside him, but this is a battle for Isaiah's heart. And it's also a battle for yours. God is not just going to work on Isaiah and show him how much he needs the Lord. God is going to work on you, sister. And He will orchestrate in His own time and His own way. I don't know how. But I do know we need to pray."

"Can we do that now?" I said.

"I thought you'd never ask."

Part 2

THE AWAKENING

CHAPTER 10

✦ ✦ ✦

Isaiah, now nineteen, slept soundly in the room his mother called "Ground Zero." There were clothes on the floor near his laundry hamper. Wet towels lay near his gym bag. Socks hung in the plastic hoop on the back of his door. The truth was, once Isaiah made it to his room, he liked to relax. He could get things looking okay in a few minutes if he had to, but he liked it this way. Anything he needed he could find. He'd heard this was the way creative minds worked. They liked things messy. Look at Einstein's desk.

The phone's buzz woke him from his slumber. He opened one eye and saw the blurry name on his phone. He picked it up and hit the speaker button and mumbled, "Jamal."

"Isaiah, we're ballin' at the park in twenty. You in?"

"Nah, man. I'm chillin'."

"Dude, come on. Me and Andre need you for three on three."

Isaiah didn't even open his eyes. "Why you playin' so early?"

"It's ten thirty, bro!" Jamal yelled. "Get over here."

Isaiah sighed. It would feel good to blow off some steam playing three on three. "All right. I'm comin'."

Isaiah had been up late playing an online game. He kept nodding off in the middle of it and finally told the others he had to go and switched off the TV and fell headfirst into bed. It was the same position he returned to after Jamal's call.

He was about to drift off when his phone buzzed again. It was his mother. She would have left for the salon by now. Why would she be calling?

"Hello?"

"Isaiah, I didn't see the trash can out by the street. You know it's running today."

"Yes ma'am, I know." He tried to sound confident. "I got it."

"You already got it or you're gonna get it? It was still by the house when I left." There was an edge to her voice. "Are you in bed or are you up?"

Isaiah threw off the covers and stood by the bed in his shorts and T-shirt. "Nah, I'm up."

"Okay. Well, you forgot last week."

Isaiah could tell she was trying to hold back and not yell or nag. She'd been trying to do that for several months, and when she slipped he called her on it, saying that nagging him never worked. But she had gently said he needed to pull his weight around the house. And in subtle ways she made it clear that he needed to get his life in gear, which meant getting a job. Was that from his mother or something inside him? He pushed the thought away.

"Ma, I got it."

Her voice sounded all sweet now. "Okay, baby. Listen, I'm just trying to help you." A sound in the background. "Oh, a customer just came in. I'll see you tonight. Love you."

"Love you, too," he said. He put the phone down and

collapsed on the bed again. His thoughts turned to the three on three and who else might be playing. In his reverie he felt a low rumble outside, like a bass drum at a playoff game. Then he heard the telltale sound of a trash truck's diesel engine and he bolted out of bed and down the hall to the kitchen. He grabbed the two full plastic bags and hit the door, flying barefoot down the concrete driveway, yelling and waving the bags.

He reached the road and saw the truck in the distance. He raised the bags, hoping the driver would see him in the side mirrors. The truck kept going without slowing.

He ran inside and got dressed in his #8 jersey and tried to make the trash bin outside look as good as he could. With two weeks of trash inside, he tried shoving the contents down, pushing with his foot to get the bags to settle. One bag burst and the smell was nauseating. He even sat on top of the bin's lid but the bags still overflowed.

Unable to figure a better plan, he turned the bin around so it would at least look different when his mother pulled in that evening. Why didn't the guy on the garbage truck see him?

He rode his bike through the tree-lined subdivision, taking the back way to the park. He ran through the scenarios of what he would tell his mother about the trash when she got home that evening. No matter what story he told, she'd blame him for not getting up. Better to be honest and tell her he wouldn't let it happen again. Bat his puppy dog eyes.

Isaiah had gotten his driver's license at seventeen. He borrowed his mom's car when she would let him, but his BMX bike was his main form of transportation, other than getting rides from friends. He wasn't proud of riding a bike instead of driving a car, but he did what he had to do. And he was able to think while he pedaled. And the ride got him warmed up for the game, working up a good sweat so when he pulled up to the court, all he had to do was stretch out and take a couple of shots and he was good to go.

Jamal and Andre were his teammates in the game to 21. Jamal had been one of his best friends in high school. He was about the same height as Isaiah and his feet were lightning. He played a lot taller than he looked because of his speed and jumping ability. Andre was taller than both Isaiah and Jamal, but he wasn't as fast. He had a competent jump shot and played well, but he had more enthusiasm than talent.

On the other side was Keenan, who was twenty-three and had several inches on Isaiah. He was an inside threat and Isaiah knew it was up to him to stay between Keenan and the basket or it would be a short game to 21.

Isaiah's team was up 18 to 16 when Keenan took a pass near the top of the key and put a move on Isaiah that froze him. Keenan drove to the basket and jammed it home and the team celebrated.

Isaiah took the ball out and Keenan got in his face.

"Where you at Zay? Tie game, baby!"

"You ain't won yet," Isaiah said. "Let's go!"

Keenan inbounded the ball in the make-it take-it game and Isaiah knew what was coming. He let Keenan get behind him and run toward the basket. Isaiah turned and cut off the pass and dribbled into the backcourt. He stepped to the three-point line, feeling Keenan right behind him. He gave a quick crossover dribble that sent Keenan flying past him, then squared up for the three-pointer and let it fly.

Nothing but net. 21-18.

Jamal went crazy, picking Isaiah up and screaming at the win. Andre joined in the celebration. Despite the trash talk during the game, the players knew this was less about winning and more about playing well and as a team. Keenan was a good sport and sat with them as they rehearsed the game and chugged water.

"Zay, we gamin' in an hour. You in?" Jamal said.

Isaiah knew he meant a continuation of last night's online game. He had nothing planned that afternoon. "I gotta eat something, first. Hey, loan me ten. I'll pay you back."

Jamal gave him a look. "You already owe me forty, bro!"

Keenan laughed at the banter, then turned serious. "Isaiah, what you doin' now, man? You goin' to college?"

The question, especially right after the news that he'd be gaming that afternoon, felt like a jab. Isaiah stayed cool and said, "Nah, I ain't doin' all that."

Keenan leaned back. "So what you gonna do?"

Another jab. Isaiah grabbed his hat and tried not to sound defensive. "I'm just chillin', man."

"You got a car yet?"

Before he could answer, Jamal said, "Yeah. His granddad left him a sweet '66 Mustang."

Keenan lit up. "For real?"

Isaiah stood and gave Jamal a derisive look. "Man, shut up."

Jamal smiled and bounced the ball. "Man, that thing is trash. Don't work. Couldn't give it away if he wanted to."

Jamal and Andre laughed as they walked away.

Several hours later, Isaiah sat in his giant beanbag chair with his headphones cranked, hearing the automatic rifle fire full blast as he played *Realm of Risk*. Movement at the right of the screen. He spoke into the microphone. "Hey, 'Dre, you got two guys coming in."

"I see 'em."

"Jamal, where you at?" Isaiah said.

"I'm picking up loot!"

"Hey, hey, shots left! Shots left!" Andre said. "Come help me!"

Isaiah twisted his body, as if it might speed things up. "I'm coming!"

In the distance he heard something. Was there someone sneaking up on him? He swiveled his player on the screen. Nothing.

Then, a voice.

"Isaiah Tyrone Wright!"

And with his mother's words yelled from the kitchen, the game was over.

CHAPTER 11

✦ ✦ ✦

Cynthia

I went home early from the salon one afternoon to buy some groceries and make dinner for Isaiah and me. Tammy and Keisha had things under control. I wanted to talk with my son about some of the things I had gleaned from a recent talk with Miss Clara. Carefully, of course. I wasn't going to unload a spiritual dump truck on him, but there were things he needed to hear.

Miss Clara had given advice for next steps with Isaiah. She said to pray hard before I made any big requests. She thought that when I owned up to some of my faults and failures, it might open the door for Isaiah to do the same.

"Being vulnerable with the people you love doesn't push them away, it can bring them closer, Cynthia. But you have to do this without strings attached. If you're looking for the perfect response from Isaiah, trying to get him to do something in return, you're trying to control him. Pray about it and let God work in both of your hearts. And let go of how he responds—you just be real and honest."

I was praying about what I was going to say, how open and honest I was going to be, as I walked the cereal aisle at Harris Teeter. I looked at the shelf and was stopped in my tracks when I saw a green box. It was Darren's favorite breakfast bars. I kept him stocked up on them because he would grab a couple on his way to work, that is, when he had a job. I just stared at those boxes, thinking about buying them and stacking them in the pantry. And the more I looked, the more I wondered if I had done that out of a sense of hope that he might stay employed, that he might be responsible. Did I buy those bars thinking one day Darren would become a better husband and father?

"Excuse me," a woman said, jolting me from my thoughts. I was in the middle of the aisle, my cart behind me, staring at those breakfast bars like a zombie, blocking all traffic.

"I'm so sorry," I said, stepping out of the way.

"Takes me a long time to decide, too," the woman said, smiling. "Too many choices."

She had no idea what was rolling around my soul, but I smiled anyway and moved down the aisle. Funny how a little box of processed honey and oats can trigger things so deep. And I wondered if God was trying to get my attention, if He was waking me up to something. Can He move a heart in Harris Teeter?

I was still angry at Darren. After all the praying I'd done, I still wanted God to give him a dose of his own medicine. I wanted his life to be miserable. I didn't say that out loud or even in the journal I started. It's hard to be honest with God. It's harder to be honest with yourself.

Something Elizabeth said came back near the dairy section. She said trusting God fully means that I can give things to Him and not hang on. I can let God, in His good time, handle Darren and repay him for the heartbreak he'd caused.

"He will settle the score," Elizabeth said. "You release him to God's kindness and mercy and also His judgment. Let Darren's name be a prayer, a cry for God to intervene."

By then I was in paper goods, that's how long it took all of this. I stopped between the toilet tissue and the paper towels with nobody around and whispered, "Darren." The name felt like acid on my tongue. I closed my eyes and remembered that night and the feeling of a ripped-open heart.

I said it again. "Darren."

Something happened that second time. I felt it in my shoulders, if that's possible. And I thought, if God really is sovereign over all my life, I could give Darren to Him like an offering. And then I thought it was an awful offering. But I felt a stirring inside to give God the pain and the hurt Darren had caused. I closed my eyes.

Lord, I'm still angry and broken over what he did. But I want You to do whatever You want with Darren. I release him to You and I let go of my anger and rage and hurt. This is my offering to You today.

It felt like my soul was lighter, somehow. I was beginning to believe that I really could trust God with every area of my life. It was a relief that He didn't need my help.

"I like the 'select-a-size' ones," someone said.

I opened my eyes and there was the same woman from the cereal aisle pointing at the paper towels. She must have thought I was either crazy or having a spell.

"I like those, too," I said.

I did the rest of my shopping without seeing the woman again or stopping in the middle of the aisle to pray, but there was something new growing inside. It was almost like I could do a spiritual waltz through that store.

Empowerment is what I would call it, this feeling that was welling. Power to live. Power to love. Power to forgive.

Well, that last one, I don't know if I can ever work up that much lightness in my soul, because just when you release somebody, the thoughts and feelings can creep back in. Forgiveness is not a one-time decision, it's a continual offering. You have to decide. And then you have to come along every day and sweep that dirty sidewalk of your mind and decide again.

I got in my car and turned on the radio, and right then this song came on that perfectly fit what I was thinking. How does that happen? Do people at the radio station know what's going on in my soul? I sang along and a tear or two leaked out and I drove up our street with all the hope in the world just glowing inside. I was ready to burst into that house singing the Hallelujah Chorus.

I was praying, *Lord, open a way for me talk with my son. You are doing something in me, I can feel it. Do the same in Isaiah's life. Turn his heart toward You. And help me listen well. Help me draw him out and get him to talk about what he's going through so that he can tell I care.*

I just knew something good was about to happen. I could feel it in my bones.

And then I turned into the driveway.

Now listen, you can be on some mountaintop with God, praising Him and thanking Him for the view, and the enemy will take that exact moment and try to knock you into the valley. Just kick you over the edge. And all it takes to remove the stirring inside is some little thing that touches some nerve about the real world and all your problems and struggles and doubts and fears.

All it took that day was the trash can.

I pulled up and stared at the overflow. It was turned around to make me think something had changed, but it hadn't. I got out and went over and the aroma of that garbage made me grit my teeth and want to move my son's bed out here so he could smell the coffee.

Lord, help me.

I grabbed three grocery bags and carried them inside, balancing them as I got the kitchen door open. The grocery bill was higher that day and that sent me down the road of wondering how we were going to make it financially. The tension was back, my shoulders tight.

"Isaiah, can you come help me?" I said it as loud as I could and tried to mix in a little sweetness.

No response from his room. I thought I heard him talking. Was he on the phone? Playing a game?

"Isaiah?"

I took a deep breath to settle me and returned to the car and grabbed three more bags. I kicked the door closed behind me and got the bags to the kitchen counter, the anger beginning to boil. I called again, this time with a little oomph in my voice.

No response.

"Isaiah Tyrone Wright!" I yelled.

That did the trick. He sauntered into the kitchen with his hat on backwards, wearing his favorite jersey. No rushing to help, no urgency. He had that ashamed puppy look like when he knows he's done something wrong.

I was trying not to lose my cool. I was trying to remember what I'd prayed minutes before. But when I opened my mouth, the boil bubbled over.

"Could you not hear me?"

"I was in the middle of a game. I can't pause it."

I grabbed the cereal box and resisted the urge to throw it at him. "Boy, I don't care nothin' about no games! You're always in the middle of a game. Do you wanna tell me why this trash can is still full?"

He looked away, then scratched the back of his head. That was the extent of his response.

"Did you at least start your laundry?"

A blank stare and an open mouth. He was searching for the words.

"Um, not yet."

I moved a little closer and lowered my voice. "Is your room clean?"

"I'm about to do that right now."

That hit a nerve I didn't know I had. I shook my head and gave him a stare. I had been waiting for a moment to bring up what was on my heart, and a little voice inside said this was not the time. But I told that little voice to be quiet.

I tried to keep from lashing out and getting emotional. With as much control as I could muster, I said, "Okay, listen. I'm tired of having this same conversation over and over again."

Isaiah rolled his eyes and looked away. The nerve inside me got pressed a little harder.

"You are nineteen years old. That means it's time for you to step up. If you're not going to go to college, that's fine. But let me tell you what, you are going to get a job, because this is what we're not doing. You're not living off your mother. Not when you're fully capable of taking on some of this responsibility yourself."

I took a breath. Isaiah looked down and around—everywhere but at me. He turned to walk away and I stopped him with one word. "Isaiah."

Finally he looked at me.

"I love you," I said. And it was true. I did love him, even if I couldn't stand him right then. "But if you're going to live here, you're gonna pay me rent here. You're not going to spend all your graduation money on sneakers and video games."

Isaiah interrupted me. "Rent?"

He said it like I had said the word in Swahili.

"You gonna make me pay to live in my own house?" he said.

Now it was my turn to act as if he'd spoken in a foreign tongue. "Your house?" I laughed at how absurd it sounded. And the nerve inside led me down another trail. "You are my son. But I'm giving you one month to find a job. Or you can find one of your little friends that's gonna let you sleep on their couch for free."

My heart was beating so fast, it felt like I had just sprinted a hundred-yard dash. Isaiah wanted to say something but instead, he shook his head and walked out of the room.

And then I wanted it all back. I wanted to rewind to the grocery store and what happened in the car driving home and look at the trash can one more time and take a deep breath and come back in the door again and do it all over. I meant all the things I had said to Isaiah—they needed to be said. But was there a better way to say all of that without him walking out of the room?

I threw up a prayer standing in the kitchen. I closed my eyes and whispered, "God, help me. And help him."

CHAPTER 12

✦ ✦ ✦

Isaiah stewed about what his mother had said, cleaning up his room by stuffing things in drawers and stacking things in the closet out of sight. What was up with her? He wanted to ask her if she'd had a bad day at work or something, but he knew that would set her off even more.

Pay rent? Who asked their son to pay rent? Was she going to pay him for what he did around the house? Taking out the trash, mowing the yard . . . There was more he did, he just couldn't think of it. None of his friends who lived at home had to pay rent. It didn't feel right. Maybe it was a phase she was going through, something she'd get over.

The next day he heard her talking in her room, which was right next to his. He wasn't sure who she was talking with, but whoever it was said stuff that made her cry as she recounted the scene the day before. He only caught bits and pieces of her side of the conversation, but it was clear that she was sticking to her "rent" idea and one month to get a job.

He went outside and called Keenan and explained what happened. "Something's not right with this. She gave me an ultimatum."

"Look, it's your mother, her house, she gets to make the rules, right? You don't like it, move out."

"Man, how am I going to do that?"

"Like she said, get a job."

"You're no help. You're supposed to have my back."

"Look, I hear you. Why don't you call your dad? Go live with him for a while."

Isaiah had told Keenan about the divorce but not much more than that. "Nah, my dad's not an option."

"Hey, what about that car? The one your granddad gave you."

"What about it?"

"You could sell it and get some cash. Or fix it up."

"You've never seen it, right?"

"No, but I'm about a mile away from you."

Isaiah was sitting on the porch in front when Keenan pulled up. He walked him toward the garage, knowing what was going to happen when Keenan saw the car.

As they walked, Keenan said, "Whatever happened with you and Courtney?"

Just the sound of her name sent a jolt through Isaiah. Courtney's breakup with him had echoed in his heart and mind and had kept him from moving toward other girls.

"We just grew apart. It happens. Why you want to know?"

"Heard she was making waves at college."

"What's that mean?"

"She and her cheer squad were in this competition I saw on TV. She looks like she's—"

"Good for her," Isaiah said, interrupting Keenan. "I'm glad she's enjoying life."

"What are you so upset about?"

"Why'd you have to bring her up?"

"You said you just grew apart. Did she dump you?"

Isaiah grabbed the garage door handle.

"Hey, hold up. Seriously, what happened?"

"I didn't like her anyway. She was up in my face about my grades and going to college and having ambition."

"You mean, like your mom?"

"That's brutal, man," Isaiah said. "Why don't we talk about you and your girlfriends?"

Keenan lifted both hands in surrender. "Let's take a look at the hot rod you been hiding."

Isaiah yanked the heavy door open. Inside sat a car covered in so much dust and rust he couldn't remember the color. Keenan laughed and stepped inside for a closer look.

"I told you, man. It's been sittin' here since I was nine."

Keenan ran a finger over the hood and left a line in the dust. He went to the passenger side and leaned down to look at the tattered upholstery, the foam coming through the seats.

"Your grandfather drove this?" Keenan sounded skeptical.

"Yeah, my mom said it was in bad shape when he got it. He was gonna fix it up with my dad. Then my dad told me he was gonna fix it up with me. This is the way he left it . . . like every-thing else."

Keenan folded his arms in front of him and looked at Isaiah. Isaiah wondered if his friend could hear the pain in his voice.

"You know, if I could get somethin' for it, I'd sell it," Isaiah said.

Keenan shook his head. "Well, if you lookin' for a job, you better find one that's close. 'Cause you ain't drivin' this." He patted the top of the car and put his arm around Isaiah and they walked out of the garage.

"I hear they need a busboy down at the diner."

"Washing dishes and rolling silverware? That ain't me."

"What is you, then? What are you looking for?"

"I don't know. I guess I'll know it when I see it."

Keenan nodded. "Good luck with that."

✦ ✦ ✦

After Keenan left, Isaiah rode his bike toward town looking for *Help Wanted* signs in windows. With his favorite hat turned backwards and an untucked baseball jersey that he wore like a cape, he pedaled leisurely on sidewalks looking for any sign of stores needing employees.

A fast food place had a *Now Hiring* notice on the door, but Isaiah shook his head. Last thing he wanted was to slip and slide on a greasy floor in front of a hot grill. He liked burgers and tacos and figured if he worked behind the curtain he'd learn too much and never eat there again.

He stayed away from his mother's salon, riding on less-familiar streets. A law office. Two insurance companies. A dentist. Another fast food place with *Now Hiring* hanging crooked on the front window. He was beginning to see a pattern.

There was no video game store on this side of town. He'd jump at the chance to be around the games and controllers all day. There was a Game On store across town, but he'd need to borrow his mom's car to apply. Other than that, he hadn't thought about where to work as much as he had thought about how much he'd be paid. The words of his former girlfriend Courtney came back to him and he shook his head, as if trying to get her voice out of his heart. He could see her frowning at his lack of direction. Funny how the negative stuff stuck.

He came to a stop at an intersection and pulled out his phone to look at a map. To his right sat Cornerstone Coffee,

a small shop in a newer stucco building. He didn't like coffee
and he couldn't imagine standing all day wearing an apron and
making drinks he would never taste. He noticed a sporting
goods store about two blocks away and was about to leave when
he glanced at a girl in the drive-thru at the coffee shop. He did
a double take. She was Black and looked about his age. She was
cuteness squared. Curly hair and a pretty face. One look and he
forgot his promise about women.

He walked inside and took a deep breath, and the coffee
aroma suddenly had a pleasing effect. He passed a customer
leaving as the girl behind the counter said, "Have a blessed
day."

Sounded like something his mother would say. He shook
that off and strutted forward in his camo pants, suddenly feeling
he wasn't dressed like he should be.

The girl gave him a big smile. "Hi there."

Something fluttered inside and he didn't care if they had any
job openings. Her face was even more inviting than the pastries
in the display case beside her.

"What can I get for you?" she said.

Isaiah lowered his voice and leaned close. "Hey, what's your
name?"

The smile disappeared and she sounded a little guarded when
she spoke. "Uh, my name's Abigail. Is this your first time in our
shop?"

"Yeah, this is my first time here." He looked at the tables
around the room. "You know how to make good coffee?" He
paused and looked deep in her eyes and added, "Abigail."

She turned her head and in a less-confident voice said, "I mean,
our customers seem to think so."

"Uh-huh," Isaiah said, thinking of the next logical question.
"You live around here?"

"Yeah, but I don't really . . ."

A tall man came from the kitchen area and walked up behind Abigail. Isaiah still had his elbows on the counter looking deep into the girl's eyes.

"Can I help you?" the man said, moving all the way into Isaiah's space.

Isaiah took a step back. "Nah, you good, man. I'm just trying to talk to the young lady here. You feel me?" Isaiah chuckled.

The man didn't smile. "That's my daughter."

A sinking feeling. He glanced at Abigail who seemed relieved her father had come to the rescue. But rescue from what?

"I'd like to know if you're interested in getting a coffee today?" the man said with military precision.

"Naw, to be honest, it's really not my thing, so . . ."

"Hmm. Then you need to move on."

Something rose up inside again, this time indignation. "What? You can't just kick me out of here. I ain't did nothing wrong."

The man didn't seem moved by Isaiah's sense of injustice. He spoke in even tones, without emotion. "Well, like I said, if you're not here to get coffee today, then you need to be on your way."

The stirring rose to boiling inside. He'd felt this way when an opposing player hit a shot and taunted him.

"What's your problem, man? You can't just come out here and threaten me. I ain't committin' no crime."

The man nodded and walked around the pastry case.

Isaiah raised his voice, yelling now. "Huh? Do I look like a criminal to you?"

Abigail stood with her hands behind her, looking shocked at his display. Her eyes followed her father as he strode toward Isaiah. He stopped a few inches from Isaiah and said firmly, "Okay, I'd like for you to leave."

Isaiah squared him up like an opposing player who had

fouled him hard. Isaiah moved closer, almost daring the man to touch him.

"I need for you to leave my shop right now."

Isaiah took a breath. "What, you think I'm beneath you? Huh?"

Forcefully, but still in control, the man said, "Get out. Go on."

Isaiah turned to Abigail. She could have stood up for him. She could have said everything was all right. *He didn't mean anything, Dad. Leave him alone. He's kind of cute.*

She didn't say a word. In fact, the look on her face told him all he needed to know. He was alone again. Instead of being welcomed, he was being ushered out.

He walked toward the door. "I'm going. And I won't be back, either. Believe that."

Isaiah expected to hear *We don't want you back.* But he heard silence behind him as he hit the door and walked outside, wondering what Abigail would say to her dad. He took one final look at the shop before he pedaled away. All he could think was how much he hated coffee.

CHAPTER 13

✦ ✦ ✦

Cynthia

I have a natural urge to do things myself, on my own, in my own strength. If I can't pull myself up by my bootstraps, I'll kick myself until I do. (And that's a sight to see, let me tell you.) Anything worth doing is worth accomplishing alone—that's how I've lived, and it's exhausting. Success is part of this equation, that I'm not really accomplishing anything unless I do it myself. Needing help cancels the accomplishment.

I'm beginning to see how hard life can be when you live this way, thinking you always have to work things out on your own. It leaves you tired inside and out. Maybe it's the need for control—that if I can't do it myself, I'm out of control, which I hate. But I wonder if it has something to do with pride. If I can't do it myself, it hurts my pride. If I'm not able to figure it out alone, I feel less valuable. Where's that coming from?

I've often asked God why life has to be so hard. Why does it feel like I'm in a constant game of tug-of-war with myself? I'm on either side of the muddy hole, pulling with all my might. And I always wind up muddy and worn out.

Elizabeth and Miss Clara got me thinking about this. My life is enriched because they've come alongside me. My helplessness, my need for advice and guidance has shown me that when I ask for help, I'm not showing weakness but strength. No, scratch that. When I acknowledge my weakness, that's when I get stronger because I ask for help instead of staying stuck in the mud. Makes me think of that verse about God's strength being made perfect in weakness. I'm not being weak asking for help, I'm humbling myself and agreeing with God.

Miss Clara touched a nerve when she asked me one day, "Do you think less of an animal that is dependent on you for water and food? Do you criticize a dog or a cat or a goldfish for being dependent? No, you care for that animal. Its dependence on you gives you the opportunity to care for it and that dependence endears you to it. You don't hate it that it's hungry every day. You love it even more because you know without you they wouldn't make it. So why would you hold back from your heavenly Father? You are much more valuable than a parakeet or a gerbil. You're His prized creation. So bring Him everything and don't ever feel ashamed about depending on Him. That's what He wants. It's impossible to have faith in someone you don't depend on."

I remind myself of that every day when I get up. Don't hold back from God thinking He has too many plates spinning. I've lived this way so long it's like a groove in a record and I'm the needle. (I still remember record players and if you don't, that's okay.) Before my feet hit the floor in the morning and I start moving a hundred miles an hour, I pray, "Lord, I need You.

Help me to see how much I need You. And to receive the help You want to give me, however You want to give it."

It's easy to slip into the other mode, motoring through life in my own power or trying to be spiritually self-sufficient. I've often felt God especially loves those who help themselves, and if I could do it on my own He would be happier because that would mean one less thing for Him to worry about. See what I mean? God doesn't worry. He's God. I make Him out to be like me when I think my problems are a great big bother to Him.

I'm beginning to believe—actually I'm choosing to believe—that I'm not a bother to Him. He wants me to cast my cares on Him instead of trying to fix everything on my own.

And that's the other change I'm seeing. Life is not about getting fixed. It's not about reaching some plateau where I've "made it" and don't have to worry about anything. Miss Clara said that God's goal for me is to conform me to the image of His Son. I thought all along that being a Christian was about not sinning as much as I do. But Miss Clara said the closer you get to God, the more sin you see. His goal is to make us more like Jesus and the bumps and bruises are part of the plan to help get us there.

I don't understand all of that, of course. And I still don't see why life has to be so hard, especially when it comes to somebody I love like Isaiah.

I brought some of this struggle to work with me one day and began to process it with my coworkers. And let me tell you, you have to be prepared for the advice you'll get when you share the struggles of your heart.

CHAPTER 14

✦ ✦ ✦

Isaiah pedaled faster to get some of the adrenaline out of his system.
The scene at the coffee shop made him grit his teeth. He didn't
look at his phone, he just rode as fast as he could, and when he
slowed he found himself in an industrial part of town. Buildings
with warehouses attached and lots of loading docks and parked
cars.

He stopped near a business that had a blue-and-green stripe
across the front of the building. Dark blue letters said *MOORE
FITNESS*. Lots of windows. The building looked relatively new.

He rode across the street, parked his bike, and wiped the
sweat from his brow. He walked inside and saw the sign behind
the receptionist. *Moore Fitness*. On the walls were posters of athletes working out on treadmills and bikes and other equipment.

The nicely dressed woman at the front locked eyes with him
as he approached. She smiled and said, "Hi, can I help you?"

He looked at the counter and kept his voice low. "Uh, I'd like
to apply for a job."

"Okay. Well, is there a certain type of job you're looking for?"

"Nah, I just want to see what you got."

His response didn't faze her. She reached for a clipboard and grabbed a pen. "Okay. Here's an application if you'd like to fill it out."

Isaiah took it without a word and sat in a leather chair beneath the posters. He couldn't help thinking that he should be on a poster, or maybe could have been if he'd decided to go to college. He focused on the application.

Name. Address. Email. Phone. Social security number. So far so good on all that.

Are you a US citizen? Have you ever been convicted of a felony?

Then came the education part and he wrote down *Montclaire High School*. Underneath that was *College*. Did he have to go to college to work here? He wanted to ask the woman but decided to leave the space blank.

A Black man with salt-and-pepper hair walked in wearing a sport coat, checking his phone. Isaiah glanced at him, then went back to the application. Previous Employment. That was easy, he had none, except for raking leaves and mowing yards for neighbors. That was years ago. There was space for references. "Professional only." What did that mean? Military Service. His stomach churned.

"Hello there, young man," the man at the door said.

There was something about his voice Isaiah couldn't place. Did he sound like his grandfather? There was almost a musical quality to it.

Isaiah glanced at the man, looked him over, and went back to the application.

"How are you doing today?"

"I'm good," Isaiah said softly.

"Well, are you interested in fitness equipment?" the man said, inching closer.

Isaiah shrugged. "I don't know, man. Maybe."

"Well, I'd be happy to talk to you, if you'd like to—"

"Look man," Isaiah said, interrupting him. "I'm just trying to see about a job, right? That's why I'm filling this out. I ain't here to buy nothing. What, you a salesman for this company?"

"I'm the president," the man said.

Isaiah looked up at him and his heart met his stomach in the middle. He'd royally messed up. He could hear his coach yelling at him and all that locker-room angst welled. He looked at the application, useless now, and stood quickly and ripped it from the clipboard. He slammed the clipboard on the reception desk, tossed the application in the trash can, and headed for the door.

The president of the company was still standing there watching him. What was up with this guy? Isaiah walked past him, wanting to leave as fast as he could.

"Whoa, whoa, whoa, whoa, whoa," the man said, like Isaiah was some horse he was trying to turn in the corral.

Isaiah stopped at the door and turned. What was up with this guy? It was like he was trying to stare a hole in him.

"Where you going?" the man said.

Isaiah shrugged and almost whined. "Well, I ain't gonna get a job now."

Quietly and with a measure of what sounded like compassion the man said, "What's your name?"

Isaiah looked away and sighed.

The man reached out a hand. "Joshua Moore. Will you tell me your name?"

He gave up. "Isaiah." He held out a limp hand and the man shook it, but Isaiah couldn't make eye contact. He felt embarrassed in front of the president as well as the woman behind the counter, who was watching all of this.

"Good to meet you, Isaiah. You got lunch plans?"

"What?" Isaiah couldn't believe what he was hearing. What was up with this guy?

"I can buy you lunch. We could talk."

Isaiah glanced at the receptionist. She gave a knowing smile. What was it with these people?

"You being for real?"

"I am," Joshua said.

Joshua suggested Isaiah put his bike in the employee parking area, where it would be secure. Isaiah left it and Joshua drove him to the restaurant. On the way, Isaiah looked up the Game On store and clicked a tab that said *Employment*. There was a position open and he got excited. Maybe they gave discounts to their workers.

At the restaurant, Isaiah ordered a rib eye steak. It wasn't the most expensive thing on the menu, but it wasn't cheap. The server asked if Joshua wanted his "usual," and he said yes. They knew him by name here, so he had to be a regular.

When the server took their menus away, Joshua sat back. "So, tell me about yourself, Isaiah."

What to share? "I mean, I'm nineteen. I just need a job, you know?"

"You have family here?"

"Just me and my mom. She owns a hair salon off Heartwood."

Joshua nodded, processing the information. "College plans?"

Isaiah laughed. "Nah. That ain't me."

Joshua responded with an easy laugh. "Okay. Well, five years from now, where do you want to be?"

Isaiah stared at the table. He didn't know where he wanted to be tomorrow, let alone five years down the road. How could he answer that? He felt tightness inside, like he was taking a test without knowing it.

"Five years? I don't know. I'm just taking it a day at a time."

He thought it was a good answer. He was proud of it. Sounded like something his mother would say. But the look on Joshua's face, the smile that crinkled his eyes, made him think he'd made a mistake.

Joshua leaned forward and kept his voice low. "Well, Isaiah, if you're available to work, we can discuss options in my company. But I want to ask you a few questions first." He reached for something in his jacket pocket. "Now, if you want to take some time to think about your answers, we can get together and talk again when you're ready."

Joshua slid his business card across the table like he was a dealer and Isaiah was the player. Isaiah studied the design and the information included. Joshua spoke deliberately, as if he wanted Isaiah to chew on the questions like he would the steak from the kitchen.

"Here are my questions. In what ways do you want to grow in the next year? What kind of man do you want to be? And what do you want people to think when they see you coming?"

Before Isaiah could say anything, the food came and he was glad. There was something about those questions that made him feel pressure. All he was looking for was a place to punch in, do a little work, punch out, and get a paycheck every two weeks. This man was asking about his five-year plan and college and who knew what? Was he expecting him to make a five-year commitment to his company?

As he cut his rib eye, Isaiah made his decision. This would be the first and last meal he'd share with Joshua Moore.

CHAPTER 15

✦ ✦ ✦

Cynthia

Think like the person in the chair.

That's my personal philosophy of hair styling. If you're coming to a shop and paying good money to look beautiful, do you want to be peppered with questions like *How's your day going?* or *Got anything planned this weekend?* Instead, think like the person in the chair. What do I want to talk about? Do I even want to talk at all?

I keep notes on all my clients. Their husband's name, how many children they have, who's off to college, who's getting married. So when they sit down and I start working, it's a relationship, not an interview. I show interest in their life, what's important to them. That's why many return—they feel I'm part of their family. And sometimes we get into some deep conversations.

I also tell my coworkers that showing interest in people and remembering things about them makes them better tippers, but never base your attitude on what they tipped the last time. Treat everybody as if they tipped one hundred percent.

When Felicia sat in my chair and I began to work on her extensions, we got into a deep conversation fast. Felicia is a sweetheart. Always has a smile. Her husband was in the military, he's retired now, and we often joke about her coming to the salon to get a little time to herself.

"How's that Isaiah of yours doing?" she asked.

Tammy and Keisha didn't say anything, but they both chuckled. It was more of a burst of air from their mouths. I gave them a look. There were two customers in the drying stations so Tammy and Keisha were able to eavesdrop.

"He's fine," I said. "I'm having a little struggle with getting him in gear."

Tammy said, "It's not about the gear, it's about starting the engine."

Felicia chuckled. "Not ready to leave the nest yet?"

"I'm trying to focus on the positives and not the negatives," I said.

Keisha had a magazine open, her hair wrapped in foil. Offhandedly she said, "I think tough love is the hardest kind to give."

"I did give him some tough love," I said. "I gave him a month to get a job."

"A month?" Tammy said. "And what are you going to do when he comes back and says nobody's hiring and the job market is too tight?"

"I'll cross that bridge when I come to it."

Felicia asked what Isaiah was thinking about college and that sent us down a whole different trail of me not wanting to push him but also not wanting to see him waste his talents.

"Failure to launch," Keisha said. "I see it all day long."

Tammy stood tall and I could tell she was ready to preach.

"I'll tell you what I think . . . You either help at home to the degree you're adding value like a job, or you get a job that funds the value of your home to the degree it equals the work at home you would have done."

Keisha gave an affirming, "Yes ma'am."

"Girl, what?" I couldn't follow her rapid-fire words. "You lost me. You're going to have to say that again."

Tammy turned and stood like a prizefighter ready to throw a few verbal punches. "In other words, if he ain't helping at home, he needs to get a *j-o-b,* where the support of you becomes the outcome of his income."

"Come on, now!" Keisha said.

I was getting more confused the faster Tammy talked.

"Cynthia, you are the owner of your home," Keisha said, "and the parent in authority of your son. Honey, I agree, you need to draw a line in the sand."

Now I felt like I was on the defensive. I had laid down the law to Isaiah, but part of me felt like I'd come on too strong.

"Well, I'm just trying to figure out how to balance helping him know I understand him but still pushing him to become an adult. And that is not easy."

Tammy nodded. "You're on the right track, girl. He's got to step up and step out. 'Cause you can step in and speak up about him not steppin' up, but you don't wanna overstep the main step of loving him."

I gave Tammy a look. She might have been right but it was hard for me to unpack what she'd just put down.

"Yes, ma'am!" Keisha said. "That's exactly what I was thinking, girl."

I laughed. "Okay, you two must be on a higher level, but I'm gonna catch up."

Keisha craned her neck, seeing something out the front window. "Here he comes now!"

Isaiah walked through the door wearing shorts and a T-shirt. No backwards hat, which I thought was an improvement. Seeing him walk through that door with an air of confidence made me smile. And I was glad he hadn't walked in a few seconds earlier.

"Hey Isaiah," Tammy said.

He smiled broadly and sauntered in. He didn't come to the shop often, and that made me wonder if everything was all right.

"Isaiah, you walk here?" I said.

"It's just one mile from the house."

I smiled. Just one mile to a nineteen-year-old was nothing.

"But I need to use your car," he said. "I found a couple of places online that are hiring so . . ."

I wanted to be happy he was out looking for a job. Although I wondered how he would get to work if he needed the car to get there.

But there was something bigger that flashed in my mind. "Well, okay, but I need you back here by five. I'm picking up a case of products from Maxwell's at five fifteen, and they're staying open late for me. So you can't be late."

"I won't," Isaiah said quickly. Too quickly for me.

I grabbed my keys and handed them to him. I saw Tammy raise her eyebrows at me as Isaiah took the keys.

Maybe it was the pressure of the other women and what we'd just been talking about that caused me to stop him before he walked out the door. With as much gravitas as I could muster, I said, "Isaiah, five o'clock."

"I'll be here."

"I'm not playin' with you," I said to his back, wagging my finger.

"Yes, ma'am," he said as he walked out and waved.

My stomach churned as the door closed. Had I made a mistake handing over the keys? Or would this be a chance for him to show his responsibility?

Tammy gave a mischievous chuckle. "He sure favors his daddy."

"He do, he do," Keisha said. "Ain't he working as a truck driver now?"

"Girl, I don't know what Darren is doing," I said, trying to get the conversation on a different track. "I don't want to talk about no Darren."

Tammy gave another chuckle and I saw Isaiah pulling out of my parking space.

"Well, you were talking about your son getting his life in gear," Felicia said. "Seems like he's showing initiative about finding a job."

"He's a good kid," Keisha said. "He's going to be fine."

Her words calmed my heart a little, but for some reason I had a bad feeling about what had just happened.

CHAPTER 16

✦ ✦ ✦

Isaiah drove across town practicing his pitch to the Game On store manager. He felt this was a much better fit than working at a sports equipment plant. Hopefully the manager of the store wouldn't ask questions about his five-year plan.

He liked the freedom of driving and being in control. But the farther he drove, the more he wondered how he would get to work each day without his own car. He parked on the street near the store and got out, silencing his phone so he wouldn't be disturbed by a call. He could see the orange *Now Hiring* signs in the window.

This is it, he thought. *I can feel it.*

His phone buzzed and he answered. "Yo, Jamal."

"Sup, man. We're headed to the park. Come ball with us."

Isaiah reached for the door. It was locked. Another sign said, *Sorry, We're Closed.* He could hear his mother telling him he should have called to make sure they were open.

"Look, nah man. I'm looking for a job."

He peered through the window at the darkened store. They had the latest equipment and games on display. It looked like paradise inside. But paradise was closed for some reason.

"Dude, you can do that any time," Jamal said. "We need you for two-on-two."

"Nah man, I can't right now." He thought he saw movement inside the store, but realized it was the reflection of the street.

"Come on, Zay," Jamal said, pleading. "Just gimme an hour."

Isaiah thought a moment. Playing two-on-two would relieve a little stress. And there was nobody at the store. He could play, come back to get an application, and still make it to the salon before five, no sweat.

"Look, one hour, man," Isaiah said.

The competition was a lot more intense than Isaiah expected and he immediately got into his zone. Jamal, Andre, and Keenan were working up a sweat too, and he was again trying to cover Keenan with his height advantage.

At the end of the fourth game, Keenan hit a three-pointer and celebrated. "That's two up. Next game wins."

Isaiah was focused now. He wanted this next game. And he had a plan on how to overcome Keenan's moves. But something felt wrong. The sun had moved to the west. He was forgetting something.

"Let's run it back!" Jamal said. "Let's get it, Zay."

Isaiah, drenched in sweat, took the ball, then stood straight. "Yo, hold up, what time is it?"

"I don't know. I left my phone in my car," Keenan said.

Isaiah let the ball fall and ran to the bench. Next to his mother's keys he saw his phone. It read *5:23. Missed call from Mom.*

"Yo, I gotta go!" he yelled and sprinted for the parking lot.

"Zay, we got one more game, bro!" Jamal yelled.

Isaiah was in the car, backing up, then driving way too fast. His heart beat faster now than during the game. He could imagine his mother's face when he arrived. He could hear her voice and anticipate her words.

He could lie to her and tell her the interview went long. No, he couldn't do that. But he sure wasn't going to tell her he had been playing two-on-two. This was not going to be good.

Sure enough, his mother was standing outside the salon with her arms crossed, wearing her jean jacket, her hair up with a yellow wrap around it. She stared at him as he rushed to a stop in front of her and jumped out. If he could get the first words in he could defuse the situation.

"I'm sorry. I lost track of time."

His mother strode in front of the car. Nothing was going to defuse this situation.

She pointed at him. "I'm driving."

He got in the passenger side expecting her to drive away. She had some kind of appointment but wasn't going anywhere. The last thing he wanted to do was look at her, so he reached around and buckled his seatbelt.

"It's 5:39," she said evenly. Then her voice got tight and rose with intensity. "Maxwell's stayed open for thirty extra minutes, only to have me not show up. And now, now I gotta push back my appointment. And I have to hope, ooh boy, you'd better hope they give me the same discount tomorrow they were planning on giving me today."

Isaiah sat silent. He knew he deserved this and he was intent on taking it.

His mother raised her fists in the air. "I called them three times asking them for five extra minutes! Five extra minutes."

He couldn't take it. He interrupted her. "Ma, I said I was sorry."

"I let you use my car! You turned around and made me look irresponsible!"

Sweat trickling down his forehead, Isaiah pushed it away with the back of his hand. As soon as he did, he knew it was the wrong move. His mother studied him, her face contorted.

"Why are you so sweaty?"

He sighed and looked out the passenger window. She made a sound, half laugh, half anger—like she was so mad she wanted to throw him out the front windshield.

"Oh no, you didn't! No, you didn't! You lied to me? You told me you were going to look for a job."

"I was! They were closed. What am I supposed to do?"

"What are you supposed to—? You're supposed to keep lookin'! Not give up at the first sign of inconvenience. That's something right there your father would do."

It felt like sticking a knife in him and Isaiah shouted back, "I ain't him!"

"You actin' like him," she said, her eyes boring a hole in his soul.

That was it. He clicked the seatbelt and was out of the car in a flash.

"Boy!" his mother said behind him. Then her voice was silenced as he slammed the door and walked across the parking lot. He moved way to the right and didn't turn when his mother drove past him. He thought he'd see brake lights. He thought she might come back and tell him to get in the car.

She kept driving.

Fine, he thought. *Go ahead. I don't need the ride. And I don't need you comparing me with him.*

CHAPTER 17

✦ ✦ ✦

Cynthia

When Isaiah got out of the car, it was all I could do not to run after him. I clasped my hands in front of me and shook with anger. The anger was at him but also at me.

I knew when he borrowed the keys there was something off. I should have told him I needed the car and he could find another way to look for a job. Instead I rescued him and because I wanted to believe the best, I gave him the keys. So that was on me.

After he drove away, I was scatterbrained, looking at the clock, wondering if he'd remember. Wanting to call him or text **Don't forget, I need the car.** I held back, not wanting to nag. I wanted to trust my son to keep his word. But the closer the clock came to five o'clock, the more I worried.

I went to the office and closed the door and laid my head on the back of it. *Lord, please help him remember. Please bring him here on time. Let this just be my fear taking over. I want to believe You are at work. Get me out of Your way. Do something in Isaiah's*

heart. And if the worst happens, help me not fly off the handle. Help
me not yell or say unkind things. Help me be self-controlled.

When five o'clock came and there was no Isaiah, I was a wet
hornet inside. At five ten, I was a wet hornet on steroids. So I
prayed again and asked God to keep me calm and try to be thank-
ful and all kinds of spiritual things you read in the Bible. But I was
less Paul in Philippians and more Paul in Romans 7. The thing I
want to do, I don't and what I don't want to do, I do. And when
that red Chevrolet came zipping across the parking lot, you could
have fried an egg on my forehead.

It wasn't until Isaiah got out of the car and started walking
toward home that I realized how far short I had fallen. It was like
something came over me and I couldn't help it.

My hands were shaking when I clicked the seatbelt. I heard
the echo of my driver's ed teacher who always said, "Never drive
angry. If you're emotional about something, wait till you have
calmed down to take the car out of Park."

I thought about stopping and seeing if Isaiah would get in,
but I didn't. I just kept driving, my heart beating and my chin
puckering.

Seeing Isaiah walk through the parking lot reminded me of
when he was three and I had taken him to the pool. He wanted
to go in the pool without his floaties on and I tried to convince
him he had to wear them. But he saw the other kids in the water
without them and wanted to be like them, I guess. He threw
them on the ground and walked back into the men's locker room
and wouldn't come out.

That was how he was walking now. Head back, shoulders
straight, like he was a soldier off to war.

I wiped away the tears as I drove, then ugly-cried when I
pulled into the driveway. I had promised God and myself that
I would never compare Isaiah with Darren and what had I just

done? I was afraid I had killed that young man's spirit. But how was I supposed to get through to him? Everything I said was the truth, but it was spoken in anger, not love.

I stewed some more when I got inside and then I went in my room and started putting away laundry, feeling like I could at least get something done while I fell apart. I called Liz and told her what had happened. She commiserated with me and said she'd blown her stack at her daughter, Danielle, over a lot less.

"You have every right to be upset," Elizabeth said. "You drew a line and he crossed it. If this helps at all, his actions today have made things clear you can't allow him to drive your car."

"But how is he going to get a job if he doesn't have a car? And he can't pay rent unless he gets a job."

"He's in a no-win situation, but he's there because of his own choices. You have to remember that. But with all of us praying, there is a lot of hope for Isaiah."

"I don't know, Liz. I mean, seriously, there are moments when I feel like I'm just going to lose it."

"Like today," she said.

"Yeah, I mean, I love that boy with my whole heart, but I literally cannot be his mother and his father."

"But you're the only one now who can speak into his life."

"No, I get it. I do get it. Yeah, I'm just asking for you to pray for him. And for me."

"And that is the key. Miss Clara agrees with me on that."

"Yeah, I know. I know." I changed the subject. "Girl, when are you comin' to see me again? It's literally been over a month since you've been to the salon."

"Well, I might just have to come over there. Can I bring a friend?"

"Oh, you can bring whoever you want to bring because I need as much prayer as I can get."

"I'll see what day works. But don't you give up hope, you hear me?"

"Okay."

"Love you."

"I love you, too. I'll see you soon. Bye-bye."

I put the towels away and the rest of the clothes, then stared at the wall. Isaiah had to be feeling awful for letting me down. But I needed him to feel the weight of his choices, as Elizabeth said. I wanted to go into the kitchen and make dinner and pretend all of that hadn't happened. But I knew I couldn't. Rather, I knew that wasn't the best thing for him. He needed to sit with what had happened.

In the meantime, I made a sandwich and took it to my room and sat on the bed. How many fights had I had with Darren that went unresolved, with the two of us going to our own corners, then not saying a word about it. The walls built up until it felt impossible for me to climb over just to have a conversation.

I didn't want that to happen with Isaiah. But how was I going to move toward him with all the anger still flowing through me?

God, help me, I prayed. *And help him.*

CHAPTER 18

✦ ✦ ✦

Isaiah heard the muffled sounds of his mother doing something in her room. He couldn't shake the feelings—letting her down was the last thing he wanted to do, but he couldn't convince her of that now.

The way she looked at him reminded him of the night his father left. When she tossed the video equipment in the trash, she had that same scowl. He didn't mind that scowl aimed at his father, but when it was aimed at him, that was a different story.

He felt dirty inside. Ashamed. Why couldn't his mom understand that he had just made a mistake? He'd lost track of time. He hadn't abandoned her like his dad. But that's where she went.

It was Jamal's fault. If he hadn't called and made him play two-on-two . . . Nah, that wasn't right. He could have stuck to his guns and said no.

That's something right there your father would do.

He still couldn't believe she had said that. Comparing him with his dad was the lowest, given all the hurt both of them felt at what Dad had done. And then he wondered if more was going on in her heart than he could know.

In high school he'd had a teacher who explained a term he couldn't remember. She said people who are hurt in the past are often triggered by things in the present that remind them of past events. They can overreact because something current hits a nerve and makes them respond.

He looked at his closet. His gym bag was big enough to fit a lot of clothes if he moved out. But where would he go? It would show her he didn't have to take that kind of treatment if he left in the night.

He put a few shirts and some underwear inside. But even as he did, his heart softened. She was doing the best she could, just like he was. She didn't need more punishment.

He glanced at his nightstand. On top was the business card Joshua Moore had given him. He picked it up and remembered the questions Joshua had asked. It took him a few minutes to recall them, but he finally did.

In what ways do you want to grow in the next year? What kind of man do you want to be? And what do you want people to think when they see you coming?

He wanted to work at the video game store, but a position at Moore Fitness would mean he wouldn't have to borrow a car—he could ride his bike. The man seemed like a good guy who gave Isaiah a chance, even after he had insulted him in the lobby of his own company.

And there was something else about Joshua that Isaiah couldn't put a finger on. What was it?

He scrunched lower in his bed and soon his eyelids drooped. All the emotion of the day had exhausted him. He turned off the light on his nightstand and closed his eyes. He didn't know how long he dozed, but he awoke with a start and sat up.

He glanced at his clock. Middle of the night.

But it wasn't the time that had awakened him. His eyes were open because he was thinking about the business owner who had taken time to ask questions and listen. The man had asked questions and even bought him a rib eye. His own father had never done anything that kind.

Was it all just a ploy to get a new worker in his warehouse, or was something else going on?

CHAPTER 19

✦ ✦ ✦

Joshua Moore prided himself on being able to read a room and sense what was going on in the minds of his employees, his managers, and the people in the warehouse. He even anticipated the moves of his competitors. He'd often been wrong, of course, mostly about what his wife was thinking, but she was quick to tell him what was going on and remind him that all he had to do was ask.

The young man he'd met, Isaiah, was a mystery. Eyes are the windows of the soul, and if that was true, Isaiah's were frosted. Joshua couldn't see a thing through them. But every time Joshua thought of Isaiah, he wondered if there wasn't some pain in his life that kept him from answering the questions he'd posed. Why did such a bright-looking kid have seemingly no direction?

He was in a meeting with Emmett Jones, a Black employee who kept track of numbers and trends and all the things Joshua couldn't. Their sports equipment manufacturing business was highly competitive, just like the athletes they served, and Emmett stayed on top of stats about other companies, sales algorithms,

Fibonacci sequences, and all the secrets hidden behind, between, and beside the numbers on flow charts. He was a numbers man, a guru who anticipated where the company would be in a month, a year, or a decade if current trends continued.

Emmett met with him in one of the larger conference rooms at Moore Fitness, and before he said a word, Joshua could tell something was wrong. Emmett was the most cool, calm, collected person on staff. Always in control of his emotions and even-keeled. On the basketball court, when they played during lunch breaks, Emmett was the one you threw a pass to when you were in trouble under the basket. He could take a long three-pointer and hit nothing but net all while close to yawning.

Today, Emmett paced in front of the video display of his device, and there was a thin line of perspiration above his lip. Joshua took note of this as Emmett continued his latest report.

"Our top three distribution accounts are the same as last year, with GymFit still number one at 4.5 million a year. But with their president stepping down, that also makes them our main concern. Our five-year agreement with them is up next summer."

"Yeah," Joshua said. "Any word on their vote?"

"They haven't announced anything yet, but we're ready to connect as soon as they do."

Joshua read between the lines and looked at the pie chart. GymFit was the biggest slice on the display. "If we lose the GymFit account . . ."

Emmett pursed his lips. "We lose the GymFit account, I'd say we have about four months before you have to start making some difficult choices."

Joshua stared at Emmett. There it was. *Difficult choices.* Two words he hated to hear. He looked at the monitor again and instead of seeing stats and graphics, he saw the faces of his employees and their families. So many people depended on the success of this business. So many people would be affected by *difficult choices.*

Emmett squared his shoulders and Joshua sensed the tension in the man's voice.

"One more thing I need to bring up. Slayer Sports. They're developing a line of niche equipment that will directly compete with us. I don't know how soon they'll be ready, but we should keep an eye on them."

"I agree," Joshua said, almost growling as he responded. "Thank you, Emmett."

And just like that, Emmett's shoulders loosened and he seemed back to his cool, collected self. "No problem."

Someone knocked lightly on the door and Grace, the receptionist stepped in. "Mr. Moore, there's a young man, Isaiah Wright, here to see you."

Joshua smiled. "Yes, I'll be right out."

Joshua found Isaiah in the lobby, on his phone, his baseball cap backwards, one leg stretched forward. When Joshua walked in, Isaiah looked up.

"Isaiah, how are you?" He reached out a hand and Isaiah stood and gave a weak handshake.

"I'm good. I just wanted to talk to you for a minute. You know, I been thinkin' about your questions."

"Okay, I'd love to hear your thoughts."

Isaiah seemed nervous, at times looking Joshua in the eyes and at others looking down. This seemed like a hard conversation for him and Joshua stayed focused on Isaiah's face.

"Yeah," Isaiah said. "Uh, you know, as far as how I wanna grow this next year . . . I guess I wanna learn how to take on more responsibility and learn some new skills."

"That's good."

"And then you asked, uh, what kind of man I'd wanna be. And I wanna be a good man, you know, someone that could get the job done."

Joshua nodded, still focusing on Isaiah. The young man had paid attention at their lunch meeting and had processed the questions well. From years of experience talking with new recruits, he had learned the best thing to do in this situation was to not fill in the silence but listen.

"Also, you asked what I want people to think when they see me comin'. And, you know, I'd want them to see someone they respect. So . . . yeah. That's it."

Isaiah smiled, appearing relieved that his speech was over. Joshua returned the smile and with a gentle tone said, "Okay. So are you looking for full-time work or part-time?"

Isaiah turned and sighed, as if he hadn't prepared for the question. "Uh, start part time?"

"Okay." Joshua took a moment before his next question. "Would you be willing to meet with me twice a week for some mentoring, before your shift starts?"

"Mentoring? Like, for this job?"

"Well, yes. But also some life principles. Things that you could use no matter where you're working."

Isaiah thought a moment. "I mean, yeah. I guess."

"Well, let's go to the factory floor and I'll show you what we have available. I'll connect you with the manager and finish the interview process. Good?"

"Cool."

CHAPTER 20

✦ ✦ ✦

Isaiah hadn't expected Joshua Moore to personally show him around the factory floor. He followed him past the lobby and the first thing he noticed was a design along the hallway walls that looked like reminders or motivation for employees.

"Compassion, Service, Dedication, Hard Work, Honesty . . ." The words continued the length of the hall.

"So, what happens in here?" Isaiah said.

"I'll show you the packing and shipping division first."

"Division? How big is this place?"

Joshua gave him a look that said, *Let me show you instead of telling you.* He swiped his access card in front of the scanner and opened the door.

Isaiah's mouth dropped when he walked inside. It was like walking into a huge arena that spread in all directions. Workers in brightly colored vests moved near pallets on the factory floor. He could see conveyer belts in the distance and the sound of motors running overhead. Some employees sealed boxes and labeled them while others wheeled full pallets to a loading area.

"We make two hundred and five different products for the fitness arena. Weights, treadmills, jump ropes, almost everything in between. We store the pieces, and we supply all the parts to our distributors so they can go ahead and assemble and sell."

The vests made the workers look like they were on different teams. The floor had the aroma of fresh metal and plastic and cardboard.

"We also produce several products for the medical and mission field," Joshua said. "Each day we fill six to eight hundred orders."

"How many people work here?"

"In this area, twenty-four."

Joshua led him to a tall man in a blue vest. His hair was tied in the back. In fact, everyone on the floor had their hair either short or up in the back. The man was focused on a clipboard he held.

"Todd, how you doing?" Joshua said.

Todd shook hands with him and smiled. "Mr. Moore, I'm fine. How are you?"

"I'm good, thank you." Joshua put a hand on Isaiah's shoulder. "This is Isaiah. When you have the time, I want you to go ahead and bring him through the interview process for part-time work."

Todd nodded and shook Isaiah's hand. "Okay. Good to meet you, Isaiah."

"Sup?"

"I'll show him around, then bring him back to you."

"Yes, sir," Todd said.

Joshua continued the tour. "It's taken me twenty-one years to get here. It's been hard, but God's been good."

Isaiah was so focused on his new boss that he didn't see a cart moving toward him. He jumped out of the way, his sneakers squeaking like he was avoiding a defender on the court. He noticed some kind of mechanism at the bottom that controlled the cart.

Joshua laughed. "It's not going to run into you. The scanner will see you and stop the cart."

Isaiah smiled and took a closer look. "That's crazy, man. How many of these you got?"

"We've got ten floor robots, and seventy-five storage robots, all programmed by our engineers." He pointed to another section of the room. "Come on."

Up a flight of stairs, they reached the factory's upper level. Containers moved in different directions as if by magic.

"I ain't never seen nothin' like this," Isaiah said. "How they work?"

Joshua turned and called to a man named Cody who stood at a control screen. "How are they rollin'?"

Cody looked to be in his twenties, lasered on the screen. He wore glasses and a full beard and was a little on the plump side. He bounced when he walked toward them like a happy puppy with a new toy, cleaning his glasses as he said, "Well, none of them called in sick today, so I'm feeling pretty good."

"This is Isaiah. Give him a quick explanation of the system."

Cody reached to bump fists with Isaiah but it turned into an awkward handshake. He recovered and said, "Well, basically when an order comes in, one of the bots will pick it up and take it to its specific port. And then it'll go down to a conveyer belt and be placed in a box specifically designed for that product. And then it's labeled and stacked for shipping." Cody smiled as he watched the boxes moving in organized patterns, controlled by the bots. "They're like my best friends."

"You got all that?" Joshua said, chuckling.

✦ ✦ ✦

Something strange happened with each person Isaiah met at Moore Fitness. Whether it was on the factory floor or in personnel, it didn't feel like Joshua was dragging a part-time employee around, it felt like he valued Isaiah and was enjoying showing him the facility. But there was no way the guy had the time to do that with every employee. And he had done it without Isaiah making an appointment.

Was this guy for real? Or maybe it was a ploy to get Isaiah to commit to the company. Joshua would no doubt pass him off to some underling soon. But Joshua had talked about mentoring, whatever that was. Was he going to do that or would someone else?

The questions lingered as Joshua led him to the office of a woman named Janelle. Her office was nicely decorated and there was a lot of natural light and plants. Her desk and credenza looked expensive. She was typing at her laptop when they entered.

"Janelle, may I introduce you to someone?"

"Of course." She stood and walked around the desk. She smiled at Isaiah, and there seemed to be some recognition on her face. Had he seen her before?

"Hello there," she said warmly.

"This is Isaiah Wright. We're talking about him working part-time with us."

"Nice to meet you, Isaiah." She shook his hand.

"Good to meet you," Isaiah said, flashing his smile.

"Janelle oversees the human resources department. She has put up with me since the first day we opened and knows about just as much as I do around here."

"But I don't work as many hours as he does and he needs to push the pause button sometimes and come home with me."

Isaiah studied her—wondering what she meant by that. Before

he could ask, Joshua put his arm around Janelle and said, "We've also been married for thirty-five years."

Isaiah laughed. "Oh, gotcha."

"You should have seen your face," Joshua said.

Joshua excused himself and Janelle gave him an employee handbook. There were forms to fill out and sign and as he did, he felt a sense of confidence. And he couldn't wait to get home and tell his mom what had happened.

Seeing Joshua and Janelle laughing together and working at the same company left an ache inside, reminding Isaiah of what he didn't have. What he would never have, which was a mom and dad who were together. He tried to push that thought away but the pain lingered. Then he wondered if he would ever find someone who would want that kind of relationship with him. He wanted to ask Janelle how they'd found each other and how they knew the other was the "right" one. Is there only one "perfect match" for each person? Is that why people get divorced, they don't find their soul mate?

The last step in the process was meeting with the guy with the man bun, Todd. Janelle said he would go over the specific rules of conduct and safety on the factory floor, which were evidently a big deal. Todd's office was smaller and looked out on the factory floor. He went through the different colored vests, rules for moving around the floor, things to never do or always do.

"This is an alcohol and drug-free space, so any infraction of that rule could lead to termination," Todd said.

Isaiah wanted to say that with his mom, alcohol or drugs would lead to him living in somebody else's house. No way she would put up with that. But he held back.

Todd looked at the schedule on his desk. "And our only open part-time spot is Monday, Wednesday, and Friday from nine to five. That'll work?"

"Yeah."

"Your training starts on Monday. Please be on time. It takes everyone here to stay on track. Any questions?"

"No."

Todd held up a plastic card with a black fob attached to the back. "And this is your key card. Don't lose it." He put it on the desk in front of Isaiah. "And be on time. The worst four-letter word here is *l-a-t-e*."

Isaiah thought of his mother's face, how she looked at him when he was late returning her car. "I get it," he said.

CHAPTER 21

✦ ✦ ✦

Cynthia

I don't know about you, but I fight a constant trust battle. I can believe something so deep and so clear that I feel it in my bones, and the next minute I'm swirling with doubt and fear and thinking of all the bad things that can happen. Maybe that's because a lot of bad things *have* happened and I don't want to go through that again. So for me, the biggest daily trust test is with Isaiah not becoming his father.

I was making dinner, and I was at the point where the mushrooms were at just the right temperature but I had to keep stirring. I had no idea where Isaiah was or what he was up to or if he was coming home for dinner. I sure wasn't going to call him or text him and be the hovering mother. But I still wanted to know when he was getting home. This is the tension I live with every day, wondering whether Isaiah is going to move toward becoming a mature man or if he'll flounder.

For so long, when I would see Darren walking in that back

door or I would come home and see him on the couch, my stomach knotted. Just the sight of him caused a negative physical reaction. I didn't want to feel it, but it was there, like a light on the dashboard telling me something was wrong.

Now, I wondered if I might react to Isaiah that way. We hadn't really talked about the things I said in the car. And I did get the discount at Maxwell's, by the way, but I could tell they weren't real happy with me.

That reminded me of Darren. I would apologize and make excuses for things he had done—or failed to do. And then he and I would argue about it and he would retreat or just leave. Things got so heated we just didn't talk about any of it. The effect of all of that, over time, was that we avoided each other. He'd see me coming and he'd move out of the way and so would I. And a marriage that gets to that point is in trouble. I can see that now.

What about a mother who feels that way about her son? And what if her son feels the same about her?

My mind went down one trail after another. Was he out playing ball all day? Would he come home sweaty? Had he gone to Jamal's house to game? The negative thoughts made me think my enemy was working overtime.

As I tossed the salad, I tried to give that to God.

"Lord, I can either trust You or not. I can either put him on the altar or not. So I give him again to You. When he walks in, let him see love on my face instead of anger and bitterness. Let love leak from my heart to my face. You have given me grace and mercy and I've wrung it out like a dishrag. I need Your help. You're going to have to squeeze the love out of me because I'm struggling. I don't know where he is and I'm worried about so many things. I want to give them all to—"

The door opened and Isaiah walked in wearing his jeans and a nice T-shirt. He wasn't all sweaty, so he hadn't been playing ball.

"Hey," I said.

"Hey."

A deep breath. Stay calm. Watch your tone, Cynthia.

"What'd you do today?"

"Not much," Isaiah said, smiling. "I stopped by Moore Fitness."

I glanced up at him and wondered why he'd been there. They sold expensive workout gear. Was he going to ask for money to buy something?

"Moore Fitness?" *Watch your tone,* I thought. "Why?"

His smile unnerved me. Like the Cheshire cat in *Alice's Adventures in Wonderland.*

"They were hiring some guy," he said.

My heart fluttered. I didn't want to get my hopes up.

"Who?" I said.

Isaiah beamed and pointed both index fingers up at his face and said, "This guy."

I turned my head and clenched my hands like he had just won a national championship. Right then I understood what "my cup runneth over" meant.

"My goodness, Isaiah! You got a job at Moore Fitness?"

He laughed, like he was planning to tell me this as a surprise just so I'd hop around the kitchen doing a happy dance. I hugged him and he hugged me back and it felt like all the anger at him being late, and all the fears I had, just washed away. Tears welled up in my eyes and I held on to him.

When I pulled back, I couldn't hold in the excitement. "Oh, I am so proud of you. When do you start?"

"Nine a.m. Monday."

He sounded so confident. And his face looked different—like

he had turned some corner in life and things were about to change.

"That's what I'm talking about—you have made my day!"

Then a thought flashed through my mind as I made the connection between the business and the owner. "Do you know that he helped your uncle Tony for several years?

"Uncle T, Uncle Tony?"

"Mm-hmm, he discipled him, helped him with his work and stuff."

Isaiah got that little crinkle between his eyes that he gets when he doesn't understand something. "Discipled him? What does that mean?"

I should have kept my mouth shut. Revealing too much about how Tony had grown spiritually through Joshua Moore's help would put Isaiah off. But I was in it now and I had to answer the question. So I did a little mental two-step and launched in.

"You know, it's when one person . . ." I waved my hands around like that would help him. How do you explain such a thing? "It's kind of . . ." I stopped and looked up at him. "You need to come to church with me."

A big sigh and a roll of the eyes. "Mom, we already talked about this. Church, that's your thing."

"Isaiah, God wants you to know Him."

"And I ain't hiding from Him. I'm right here. And He can find me if He wants to. But I ain't gotta go to a church building for Him to see me."

I felt like I'd overstepped. I was just so excited to hear that Isaiah had not only found a job, but at a place where I knew there was a strong believer who owned the company. I had jumped ahead because of that excitement, so I took another breath and collected myself.

"Okay. Well, are you going to see Mr. Moore regularly on your job?"

"Yeah, he wants to meet twice a week before my shift for . . . uh . . . mentoring or something like that."

Now my heart was on a roll. I wanted to call Elizabeth and Miss Clara. I could have run to both of their houses in my flip-flops I was flying so high inside. But I kept a lid on my excitement this time and kept stirring those mushrooms.

"Oh, okay. Dinner will be ready in ten minutes."

Isaiah walked to his room. When he was out of sight, I put the lid on the pot of rice and clasped my hands and looked toward heaven. "Okay, Lord. I see You working. Draw him to You, Jesus. Just draw him to You."

That was the best tasting dinner I've ever eaten because it felt like we were eating the bread of angels. And before my head hit the pillow I prayed a prayer of thanksgiving and then gave Him one more request.

"Lord, I don't want to get in the way of what You're doing. Help me trust You. Help me believe in Your power."

I don't remember falling asleep. There was such a sense of peace in my heart that I just drifted off with hope like a cloud underneath me.

CHAPTER 22

✦ ✦ ✦

Isaiah's alarm went off and he jumped out of bed and into the shower. He dressed for work and grabbed a piece of toast as he hurried through the kitchen.

"Don't you want some eggs and hash browns?" his mother said.

"No time, Mom. Thanks."

He finished the toast as he got on his bike. He glanced at the garage and wondered what it would be like to have a working car.

He was to the end of the street when he remembered his key card. He raced home, found it in his room, and headed back out. He parked the bike behind the Moore Fitness building and swiped his card.

Joshua Moore was in the conference room waiting with two plates in front of him. "Brought you some breakfast. Hope you're hungry."

"Didn't know breakfast was part of the deal."

Joshua smiled as Isaiah settled in and put some butter on his biscuit. Hash browns, sausage, eggs, and a bottle of orange juice. If this was mentoring, he could get used to it.

"My mom said you know my Uncle Tony," Isaiah said.

"Tony Jordan is your uncle?"

"Yeah, man. She said you helped him a lot."

Joshua got a far-off look, like he was reliving something. "Tony's a good man. I'm glad to know about your connection with him."

"Yeah, I was asking her about the mentoring thing. Do you do this with all your employees?"

"Only the special ones," Joshua said, smiling.

"So about how many?"

"Isaiah, everybody is special. We all have unique abilities and skills, hopes and dreams."

"So the mentoring . . . What is that exactly?"

"I like to spend time sharing my vision for the company and helping employees—you—understand more of why we're here and what our purpose is."

"The purpose is to make money, isn't it? I mean, you gotta make a profit to stay in business."

Joshua pointed at him. "You got that right. You don't make a profit, the company goes under, and all the workers who depend on the company are looking for a new job." He took his last bite of eggs and pushed the plate away. "But it's not enough to make a profit. This is not just a business to me. It's a calling."

"What do you mean? What's a calling?"

"It's something in your life that goes deeper than just making enough money to pay the bills. When I come to work, I have a sense of purpose. That I was made to run this company and make the products we sell so that others benefit and get health- ier. What we make enhances other people's lives. So the calling on me is to make this company as successful as I can, not just to make money, but to make a difference in the world."

Isaiah tried to wrap his mind around what Joshua was saying.

He just needed to pay rent to his mother and have some spending money and this man was talking about purpose and calling.

"That takes me to how I want you to see Moore Fitness. Part-time, full-time, we're all part of the team. And of course, I want each employee to remember that they don't just represent themselves. They represent this company, our products, and me."

Isaiah finished his orange juice and screwed the cap on. The chairs around the table were leather high-backs.

I could do some serious gaming in these.

Joshua faced Isaiah. "I want you to think about something. Let's say you own a sports network. You hire on-air talent but they wanna go in a different direction than you wanna go. They have their own idea as to what will work on-air. If they dishonored what you told them to do, as paid employees, what would you do?"

Isaiah didn't have to think long. "And they did this on the air?"

"Yeah."

"Then they're off the air."

"You'd fire them?"

Isaiah scoffed. "They're gone."

Joshua leaned back and took in the answer. "So you'd want them to honor your authority, right?"

"It's my network."

Joshua became animated, leaning forward and moving his hands. "Then you already understand what I want for each employee here. I'm responsible for this company. And I want those under my leadership to help me do well. The same way they will want others under their leadership to help them do well in the future."

Isaiah felt like he was at a personal TED Talk. And there was a feeling that Joshua wasn't all talk. He didn't just say he valued each employee, he was doing that in real time here in the conference room. As the man talked, Isaiah remembered that Joshua knew every person on the factory floor by name. Did every employer do that?

Joshua sat back. "So, treat others the way you want to be treated. Even if you don't like them, give those in authority the same respect that you want them to give to you. Got it?"

Isaiah couldn't help thinking of his high school coach right then. "Yeah. I got it."

Isaiah followed Todd to the main factory floor where boxes were being taped by crew members. Blue bins were lined up waiting to be filled and moved to the shipping area.

"All right, this is where the magic happens," Todd said. He pointed to a woman with blond hair and blue eyes wearing a red vest. She looked about thirty, and when Isaiah approached she turned and smiled.

"Wanda has to make sure each box is properly sealed for delivery. Then, Diego and Carlos, they add a label and stack each box for shipping. But each of them knows how to work every station, so they can rotate if need be."

One of the men fist-bumped Isaiah and said something in Spanish he didn't understand. Probably, "How's it going," or something like that. They returned to labeling and stacking boxes.

"So we're going to start you in this section for now. I want you to watch these guys and try it out for experience. Then, once you get the hang of it, we'll move you to the next section."

Another worker approached in a gray vest. He looked like a football player with an athletic build. He was taller than Isaiah and strutted like a rooster.

"Hey, if you want him to learn quick, let me train him."

Todd turned. "Wyatt, I got it. And you're on storage prep anyway."

Wyatt stepped back, his arms open. "I'm just sayin'. I own the record for this section." He raised his voice and it echoed through the factory. "948 in one day! Boom!" He laughed as he strutted away.

Isaiah noticed the reaction of Wanda and the others. They smirked or scowled and it seemed like there was some history with Wyatt.

Todd turned to Isaiah. "We had a large order come in last year and he led the team to finish with 948 boxes. It was impressive, but he reminds us every day."

Isaiah gave him a knowing smile.

"Come on, let's get you started."

Isaiah got his vest and returned to the station where Wanda showed him what to do. The *clack-clack-clack* of peeled tape was everywhere and Isaiah settled in. He wondered if workers could wear earphones to listen to music, but he didn't ask. He figured the answer would be *no* because there was a lot of communication that happened between them on the factory floor. Probably a safety issue, too. If something went wrong, you had to be able to hear a warning.

Two hours later, Isaiah felt the tightness in his shoulders. There was a lot of standing and moving around to the job and he was glad he had good shoes with strong support. But he had to really focus on what he was doing to keep up with the others. And when the fatigue came, he thought of how nice it would feel to get home, relax in his room in his gaming chair, and veg out.

Part 3

ANOTHER LAYER
OF SURRENDER

CHAPTER 23

✦ ✦ ✦

Cynthia

That Monday morning I was so excited. I couldn't wait to get home and talk with Isaiah about his first day at Moore Fitness. I wanted to tell Tammy and Keisha the good news before we opened because I knew they would whoop and holler and celebrate. I imagined Keisha doing a little dance and Tammy saying, "Now he's going to be bringing home the bacon, and his income is going to be part of his outcome," or something like that.

But I didn't tell them. I guess I was afraid things might not work out. Maybe Isaiah would work for a day and then wind up at the house saying his boss was mean or the work didn't "fit him." Fear will keep you quiet, even when you have good news to share.

When I got home that evening, I had big plans. I was going to make a nice dinner for the two of us. Go all out with pasta and salad. I had bought a frozen tiramisu I needed to thaw. But I walked into the kitchen and saw dishes in the sink. He'd already eaten.

His door was closed and I listened and it sounded like he was playing a game. He probably needed a little downtime, so I didn't knock, even though I was bursting from curiosity.

An hour later, as I was finishing my reheated casserole from the night before, he came out and stood at the sink and started cleaning his dishes. I thought that was a good sign.

"How'd your first day go?" I said.

"It was good."

"That's it? Just good?"

"To be honest it was a little overwhelming. There's a lot to learn."

"I'm sure you'll get the hang of it. You catch on quick." I tossed in a little encouragement to let him know I was behind him.

"Yeah," he said.

"What did Joshua have to say?"

"He just went over his goals for employees. Stuff like that."

"Mm-hmm."

"Bought me breakfast. I'm glad I didn't eat much before I got there."

"That was nice of him. So you're going to meet with him—"

"Look, Mom," Isaiah said, turning off the faucet. "I just want to veg out. I've been thinking all day. I need a little downtime, you know?"

"Sure, I get it."

I tried not to show how disappointed I was that I wasn't hearing more. Then I pulled out the secret tiramisu weapon and put it on the counter, thinking I might coax some words from him with a little dessert.

"I'll have some later. Jamal and the guys are starting a new game. Gotta get back."

"Okay. Well, have a good time."

I tried to sound like I meant it. As I did my own dishes,

I realized my expectations were high. I wanted Isaiah to sit down and open up about everything and show me how excited he was about being employed and even tell me he wanted to work full-time instead of part-time.

I knew from Tony's experience that Joshua was a strong believer, and I also thought Isaiah might say something about that and what had happened in their mentoring meeting. Did Joshua talk about spiritual things? That's what I'd been praying for, that Isaiah would have a change of heart about God and coming to church with me.

I opened my Bible and looked at the notes I'd taken the Sunday before. Sitting there I had thought, *Lord, my son needs to hear this.*

Our pastor had been talking about Psalm 23 and focusing on God as our Shepherd. "God's goal for you is not to make you feel better and make things easy in your life. His goal is maturity." And he used Moses as an example. Moses was asked to trust in God's power working through him rather than trusting in his own power to do what God asked of him.

I don't know if you've ever experienced this, but it dawned on me while I was reading my notes that I listened to the message thinking it was for Isaiah, when the whole time I should have been listening for me!

There was a section in the sermon where our pastor talked about going through the valley. "Some of you are going through a valley of conflict right now," the pastor said. "And I want to gently say that conflict is not necessarily a bad thing. It feels bad and you want it gone, but God works in the discomfort of your life. He uses the valleys, the losses, the pain, and the struggle to do things inside of us."

I stared at the words I'd scribbled two days earlier and something stirred inside. What if Isaiah was a gift to show me how far from trusting God I am? What if Isaiah is pointing out how much I am controlled by my fear and how I try to make things work out in my own strength? I was looking at another layer of surrender to my life. I had laid Isaiah on the altar, but I hadn't put myself fully there. Or, if I did, I had crawled off.

What are You teaching me here, Lord? I've made this all about Isaiah and I think You're showing me something about me. And I don't like it. So I need You to shepherd me through all of this.

I went back to Psalm 23. It's something how a different life situation can cause you to look at the same verses you've read—and even memorized—in a totally different way. I had been through so many raging rapids with Darren that I craved the still waters. Were those available to me in the middle of my doubt and confusion now?

I went to sleep with those verses running like a stream through my soul. And when I woke up I felt like God had done something, that my contentment didn't rest with Isaiah's employment status. And I didn't have to hear every little tidbit about his day in order to make me feel better.

When I left, Isaiah was still asleep. He had the day off. I was going to trust God today with all my heart. And when I got to work I felt the Shepherd near me. And when Tammy and Keisha asked about Isaiah, I didn't tell them about his new job, but I did say that the Lord was doing something good in my own heart to make me trust more.

"Mmm-mm," Tammy said. "That kind of trust sounds like a full-time job."

She was right. Trust is a full-time job in a part-time world.

And then I drove home.

Why does it seem like you have to go through the same things several times in order to learn and grow? I am beginning to understand why David wrote that Psalm. He knew sheep. He knew how slow they are to trust. I am a sheep from head to hoof.

I didn't see Isaiah at dinner. I was getting ready for bed when I couldn't stand it anymore and pecked on his door and opened it. There he was with his headset on and snuggled down into his favorite beanbag chair. The sound effects of gunfire leaked into the room and I noticed his dinner plate on the TV stand.

"Isaiah, you've been on that game all day."

He didn't even turn his head. "It's my day off."

"Don't you have work tomorrow?"

He sat forward all of a sudden with his controller, trying to shoot something or catch somebody, focused in like a laser. Some of the old feelings crept in from Darren and it was all I could do not to grab his dirty clothes strewn about the room and throw them at the TV.

"Yeah, I got it," he said.

"Well, it's after midnight." I said it in kind of a whine, though I didn't mean to.

"Mom, I got it."

I closed his door, turned off the hall light, and felt totally defeated. I told myself that tomorrow was another day. Another chance to trust the Shepherd. But I have to admit, I was not a restful sheep that night.

When I woke up the next morning, I forced myself not to check on him. His door was closed when I left for work. I heard no movement inside. And I thought about the pastor's words about conflict doing its work in a person's heart.

Now, maybe you would have done something different in that situation and I wouldn't criticize you for it. Maybe you think I ought to have banged on his door before I left. Or even slammed the back door or called his phone as I was driving to tell him I loved him or something like that. But I didn't. And it's because sometimes you have to let someone you love experience the pain of their own choices, even if those choices are ones that bring you pain.

I'm not saying it was easy. It wasn't. It was so hard. I wanted to protect him and wake him up and rescue him. But that morning, I began to put feet to my faith that God was at work.

CHAPTER 24

✦ ✦ ✦

In the wee hours of Wednesday morning, Isaiah awoke with a start, snorting himself awake. He had fallen asleep in his beanbag chair with his headset crooked—one ear pad on his ear and the other over his nose. He pulled the headset off and sat up, rubbing his eyes and trying to remember what had happened in the game. Had he said goodbye to the guys?

He turned off the monitor and stood halfway, his back aching from the position he'd been in for hours. The clock said 3:16 a.m., so he could still get a few hours of sleep. He fell into bed headfirst on top of his covers.

The next thing his brain registered was a far-off noise that seemed in some other world or maybe a video game. It was an annoying buzz that wouldn't stop.

Maybe if I stay in this position, it'll go away, he thought.

When it didn't, he rolled over in bed and sat up. He was now fully under his covers, wrapped like a mummy. He blinked, trying to see the origin of the buzz, but noticed something strange. The room was filled with light.

Groggy, he leaned over to his nightstand to look at his phone. The screen said Moore Fitness but all he could focus on was the time.

9:12.

It's Wednesday.

Isaiah threw off the covers and flew out of bed without answering the call. He grabbed a shirt and pants from his closet. His heart racing, he dressed, grabbed his phone and ran to his bike. If he had a car, he wouldn't be in this spot. He'd be late, but not too late.

He couldn't believe his mom hadn't woken him up before she left. He was sure he had set his alarm the night before. What had happened?

He pedaled as fast as he could, cutting through parking lots and taking every shortcut. He ran through a stop sign at the end of a street and a car honked at him. He didn't slow.

He pulled up to the back of Moore Fitness and leaned his bike against the railing and ran to the back door. Out of breath, he reached in his pocket for his key card. His heart sank. Had he forgotten it? He reached deeper into all his pockets. No card.

Panicking, frustration at a boiling point, he put his hands on his head and walked away, trying to think. He didn't want to go to the front and walk through the lobby. He turned and saw a sign that said, *All Activities Monitored by Video Camera.*

Somebody had to see him moving out there. He knocked on the door, checking his pockets again for the missing card. He knocked repeatedly until the door opened and a coworker was there—what was his name? Carlos? No, Diego.

"Thank you," Isaiah said, running past him.

The factory floor buzzed with activity. He didn't have his vest. You weren't supposed to be on the floor without a safety vest, that was a rule. But what was he supposed to do? He slowed to a walk, not wanting to call attention to himself, but walked as quickly as possible. Sweat poured down his face and he saw Todd and ran to him. Todd was at Isaiah's station, stacking boxes.

"Hey, sorry, man. I can take over." He bent down to lift some boxes.

"You got an emergency?" Todd said.

What to say? Tell him his mother didn't wake him up? Make up a good-sounding excuse? No, just tell the truth.

"Nah, man. It's my bad."

"Where's your work vest?"

"Uh, yeah, I gotta go get that."

"Have you even clocked in yet?"

"Not yet."

"You serious?" Todd said. He moved closer and lowered his voice. "Isaiah, you're forty-five minutes late and it's your third day."

Isaiah took off to clock in, his shoes squeaking.

"I can't do my job when I'm covering for you," Todd called after him.

Isaiah clocked in and retrieved his vest and tried to make up for lost time, but he was kicking himself the whole morning. He felt like at any moment Joshua would walk onto the floor, tap him on the shoulder, and show him the door.

When their lunch break came, he bought a protein bar from the vending machine and grabbed a free bottle of water. The company made it available and Isaiah wasn't sure why, but he was glad to have it.

At the other end of the lunch table two guys were arguing about something. Others joined the fray. He picked up on the age-old comparison of two NBA greats, Michael Jordan and LeBron James.

"That doesn't matter!" Wyatt said, his face red and the veins in his neck bulging. "LeBron has a championship with every team he's played for."

"Okay, how is that impressive?" another man said. Isaiah saw his ID tag said *Curtis*. "Okay, Jordan made it to the Finals six times. How many times did he win? Six times!"

Several others joined Curtis in the "six times" chorus.

Wyatt was more animated, smacking the table as he said, "But only with the Bulls. Okay? LeBron won with Miami, Cleveland, Los Angeles . . ."

"Why does that even matter?" Curtis said. "Okay, Michael Jeffrey Jordan elevated the whole basketball game. And he impacted an entire generation!"

"LeBron was *the* best player on every team he played for," Wyatt said, standing. "He was a record holder, like me." Wyatt pointed to himself and yelled, "948!" He took a bow in front of the group.

"Okay, good for LeBron, but he ain't Jordan," Curtis countered. "And neither are you."

Wyatt was at the door and imitated Curtis's final words. As he exited, Curtis said, "Hey, you've got too much dip on your chip, Wyatt."

Isaiah liked the free flow of arguing and he finally felt some of the stress of being late leave him. Just as their break was ending, someone put a hand on his shoulder and he glanced up to see a well-dressed woman he hadn't met.

"Isaiah, Mr. Moore would like to see you in the conference room."

The room got quiet as Isaiah stood. He noticed a fire extinguisher on the wall. Was there a way to extinguish the fire he'd lit by being late?

In the hallway, he paused and thought about taking off his vest and turning left and sprinting toward the back door. He could jump on his bike and let the wind take care of his troubles. Avoid facing the reprimand, the stern words, the disappointment, and whatever else Mr. Moore had in store.

He hated that prospect the most. His mother had given him that disappointing look that took his guilt and put it under a magnifying glass so that he felt it all the way to his toes. When he was late with the car, he already felt ashamed for what he'd done, like a little kid who wanted a cookie from the jar on the table, and his mother had walked in just as the jar tipped and fell and shattered on the floor. He hated that feeling. He hated that look. It didn't just say, *You messed up, Isaiah.* It said, *You are a mess-up.* And as he walked the long hallway, that was what he prepared to receive.

And then he thought of his mother and what she would look like if he ran away from his first job.

He didn't want to face Joshua Moore, though. Leaving would mean he'd avoid the pain and whatever his boss had prepared for him.

Then Isaiah thought of his father. Leaving was something *he* would do. Hit the door and not look back. No, Isaiah couldn't do that. He'd promised he would *not* turn into his father.

Gotta man up, he thought. *Take the pain. At least see what Joshua says.*

If his boss canned him, kicked him out the back door, he could tell his mother it didn't work out. And then he'd restart the job search, maybe try Game On again. He took a deep breath and headed toward the conference room.

CHAPTER 25

✦ ✦ ✦

Joshua Moore stood in the conference room with Emmett Jones, listening to a report he didn't want to hear. Emmett held his iPad in front of him like it held all the secrets to life. And the secrets Emmett shared were bad news for Moore Fitness. Was there any good news on that little screen?

The news was about Slayer Sports. They were selling equipment similar to Moore Fitness, but less expensive. Joshua had inspected a few of the products and couldn't see how they were selling at such a discount, unless they were simply trying to put others out of business.

"This is way more aggressive than we expected," Emmett said. "I mean, it is a smaller account, it's forty thousand a year, so it won't hurt us much. But we need to shore up our larger accounts."

"Yeah," Joshua said. "I had never even heard of Slayer Sports six months ago."

"They've got backing, and they're hungry," Emmett said.

Joshua noticed Isaiah in the hall and waved him inside.

Emmett concluded his report. "But we don't want them taking any more from us. I'll keep you updated."

Emmett left as Isaiah walked in and Joshua could see it in the young man's face. Like a scared rabbit. He put his hands on the backs of two chairs and leaned forward.

"I had breakfast for you this morning. What happened?"

Isaiah paused, as if trying to come up with an answer that would satisfy. Finally he said, "I, uh . . . overslept. I forgot to set my alarm."

Joshua nodded. "Okay. Well, you have a lukewarm breakfast burrito, orange juice, and cold hash browns if you want."

"Nah, nah, I'm good," Isaiah said quickly.

Joshua figured if the kid overslept he probably had jumped out of bed without eating. And then he rode his bike to work.

Isaiah glanced at the plate and said, "Actually, yeah, I'm starvin'." He pulled back the chair and sat, unwrapping the burrito.

Joshua gathered himself and measured his tone and his words. Not too harsh, but firm. He needed Isaiah to hear what was in his heart.

"Some thoughts for today. When you miss your commitments, it's hard not to see it as disrespectful. When you're forty-five minutes late for work, it forces people to have to cover for you. Now, if you have a good reason, they'll be fine. If not, they'll feel disrespected."

Joshua locked eyes with Isaiah and watched him eat the burrito, recalling a day in his own teen years when he had overslept. His manager had yelled at him, berated him like a coach throwing chairs across a basketball court. Joshua had promised himself that if he ever ran his own company, he would treat people differently. That was the power of influence. You could learn something valuable even from someone you didn't want to emulate.

"You don't need people wondering if you can do your job. You need them believing that you can do your job and respecting you for doing it well."

Joshua paused and let his words sink in. He walked to the edge of the table, closer to Isaiah. "So let me be blunt. A big part of becoming a man is showing up. Can you do that, Isaiah?"

Isaiah looked like he was taking this correction in and thinking hard about it. Finally he said, "Yes, sir."

"So I suggest that you plan ahead. Get the rest you need, set your alarm, and give yourself time to get here. That shows respect for others. And whenever you're supposed to be here, *show up.*"

He said those last two words forcefully, dramatically, hoping they would stick. And he sensed Isaiah had received the words well. He drank them in like a cold bottle of orange juice. Joshua thought it was almost as if he had been waiting for someone to say those words, to call him out, to coax him toward something better. Joshua didn't want to berate or scold, but teach and encourage and model.

Isaiah had probably received plenty of harsh words. What he needed was someone to communicate they believed he could rise up and meet the challenge he was being offered.

The rest was up to him. The ball was in his court.

CHAPTER 26

✦ ✦ ✦

Cynthia

Wednesday night I could tell that something was bothering Isaiah. I tried a few questions about work, but every time I did he clammed up, so I had to let it go and say another little prayer of surrender. I was doing that a lot these days.

That night I called Elizabeth and let her know about Isaiah's new job and where it was and the connection we both now had with Joshua Moore.

"I was just getting ready to call you and ask if tomorrow would be a good day to drop in?"

"Girl, you have an open invitation—you don't even have to call and make an appointment. We don't have anyone on the schedule for the first hour after we open, so tomorrow is perfect."

The next morning I couldn't hold back with Tammy and Keisha, so I gave them the good news about Isaiah's job and I was right, they did whoop and holler. Then things settled a little and I told them about my fears, trying to head the negative off at the pass, if you know what I mean. Tammy was not usually the most encouraging person. She was often the prophet of the half-empty glass. But to my surprise, Tammy stuck up for my son.

"Cynthia, once Isaiah sees the value of work, he's going to be like a rocket taking off," Tammy said. "You watch. And I don't just mean he's going to work to get a paycheck. I think he's going to throw himself into that factory and be one of their best employees."

"Unless he takes after his daddy," Keisha said. She saw the look in my eyes and added, "No offense, Cynthia."

Keisha had nailed my recurring worry. I told them how anxious I was that something bad might happen at work and he'd quit and hop from one place to the next. Or just give up and stay home.

"Girl, that boy has seen his father's example and he's seen your example," Tammy said. "Which one do you think he's caught more of, you or Darren?"

I hoped the answer was me, but I wasn't sure.

"So he just started working there?" Tammy said.

"Yes! And he didn't even want to tell me what happened yesterday. But you know what? I could tell by the look on his face that somethin' was wrong."

"See, when it's your child, you can tell it on their face," Keisha said.

"All I'm sayin' is, Darren was way too flippant with his jobs, and he kept losing them. So I'm gonna tell you what I'm not gonna do is sit back and watch Isaiah do the same thing. It's not happenin'. He's already dealing with so much anger in his heart toward his father, so seriously, I just need some prayer support."

"Well, that's why you called your sister," Tammy said.

"Yeah, that's exactly why. And she's going to be here any minute."

Right about that time the door opened and I caught a glimpse of my beautiful niece, Danielle. It seems like every time I see her, she grows a little taller.

"Hey, Aunt Cynthia!"

"Danielle, oh my goodness, I did not know that you were coming. What a surprise. I thought you were in college. Girl, how are you doin'?"

"I'm good. I'm just on break. Mom's parking the car."

Tammy and Keisha doted on Danielle and the bell above the door dinged. I turned to look in the mirror of my gorgeous sister, who was wearing a white blouse and a pretty pair of pants. I hugged her tightly, my heart nearly bursting from gratitude that she'd come all that way to see me. There's something about seeing the person you grew up next to, all the conflict and bickering we'd been through, walk through a door because she knew I just needed to see her. It's a feeling I can't describe.

After we got through our hug-fest, I told her to have a seat and went to get her a cup of coffee. Keisha commented on Elizabeth's pants, saying she would never be able to get her thighs in them, and that made me chuckle.

I asked Danielle if she still liked caramel and she was surprised that I remembered.

"Of course, I did!" I said, handing my sister a cup of coffee. "Now Liz, is she comin'?"

"Yes, she's here. She's just in the car finishing up a phone call."

"So, who is this again?" Keisha said.

"Well, when my sister tells me that she needs prayer support, honey, I bring prayer support."

The bell dinged again and I turned to see Miss Clara peeking in the door. "Hey, am I in the right place?"

My heart leapt at the sight of this gray-haired woman in glasses and a pretty blue sweater. She walked with a halting gait, sort of a half shuffle, half strut with her head held high.

I greeted her and gave her a big hug and it felt like hugging a beloved parent or grandparent. Keisha and Tammy had no idea how much this woman meant to Elizabeth and me, but they were about to get a big dose of Miss Clara.

"Hello, Sweet Cynthia," she said in that lilting voice of hers. "How you doin', Darlin'?"

"I'm doing better now that you're here. Please, come sit with us. How would you like your coffee?"

Elizabeth spoke up. "Oh, I know how she'd like it. She takes it very hot with one cream and two sugars."

"Now see, that's my girl," Miss Clara said, laughing with a cackle and patting her foot as she sat near Danielle.

I introduced her to Tammy and Keisha and explained a little of how we met Miss Clara and what a big help she'd been to us both. Miss Clara asked me to bring her up to speed with Isaiah's life and I gave her a flyover of his situation. She pondered a moment, then began to speak, and the whole room hung on her words.

"So, Isaiah is not running away from responsibility, he just hasn't learned how to embrace it," she said.

Tammy shook a finger in her direction. "That's good. He's got to embrace it."

I agreed, but I had to add, "But what I'm sayin' is, he hasn't had a good man in the home to be a role model. So he just sees me taking care of everything. But no matter how much I do, it's hard for a woman to call out the man in her son. You know, Tony's been helpful, but he lives an hour away on the other side of Charlotte."

"Girl, I know," Elizabeth said. "Let me tell you something. He has wanted to spend more time with Isaiah. He really has."

"Liz, I know," I said. "I know. I just want to cover him in prayer."

"But, it's not like it's an emergency," Keisha said. "Like, he has time. We don't have to act like this is overly urgent, right?"

Miss Clara jumped in, like a wild horse bumping against a fence. "Oh yes we do, dear heart. We can't treat prayer like it's some spare tire that you only pull out in an emergency. No! Prayer has to be more like the steering wheel that you hold tightly every day, no matter where you are going."

Tammy rocked back and forth as Miss Clara spoke. "Mmm, mmm, mmm, now that's good."

Keisha leaned toward her friend. "Well look, all I meant was that—"

Tammy cut her off and lowered her voice. "Shh. Shut your mouth, now. This woman's at a whole nother level."

Keisha made a gesture of locking her lips and tossing away the key. "Okay."

Miss Clara was deep in thought. "Well, if I may, I suggest that we start by praising the Lord for who He is." She raised her fists and shook them. "And then we pray that the Lord will open Isaiah's eyes so that he could see himself the way that the Lord sees him. And that he would realize his need for the Lord and he would draw near to Him. And that the Lord would capture his heart and build him up to be the man the Lord wants him to be."

As Miss Clara spoke, tears came to my eyes. And I saw the same thing happen with Elizabeth. It was as if this old woman was seeing something we couldn't see and accessing power from on high to change the script Isaiah was following.

Tammy was fired up and raised a fist. "Now that is good! Miss Clara, I need you to come by here more often!" She added, "Keisha needs you."

I got a chuckle out of that. And then we got to business with God. I love listening to Miss Clara pray. She did exactly what she suggested—she praised God for the power of His might. And she gave thanks for the answers to prayer He had given in the past. And then she paused and Keisha picked up on that and thanked God for a country where we can still gather and pray and give Him glory.

Danielle spoke up with her tiny voice that got stronger and stronger. "Lord, thank You for the change You have made in my family. The way my daddy is following You now."

"Yes, Lord!" Miss Clara prayed.

"Thank you that we can boldly come to You, not because we're good, but because of Jesus, who gives us His righteousness," Danielle continued.

I stole a glance at Liz and she lifted a hand and kept nodding. Truth is, we got lost in prayer in that salon, among the dryers and the clippers and hair care, which is exactly where prayer ought to be—right where we live and breathe and work. We turned the salon into a place of praise and thanksgiving—and then petition for Isaiah.

"And now Lord, we bring You this one who is dear to us. You know what Isaiah has been through. You know what You created him to do. Thank You for knitting him in his mother's womb. Thank You that You care for him infinitely more than we do because You sent Your only Son to die in his place on the cross. So we call out to You now and pray in Jesus' name, to draw him to You, O God. Touch his heart and show him his need for You. Let him know Your love for him, and that You want to walk with him, to guide him, to teach him, and to use him for Your glory.

"You say in Your Word that we are your masterpieces, Your workmanship, created in Christ Jesus to do the things You planned long ago for us to do. So we ask You to grab hold of

Your masterpiece Isaiah and help him to see the purpose You have for him. Show him the things You want him to do for Your glory."

We were so deep in prayer that I barely heard the bell at the front. I looked up to see a customer walk in wearing sunglasses and carrying a purse, several shopping bags, and a cup of coffee. As if that wasn't enough, she was texting on her phone when she stepped through the door. Some people take multitasking to a whole new level.

"I pray for protection against anything and anyone, Lord, that the enemy might try to use to pull him away," Miss Clara continued. "Lord, put Your hand on his life and guide him."

The woman at the door froze for a minute and I walked over to her. She whispered, "Is this a hair salon or a prayer salon?"

"Well, today it's both," I said, as Miss Clara and the others gained momentum and volume. "What do you need?"

"Stir him up to want to know You, Jesus!" Miss Clara prayed.

The woman's face grew pained, the corners of her mouth inching down with emotion. "I need both."

"Girl, you want to join us?" I said.

"Yeah, my edges need to be delivered and set free," she said. "I need both."

I led her to a chair and she sat. When we paused, she said her name was Brianna. She said she was shopping in the area and saw my sign and felt drawn to the place.

"Sweet Brianna, the Lord knew you needed some support today," Miss Clara said. "What's on your heart? Is there a load you're carrying that you weren't made to carry alone?"

Brianna burst out crying and the six of us gathered around her and listened to her story. I won't go into what she shared, except to say that her edges weren't her biggest problem. And when she left that day, with her edges looking a lot better by the way, I told her that she had not stumbled across my "prayer salon" by accident.

"Sister, I believe I just had a divine appointment with you people and God. And I thank you for what you've done for my heart today."

CHAPTER 27

✦ ✦ ✦

Joshua Moore drove home with Emmett's report weighing on him.
He had looked up Slayer Sports online after meeting with Isaiah,
going through their catalog of products and how each of them
was less than the prices at Moore Fitness. They had to be inten-
tionally undercutting them. He tried not to be paranoid, but
as he did the numbers, almost every item from jump ropes to
treadmills was ten percent less, almost to the penny.

*Lord, I'm going to choose to trust You rather than fear, but I have
to be honest. This company looks like it's trying to take us out. Give
me the faith to believe You are in control of this. Help me see it as a
way to make my trust in You stronger.*

He had these impromptu prayer drives when things at work
weighed on him. He parked in the garage and as he entered
the house he stopped short when he encountered the aroma of
salmon baking. Janelle's signature dish was parmesan-crusted
salmon with roasted vegetables. He hung his briefcase on the
back of a chair and gave her a hug.

"What did I do to deserve a dinner like this or a wife like you?"

She shook her head and laughed. "Not a thing. It's all grace."

They ate together and went over the day. Janelle said she had spoken with Emmett about a personnel matter. "And at the end, he warned me that you might not be in the best mood after the news he shared."

"I can't lie. It troubles me. But maybe it's an opportunity disguised as something else."

"We've had our share of those, haven't we?"

The conversation turned to Isaiah and Joshua's meeting with him. "I was upset that he was late, but when he came to the conference room, I could tell he was sorry."

"Did you read him the riot act?"

"No, I didn't threaten him. I don't think he needs that. I think he needs some kindness. I'm sensing his relationship with his dad has probably affected him."

"Why don't you talk with Tony? He probably knows a lot more about the situation."

After dinner, Joshua retreated to the living room and Face-Timed with Isaiah's uncle, Tony Jordan. Joshua caught up with what was going on in Tony's life, then the conversation turned to Isaiah. Tony told him more about the marriage struggles between Isaiah's mom and dad, culminating in the man moving out and the couple's eventual divorce.

"I don't think Cynthia wanted it. She really tried to work things out between them, but it takes two to do that. And Darren was AWOL."

"Has Isaiah had any other male role models, other than you?"

"I'm not sure. He's talented at sports. Off the charts on the basketball court. But I think most of his coaches have been more hard-nosed than encouraging. For some, it's all about winning and losing and not the heart of the player."

"If he's so good at basketball, why wouldn't he consider college?"

Tony shook his head, his lips pursed. "You got me on that one. Maybe he's afraid of failing. You know, you get beat down enough and you can be scared to try again. How is he working out at your factory?"

"He's had his ups and down. If I'm honest, I see a whole lot of me in him when I was nineteen. I had a little bit more ambition."

"Yeah, he just needs a little bit of guidance. But he's a good kid. You know, I reached out to his dad a few times, but he stopped returning my phone calls so we don't know where he is right now."

Joshua studied Tony's face for a reaction to his idea concerning Isaiah. "I'm considering bringing him into the next meeting."

"Yeah, bring him. Let us introduce him to the guys. You know, the more we can invest in him the better."

"I'm thinking about it."

Janelle sat on the couch beside Joshua with two mugs of decaf, the perfect end to their meal. She put his mug on the coffee table in front of him.

"Hey, tell your family I said hello."

"I'll do it," Tony said. "See you soon."

"All right, take care Tony."

"All right, brother."

Joshua ended the call and felt he knew Isaiah a little better. Would he respond to joining The Forge?

"So, do you think Isaiah's ready?" Janelle said.

"I don't know, babe. He's a little raw. I see elements of a desire to grow."

Janelle leaned closer. "He would be your seventh."

"Yeah." Joshua ran through the faces in his mind. She was right, Isaiah would be number seven. "But as long as God keeps bringing them to me, I'm going to keep on going."

Janelle smiled and put a hand on his arm. "I am so proud of you."

He leaned back, thinking about the long road they'd been down together. And the way the hard times had brought them closer instead of creating distance. She rubbed his back and her touch was like an invitation to continue. His eyes grew misty.

"Each time I . . ." he thought of the meetings, the victories won, the struggle those men had been through together. "I heal a little more."

Janelle inched closer and whispered, "Then let's just keep walking."

It was just what he needed to hear. Funny how she knew the words that could propel him.

The next morning, by faith that Isaiah would be on time, Joshua stopped at a restaurant near work and ordered two breakfasts to go. He carried the Styrofoam containers to the conference room and as he turned the corner he abruptly stopped. Isaiah waited by the door.

"Whoa, Isaiah is in the building! You're fifteen minutes early."

Isaiah flashed a smile. "Yeah, I'm tryin' not to be late again."

"No, we're not going to do that again."

"No, no sir."

"All right. Guess what? You've got a hot breakfast this time."

"Okay," Isaiah said. "I could've smelled it from the parking lot."

Joshua laughed. "From the parking lot!"

They sat at the conference table and ate their meal, talking about everything from the latest sports news to what was happening on the factory floor that day. The only reference to Isaiah being late was what Isaiah said when they'd begun their meeting. Joshua wanted the young man to feel that mistakes weren't held over him.

As they ate, Joshua opened up about some of the mistakes he had made when he was younger. He wanted to grab the world by the tail and not let go until he had climbed the mountain of success.

"The problem was, I was climbing the wrong mountain. I was scrambling and searching for something that I couldn't find on my own."

"What do you mean?" Isaiah said.

"I would have some success, make more money, buy a new toy, but it always felt empty. I'd get to the top of the mountain, take a look, and see another in the distance, so I'd run after that one."

"There's a quote by Thoreau I keep on my desk."

"Who's that?"

"A poet and philosopher who lived in the 1800s. He said, 'Some men fish all their lives without knowing it is not really the fish they are after.' That describes my life early on. I was in a constant search, trying to catch bigger fish, when it wasn't fish I was after. And it took me a long time to figure that out."

Isaiah was locked in on Joshua's words, finishing up his breakfast. He pushed the Styrofoam container to the side and Joshua leaned back in his chair.

"I wasn't much older than you when this happened."

"When did you get married?"

"I was twenty-three." Joshua chuckled. "I was so in love, but I had no idea how to be the husband Janelle needed. I thought my job as a husband was to tell her what to do and how to do it. And she was a lot smarter than me in a lot of areas. I was a knucklehead."

Isaiah laughed. "You two seem good now. I mean, thirty-five years?"

Joshua nodded. "She's put up with a lot from me. My idea of leading well was being right and telling people what to do. Over time, I realized there's strength in bringing others alongside you. You're stronger together. So eventually, I learned to listen.

"It's embarrassing to think about it now, how at twenty-four I thought I could figure out life by myself. But when you fall on your face as many times as I did, you finally realize it's better to learn from the mistakes of other people than to continually make your own."

Isaiah laughed. "Yeah, I get that."

"Aw, man. I used to get into arguments all the time. Like a big man standing my ground. Then, my mother said something to me that I've never forgotten. She said, 'You need to be more of a fountain than a drain. And you need to start giving more than you're taking.' The more I thought about it . . . I was using people to reach my own goals, without loving them at all. And that's the thought that I have for you today. Adopt that mentality. Be a fountain, not a drain."

Isaiah sat in silence, as if soaking in Joshua's words. Joshua turned and opened his Bible sitting on the table. Isaiah stared at it.

"I want to read you something. It's out of Galatians 5." He turned the thin pages and found the passage and in a clear voice read the words as if he were proclaiming something to both of them. "'For you have been called to live in freedom, my brothers and sisters. But don't use your freedom to satisfy your sinful nature. Instead, use your freedom to serve one another in love. For the whole law can be summed up in this one command: Love your neighbor as yourself.'"

Isaiah leaned forward, his elbows on the table. "What do you mean by 'sinful nature'?"

Joshua turned in his chair, leaned back and crossed his legs. "Well, the Bible tells us that we all have a sinful nature. Selfishness, pride, greed, bitterness. Yet God still loves us. So He sent His Son, Jesus, to die on the cross to pay the debt that we owed for sin. Then He raised Jesus from the dead, so that we could be in right relationship with Him, if we put our faith in Jesus. He's our way to freedom."

Joshua watched Isaiah as he spoke, trying to read his face, his reaction to his words. He didn't want to say too much or too little, but he felt, by the questions Isaiah asked and the quietness of the room, something was happening in this exchange.

"When we follow Jesus and devote ourselves to Him," Joshua continued, "He bears fruit through us that gives God glory. Love, joy, peace, patience, kindness, goodness, faithfulness, gentleness, self-control. That's what He wants us to do. That's the kind of man I wanna be."

Joshua could tell he had put a lot on Isaiah's plate other than breakfast. He had one more thing to give to encourage him.

"I'll tell you what. If you're interested, join me this Saturday. My church does an outreach downtown. We get together every month, give out food to people who are struggling. We usually start at nine a.m."

Isaiah looked surprised. "You do this?"

Joshua chuckled. "Every month. We help sponsor it. Come on, man." Joshua remembered Isaiah's bike he rode to work. "If you'd like, I'll pick you up."

Isaiah mulled it over and Joshua was about to say, "No pressure," but Isaiah beat him with a simple, "Yeah. I'm down."

"All right," Joshua said.

175

CHAPTER 28

✦ ✦ ✦

Isaiah and the guys usually played ball on Saturday mornings, not too early. As he waited in front of his house for Joshua, he shot a text to Jamal.

I got something to do today. Can't play. Sorry.

There was no response, which meant Jamal was probably still asleep. He put his phone away and paced the sidewalk in front of the house. He heard his mom moving around in the kitchen and he didn't want to tell her what he was doing.

When Isaiah saw Joshua's Bible on the table the day before, he wondered why the man had it there. Then, when he opened it and read from Galatians, he thought of his mother and all the times she'd dragged him to church. Then came the day he dug in his heels and said he wasn't going. That was her thing, not his. He still remembered the look on her face.

He knew enough from attending Sunday school that Galatians was a letter in the New Testament, but that was about it. But when Joshua read the verses, there was something about them. He couldn't put his finger on it. The pastor at his mom's church said about a million times that the Bible was alive and unlike any other book. Isaiah had found it boring when he tried to read it, but he had to admit he hadn't tried very hard.

The Moores pulled up in their car and Janelle got in the back. "You sit up front."

Isaiah protested but Janelle wasn't having it. He could tell Joshua was glad he was outside and ready rather than having to park and wait or go to the door. Isaiah rubbed his hands on his jeans.

"Nervous?" Joshua said.

"A little."

"Don't be," Janelle said, leaning forward. "This is easier than anything you'll do at Moore Fitness. And twice as rewarding."

"You won't get a paycheck," Joshua said, "but the feeling you get from really helping people who need it is its own reward."

"I just don't know what I'll be doing."

"Think of it this way," Janelle said. "You're the conveyer belt to the food people need. And you will be busy every minute you're there."

"Think you can handle it?" Joshua said.

"I can try."

The Food Donation Center was an older brick building and when they parked, Isaiah noticed families lining up in front and volunteers streaming inside. The main room was a large, open area filled with tables and boxes and pallets of just about every kind of packaged food. Peanut butter, jelly, canned fruit and vegetables, bagged chips, and muffin mix.

As soon as he got his name tag at the front, he was put to work opening boxes, moving boxes, and doing whatever a man named James showed him. As he worked, Isaiah noticed something in the room. What was it? There was an overwhelming sense of peace and joy. That was the only way he could describe it. There was constant conversation and direction, but in some areas people laughed together and it looked like just about everybody was smiling. It was contagious.

As the line of people snaked through the building, he noticed Joshua taking time with one older couple carrying a full box of food. He had his hands on their shoulders and it looked like he was praying with them.

Families came through the line together with younger children. Some moved to the back where there were racks of used clothing. He couldn't believe that all these supplies were being given to people. This was all going on every Saturday and he'd had no idea of the need or those who were serving others without fanfare.

James asked him to bring a package of rolled blankets to the table and when he placed them there, Isaiah noticed a pamphlet that said, "The Romans Road: Path to Salvation." He folded it and put it in his pocket.

He couldn't stop watching Joshua move around the room. It was interesting to see him in this context—outside of his Moore Fitness world and interacting with others. And he realized that Joshua was the same here in the food distribution center as he was in the conference room or on the factory floor.

By late afternoon the lines were gone and so was most of the food. Isaiah helped move what was left to a secure area, then watched the volunteers hug and say goodbye.

James came up to him as he was getting ready to leave. "You were a big help today, Isaiah. I'm really glad you took the time to join us."

"Mr. Moore is the one who invited me."

"Yeah, Joshua's a friend of mine. He's a good man. I've learned a lot from him. You work at his company?"

"Just started. Learning the ropes."

"Well, you're learning from one of the best. Thanks for pitching in and I hope you'll join us again."

Clouds had moved in and there was rain. Isaiah stood by a loading dock and watched the last of the families leave, hugging their full boxes as they walked through and around the puddles on the sidewalk. He reached in his pocket for his phone and realized he hadn't checked it all day. He had several messages from Jamal, all asking where he was and why he wasn't at the park.

Joshua and Janelle found him.

"Hey, you okay?" Joshua said.

"Yeah. I just never did anything like this before."

"Well, you did good. A lot of people got helped today."

Joshua put an arm around Janelle. "Isaiah, you want to join us for dinner? It's my turn to cook. I'm not as good as Janelle, but it shouldn't be too bad."

"Don't believe that," Janelle said, laughing. "He's very good."

"Hey, yeah, I'm down," Isaiah said.

"You guys wait here," Joshua said. "I'll get the car and we'll head to the house."

The Moores' house wasn't a mansion, but it was huge and in a nice section of town. They had a pool in the backyard with a shiny grill. The rain had let up and Joshua went out and fired it up. While he flipped steaks he took a phone call and Isaiah wondered if it was about work. There was a rumor going around that the company might be in some kind of financial trouble, but Isaiah didn't know much more than that.

There was a grand piano in the living room and a guitar, so someone in the family played music. Isaiah moved to the ornate fireplace and studied the pictures displayed.

Mrs. Moore walked into the living room and handed Isaiah a glass of iced tea. "Sometimes being the president means you have to take business calls on the weekend."

"Nah, I understand." He took the tea and pointed at a picture on the mantel. A young man smiled at the camera. "Hey, who's this?"

Janelle grew quiet, then said. "That is our son, Jalen."

"Oh, I didn't know you had a son. Where's he at?"

Janelle paused and Isaiah regretted the question immediately. There was some pain in her face.

"Jalen died at seventeen."

The air went out of the room. Janelle turned and sat on the couch. Isaiah collected himself and sat across from her. "Oh, I'm sorry. I didn't realize . . ."

"It's okay, Isaiah." The words were coming slowly now, as if telling the story was like mining the pain of her past. "When Jalen was growing up, Joshua was so driven in business to be a success. And it tested our marriage."

There was a mist in her eyes now. Isaiah sat frozen on the couch.

"One evening, Jalen went with his friends to ride to a party, and a drunk driver ran a red light and hit them on his side. We never got to say goodbye.

"For a while, Joshua blamed everybody, even me. It almost ended our marriage. One of the older men in our church, a mechanic, reached out to Joshua and started meeting with him. He helped Joshua reshape his entire view of life and faith according to the Bible. And that's when I saw my husband become a disciple of Jesus Christ. It changed him.

"So we don't just call ourselves Christians. We are devoted to Jesus, and we will do anything He calls us to do."

✦ ✦ ✦

The steak was excellent, but dinner was quiet. Isaiah couldn't get the face of their son, Jalen, out of his mind. After dinner, Joshua suggested they play a game, but Isaiah said he was tired, so Joshua drove him home.

"Janelle mentioned she told you about Jalen."

"Yeah, I had no idea. I'm sorry for your loss."

"You would have liked him a lot. He had a good jump shot like I hear you have." Joshua laughed at the memory and grew quiet.

"Do you ever get over the loss?" Isaiah said.

Joshua watched the road as he spoke. "No, I think when you lose someone you love you don't ever get over it. You go through it. And God picks you up when you can't get out of bed because you're hurting so bad. I think the enemy meant to use Jalen's death to get me mad at God. Separate me from Him. And I'll admit I don't understand why God let it happen. But I finally realized that walking through the valley with God at your side is better than climbing a mountain alone. Even if it's the valley of the shadow of death."

At a stoplight, Joshua turned to Isaiah. "I've been talking a lot. What about you, Isaiah? What's going on with you?"

Isaiah had a million thoughts. Giving out the food to all those people and the feeling it gave him. Feeling bad about asking Mrs. Moore about her son. Thinking about his own father. And the fight he'd had with his mom.

"You mean about work?"

"I mean about anything. What's rolling around in that brain of yours?"

"To be honest, I was thinking about my mom."

"What about her?"

"She's been trying to be both parents since my dad left. Good cop and bad cop, you know? The other day she got mad and said I was acting like my father."

"How did that feel?"

"Felt like she slapped me. But I understand why she said it. She was ticked. And she had good reason."

Joshua kept driving and Isaiah looked out the passenger window, away from him, and said, "My mom has wanted me to come to church with her. I keep telling her it's not my thing."

Joshua pulled up to Isaiah's house. Isaiah grabbed the handle to open the door. "Thanks for dinner and the ride."

"Hold up a minute," Joshua said. "Have you ever thought that maybe the conflict with your mom is a natural thing? You're becoming a man. And she wants to help you, but she probably is at a loss about what to do."

"I haven't thought about it that way."

"Was she happy about the new job at Moore Fitness?"

"She was bouncin'-off-the-walls happy."

Joshua nodded. "She's for you, but she doesn't know how to coach you. And when you make a mistake, she gets afraid. So the best thing you can do is make good life decisions and let her see she can trust you. Her trust will grow with time."

Joshua held out a hand and Isaiah shook it.

"Hey, I'm praying for you," Joshua said.

"Thanks, man."

CHAPTER 29

✦ ✦ ✦

Cynthia

I was able to close the shop a little early and switch from hair to prayer again. Liz drove over and brought Miss Clara again, as well as two ladies from her Bible study. Brianna, who had just happened onto our first impromptu prayer meeting, returned and this time I didn't do a thing with her edges. I figured we would share requests and go around, but the whole meeting centered on Isaiah again. I shared a little of my story and what I'd been through, then we began to ask God for His favor on Isaiah's life.

"Thank You, Lord, that Isaiah has a good job with a godly boss who wants to please You," Miss Clara prayed. "Lord, bless that company and let Isaiah be an asset to the people who work there."

Liz read a verse from Ephesians and prayed, "Open the eyes of his heart to You, Father. Don't let the enemy take the seeds that have been planted in his life. Make his heart good ground."

One of Liz's friends had a soft voice and I had to lean

forward to hear her. "Lord Jesus, thank You for being with Cynthia in the waiting room of life. Give her perseverance. And help her cling to You as she asks for Isaiah to follow You. Thank You that this is his testimony with You and we surrender him into Your lovingkindness and Your mercy. Give us the faith to trust You, Jesus, and trust Your timing as You work on Isaiah's heart. Change him from the inside out, we pray."

The tears were streaming down my cheeks as I listened. And that prayer hit home with me. This wasn't my testimony or anyone else's, this was Isaiah's life and his choice. So I put him on the altar again, overwhelmed by the love in that room. The fact that these women would come together and storm heaven's throne room stunned me. I could only choke out one simple prayer, "Help him, Father. Help him."

Before Miss Clara left, I got her alone at the front of the salon and told her I felt bad that I couldn't pray anything better than I did.

She took my hands in hers. "Sweet Cynthia, that was the best prayer you could ever pray. You are fully dependent on God's power to work in your son's heart. And God is moving. There's no doubt in my mind He's up to something good for Isaiah. And for you, sister."

She toddled out of the salon and got in Liz's car and I closed up and headed home as the night shadows fell. A car with a loud muffler passed me, and when I saw the make and model and how rusted it was, I immediately thought of the night Darren left. Funny how those old wounds can come back with a sound or an aroma, a song or a film or a meal that reminds you of a moment when calamity struck.

Then I passed a Chinese restaurant, which was one of Isaiah's favorites. He likes a good steak, but he also loves fried rice. I smiled at that thought, but I knew my bank account was getting lighter by the day, so I kept driving.

I had gone several streets when, in a move of the Spirit or maybe a bit of defiance on my part, I gave my signal and made a U-turn (it was legal) and said, "Not today, Satan. You are not going to steal something good from my son and me."

I drove right back there and ordered his favorite on the menu and drove home feeling like I'd just won a victory.

CHAPTER 30

✦ ✦ ✦

Isaiah sat on his bed and replayed the things Joshua had said. It made a lot of sense that his mom was scared. He did the same thing when he was afraid. He lashed out and yelled. Sometimes he clammed up and didn't say a thing.

But one thing troubled him. Joshua ended their conversation by saying he was praying for him. The troubling part for Isaiah was that instead of Isaiah rolling his eyes and dismissing the man's words, he welcomed them. Why was he strangely warmed by the man's sentiment? Joshua didn't talk about prayer as something he tacked on at the end of the day. He sounded like he really thought it worked.

Isaiah had always looked at church people as pretenders. Something bad happens to them and God will make a way. And if He doesn't, praise Him anyway. Put on a happy face. Faith, to Isaiah, was just some positive mental attitude you slipped on and walked around in so you could be in the club.

But the Moores weren't just pretending. Something real had

happened to them. And Joshua's faith didn't take away the pain of losing his son. He was still grieving, but there was something . . . What was it? Hope? Maybe it was tied up in what Joshua had talked about at their breakfast—the calling and purpose he mentioned.

Isaiah remembered the pamphlet he'd picked up earlier in the day. He pulled it from his pocket. It was just a sheet of paper folded lengthwise. Inside it listed Romans 3:23. "For all have sinned and fall short of the glory of God."

Isaiah read the verses aloud. Then he moved to the next, Romans 5:8. "But God demonstrates his love for us, in this: While we were still sinners, Christ died for us."

Romans 6:23. "For the wages of sin is death, but the gift of God is eternal life in Christ Jesus our Lord."

Romans 10:9-10. "If you declare with your mouth, 'Jesus is Lord,' and believe in your heart that God raised him from the dead, you will be saved. For it is with your heart that you believe and it is with your mouth that you profess your faith and are saved."

Romans 10:13. "For everyone who calls on the name of the Lord will be saved."

He read through all of the verses, then folded the page. He believed he was sinful, no question. From these verses it was clear everybody was in the same boat. But could it be as simple as believing and doing what it said on the page? Surely there had to be more than that.

But what if it was that easy? Was he supposed to close his eyes? Keep them open? Kneel? Sitting on his bed, his eyes misty, he took a deep breath and let it out.

"Jesus, I don't know exactly how to do this. But I believe You see me. Would You do this for me? And forgive me? I mean, You say that . . ." He opened the page and read the verse. ". . . if

I believe and confess that You are Lord, then You will save me.
So, I confess . . ."

The tears came and clouded his eyes, but he kept going.

"*You are Lord.* Please, help me, Jesus. Please."

Isaiah couldn't remember the last time he had felt tears falling. But he couldn't control them. He couldn't stop them. And he didn't want to. Instead of being a bad thing, he believed the emotion was a confirmation. God had heard him and was answering his prayer at that moment. A sense of peace flooded him. A comfort came that no matter what happened from that moment on, he was a different person on the inside.

Now what am I supposed to do? he thought.

CHAPTER 31

✦ ✦ ✦

Cynthia

The prayer meeting had calmed my heart and gave me hope that God was doing something, but I was also guarded. I've been so fired up and encouraged at times that I let my emotions run when I needed to corral them.

I knew Isaiah had gone somewhere with Joshua earlier in the day, but I wasn't sure what they had done and I wanted to hear more about it without badgering Isaiah.

I got home with the food and called for Isaiah as I entered the kitchen. I hoped he hadn't eaten yet, but even if he had, he could heat up the Chinese for his Sunday lunch if he wanted. He says Chinese is even better the day after. I figured I might have to call him a few times to break through any video game he was playing, but to my surprise he came on the first call and walked into the kitchen with a strange look on his face.

"Hey, I'm sorry I'm so late. I've got a plate for you."

"Nah, it's cool," he said, his voice low. His eyes looked a little red and I wondered if he might be coming down with something.

"I was with your aunt and a bunch of women at the salon and we were praying and I just completely lost track of time."

I saw Isaiah was looking at me. I thought maybe something had happened, like he'd quit his job or wrecked his bike.

"Are you okay?" I said.

"Yeah, I was, uh . . . praying too."

I had silverware out and nearly dropped both forks. When you hear something you're not expecting, you have to ask the next question. "What were you praying about?"

"Um, you know, I've been trying to figure things out. By myself. And now I realize that . . . I need Jesus . . . you know, to save me."

He said it with such emotion, my knees nearly buckled. But I kept looking at him, his eyes filling with tears. Real tears. And I couldn't believe what I was hearing.

"Yeah," Isaiah continued. "So I asked Him."

I don't know how long I stood there staring at him. It felt like several days, me just thinking about all the women who had prayed and all the hopes I had for my son. Wrap up all the hopes and dreams of a mother for her son, success or awards or a championship team or becoming rich, put all those together, and add a million more and nothing could come close to the feeling shooting through me right in that kitchen.

I finally came to myself and dropped the forks and moved around the counter and hugged him so hard I don't think he could breathe.

"Isaiah," I whispered, my tears falling now. "I have prayed for this."

I felt his chest heaving, the emotion overcoming us both. I realized I was hugging a new man, a new creation in Christ Jesus.

"Praise the Lord," I whispered. "Oh, thank You, Jesus."

I pushed back from him and took another look. "Oh my goodness, I've been looking forward to this for so long. I'm sorry. I just . . ."

"It's all right," Isaiah said, wiping at his tears. "It's cool. I don't know why it took me so long."

"Do you know what we were praying for?"

"What?"

"We were praying for you."

Isaiah was overwhelmed with that news, right there in the kitchen, more tears welling. And then I heard the other words I was longing to hear. He said, "Thanks, Mom. I love you."

"I love you so much, baby," I said, and we hugged again. "I love you so much."

He sat down at the table with that take-out box. He said the Moores had made steak and fed him well, but all the crying had made him hungry again. And I laughed at that and sat down and kept looking at him.

You can pray and pray for something and give it to God and never expect anything to happen. *O ye of little faith,* I thought. When I finished I excused myself and went to my bedroom and called my sister. She had the same reaction as me, just silence on the line and then big sobs of joy.

"Hold on, I want you to tell this to Tony," she said.

And I told him the same story. And then he passed the phone to Danielle and she was so happy she couldn't contain herself.

Then I dialed my dearest prayer warrior on the planet. She answered on the first ring and when she heard my voice she said, "Tell me some good news, Sweet Cynthia."

"I have good news of great joy for you, Miss Clara. The Lord has answered our prayers about Isaiah."

Before the words were out of my mouth I heard her shout,

"Thank You, Jesus! Hallelujah!" She went on for about five minutes and I could tell she wasn't just saying words, she was dancing in her room, praising God from whom all blessings flow.

When I went to bed that night, it was as if I were floating on a cloud. I was almost afraid to go to sleep, thinking I was already dreaming. But I wasn't. It was real. My son was now a member of the body of Christ.

I went to sleep with these words on my lips. "Thank You, Jesus."

CHAPTER 32

✦ ✦ ✦

Isaiah couldn't wait to talk with Joshua on Monday and instead of pacing outside the conference room, he went to Joshua's office. When the man came around the corner he stopped and did a double take, then looked at the clock on the wall.

"You are *way* early today," Joshua said.

"That's because I have some news."

Joshua looked concerned. "What kind of news? The good kind or the bad kind?"

Isaiah raised his eyebrows and tried to hide his smile. "I think it's pretty good. You'll have to be the judge."

"Well, come on in my office."

Joshua opened the door and Isaiah walked in. It was nicely furnished with a cherry-colored desk and white cabinets and bookshelves along the wall. One look and he thought it was probably Mrs. Moore who had decorated it. Joshua had a laptop on his desk and files, and, of course, his worn Bible. Behind him, on the credenza, was something Isaiah figured

Joshua had decided to put there himself. A long sword was mounted on a stand. It looked like something a medieval knight would wield, with a silver blade that glinted in the light of the room.

Joshua put his briefcase down and turned, leaning back against the desk. "So what good news could bring you here this early?"

"That's what brought me. The Good News."

Joshua squinted. "I don't understand."

"On Saturday, I found a little flyer by some of the supplies we were giving away. I picked one up and put it in my pocket."

"The Romans Road pamphlet?"

"Yeah, that's it. Man, what I saw happening with everybody on Saturday got me to thinking. I mean, the people who were volunteering had something I didn't have. I could see it in their faces. I could hear it in their voices. And, to be honest, when I watched you praying with families, it finally made me think more about me. More about what I don't have."

Joshua crossed his arms. "Isaiah, what happened?"

"There's a prayer in that pamphlet. I prayed it. I meant it. I asked Jesus to forgive me and asked Him to change me. I believe Jesus is Lord."

The look on the man's face was priceless. It was as if Isaiah had told him he'd won a billion dollars in some spiritual lottery. His eyes watered and he opened his arms and he brought Isaiah in for a big hug, slapping him on the back and laughing from joy.

Joshua pulled back from him. "When I saw you in the hallway there was something different about you. Did you tell your mother?"

"She was the first one I told."

"And what did she say?"

"She couldn't stop hugging me. And then she called some of the ladies who had been praying for me. Then, yesterday, I went to church with her."

"You did not."

"Yeah, I can't hardly believe it myself."

Joshua shook his head in amazement. "Young man, you have had a lot of people praying for you this weekend. After I dropped you off at your house, Janelle and I spent some time asking God to touch your heart and draw you to Himself. And look what happened."

Joshua gave him another hug, then sat in his executive chair while Isaiah sat on the other side of the desk. It felt like the two of them were the only people in the building and this was the most important thing they could be doing.

Joshua gave another laugh as he pulled his chair toward the desk. "Isaiah, you are my brother in Christ!"

"All right," Isaiah said. "But there's more, right?"

"Yes, yes. For one, you should be baptized. And we need to talk about discipleship."

"Yeah, I want to talk about that," Isaiah said. "So, I read, like, half the New Testament yesterday. And all of the faith-miracle stuff was done by disciples or people close to Jesus. So, if I'm doing this, I want all of it."

Joshua lifted his index finger and pointed at Isaiah. "Not many people think the way that you're thinking. People want salvation—believing in Jesus. But very few people want to follow Him into discipleship."

"Why?"

"There's a cost to discipleship. Jesus says in Luke, chapter 9, whoever wants to be my disciple must deny themselves, take up their cross daily, and follow Me."

"Take up their cross daily? What does that mean?"

"That means something's gonna die. It could be a number of things. Habits, agenda, goals. Whatever stands in the way of your relationship with Him and your obedience to Him. Your main priority as a disciple is not living to please yourself, it's living for Him. Being devoted to Him. Knowing Him."

Isaiah drank in the words of this man who seemed to speak from a quiet confidence. It felt like Joshua wasn't so much coming up with answers to Isaiah's questions but speaking from the overflow of his life.

"When I put my faith in Jesus and became a Christian, I wanted to grow as a disciple," Joshua continued. "But I had so many other things in my life. It's as if my plate was already full. But He did something that I just didn't expect." Joshua shook his head and laughed.

"What?"

"He asked me to give up golf." Joshua laughed again.

"Golf?" Isaiah said. "That ain't a bad thing."

"No, it's not. But I loved it. It had too high a priority in my life. I played it every chance I got. And one day, the Lord reminded me of my request, and I wasn't making any more room for Him in my life."

Isaiah studied the man's face. He wasn't speaking about a regret. Giving up golf seemed to have given him more life.

"So I gave up my devotion to golf. And I replaced it with more time with Him and His Word. I went from playing two to three times a week, to two to three times a year."

Isaiah chuckled and was incredulous. "Whaaaaat?"

"I'll say this," Joshua said. "There's a cost to following Jesus. But it is one hundred percent worth it."

Isaiah thought about the man's words. "He died for me. So, how could He not be worth everything?"

"He's worth everything," Joshua said, repeating the words.

"You know what? I want to introduce you to a small group of men that mean the world to me. I think you'd enjoy meeting them."

"Yeah," Isaiah said.

Isaiah wanted to ask more questions about things he had read the day before, as well as about changes he needed to make in his life. Before he could, Joshua stood and said, "Let's do a quick greeting exercise. Come on. Stand up here with me."

Isaiah smiled but wondered if he'd heard correctly. "A greeting exercise?"

Joshua stood facing Isaiah and locked eyes with him, a playful look on his face. "When I met you, I could barely get you to look at me in the eye and give me a handshake. I want to practice that right now."

Isaiah raised his eyebrows. "Are you for real?"

"Walk up to me and introduce yourself."

Isaiah took a breath and played along. He reached out a hand as he said, "Hey, I'm Isaiah." It felt awkward, but he could tell Joshua was enjoying the results.

"Okay, I guess that's all right," Joshua said. "But something to remember. When you meet someone, you're communicating something about yourself and how you see them. Everyone wants to be valued. And men, especially, want to be respected. So, when you greet someone, look at them in the eye as a confident young man. Not arrogantly, but confidently. Say your name and give them a strong handshake, then respect them by learning their name. Okay, we're going to do that like it's the first time."

"Okay." Isaiah gathered himself, as if stepping into a new role Joshua was offering. With a confident stride, he moved toward Joshua and grasped his hand. With a voice that surprised even himself he said, "Hello, sir. Isaiah Wright."

Joshua leaned in, mist in his eyes. "Nice to meet you, Isaiah. I'm Joshua Moore."

"Good to meet you, Mr. Moore."

Joshua smiled broadly. "Yeah, much better. Much better!"

CHAPTER 33

✦ ✦ ✦

Isaiah settled into his work on the factory floor, trying to learn as much as he could from his coworkers. He saw the wisdom of learning each section. Since he was part-time, if Isaiah was needed to fill in for someone, he could easily plug in and go.

In their most recent morning meeting, Joshua had given Isaiah a three-by-five card with a Bible verse on it. "This is something you can use at any worksite, today or thirty years from now."

Isaiah studied the card. "Colossians 3:23-24. Work willingly at whatever you do, as though you were working for the Lord rather than for people. Remember that the Lord will give you an inheritance as your reward, and that the Master you are serving is Christ."

Joshua had underlined the words *whatever you do*. "This means it doesn't matter what job you're given. You're not just doing it for those who employ you, you're working as if God were your boss. So if you please Him by putting your whole heart into everything you do, you're more than likely going to please your employer."

"So there are no meaningless jobs if you're a Christian?"

"Exactly. Working the factory floor or owning the company, it doesn't matter. You put all you have into what you're given to do."

Isaiah thought back to the teams he'd played on and how many guys had not worked as hard as they could during practice. Then he remembered his high school classes when he'd done just enough to pass rather than study hard. The idea that he worked for God changed every assignment, every job.

Across the factory floor he heard Wyatt jawing with someone. Isaiah couldn't make out the words, but he could tell Wyatt was showing off and bragging about something. That grated on Isaiah, but he shrugged it off and tried to ignore him. The more attention Wyatt got, the more he fed on it. When Wyatt said something, he looked around to see who had heard what he'd said, as if he were looking for people's approval. He wondered if Wyatt would try to single him out at some point to score points against "the new guy."

He scanned a stack of five boxes with one swipe, holding down the trigger on the scanner so that the boxes beeped in succession.

"Wow, you're getting really good at this, Isaiah," Wanda said. Wanda was one of Isaiah's favorite coworkers. She had a good attitude and seemed to follow Joshua's idea of "working with all your heart."

"Not as good as you. You're the fastest one here, Wanda."

"Wyatt says he's the fastest," Wanda said, giving him a look.

"I don't know about that," Diego said. "He's no Superman."

Isaiah smiled and said, "But you can be Wanda Woman."

She laughed and Diego joined in. "Yeah, that's right!"

"Wanda Woman, that's funny," Wanda said.

As Isaiah studied the monitor in front of him, Todd walked up to him. "Okay, Isaiah, you're doing pretty good here. Let's move you to a new section. Get you some more experience. Follow me."

Isaiah smiled when he heard Todd's last words. That's what Jesus had said to His disciples when they dropped their fishing nets and went with Him. Of course, since Isaiah was on a roll in the current section, he wanted to protest and ask if he could stay where he was till the end of the day. Then he remembered the verse in his pocket and followed the man. Working with all your heart meant you had to adapt and go where you were needed, not where you wanted to be.

After work, Isaiah rode his bike home, showered and dressed. His mother came home and turned the stove on and rummaged through the refrigerator.

"Hey, don't make anything for me. I'm going out."

"With who?"

"Joshua invited me to a meeting with a men's group. He seems pretty pumped about me being there."

"Are you sure they're going to serve dinner?"

"He said to come hungry. And it's at a restaurant. Those were my big clues that we're eating together."

She smiled and dipped her head. "Do you need a ride?"

He looked out the front window. "There he is now. See you later, Mom."

In the car, Isaiah noticed the radio station Joshua listened to was the same one his mom had programmed in her car. Joshua turned the volume down on a worship song as they drove. The man wore his sport coat and Isaiah felt a bit underdressed in just a shirt and jeans. Joshua also had his Bible and Isaiah wished he'd brought the one he'd been reading.

"You look pretty jazzed about tonight," Isaiah said.

Joshua smiled. "You got that right. I'm excited for you to meet these guys. And they're excited to meet you."

"Who are they?"

"You'll see."

They pulled into the restaurant parking lot and immediately Isaiah felt out of place. This was not a diner or a family restaurant. This was a fancy redbrick place with lights in the shrubs outside and a woman at the front desk who greeted Joshua by name. She asked him how he was.

"I'm good, Amy. And you?"

"Fine, thank you," she said. "Your guests are here. I can take you back if you'd like."

"That'd be great," Joshua said.

Isaiah looked for a name tag that said *Amy* but the woman wasn't wearing one. He made a mental note to ask Joshua how he remembered so many names. He'd never seen anything like it.

Isaiah followed him toward an elegant-looking dining room with a long U-shaped table with sparkling plates and silverware. There were a dozen guys already there, talking and laughing with each other like they were old friends. He noticed there were six younger men in the room, as well as six middle-aged guys.

Isaiah heard a familiar voice say, "There he is!" It was his uncle Tony. Joshua smiled broadly and gave the man a huge hug.

"How you doin'?" Joshua said.

"Just tryin' to keep up," Tony said. Then he turned to Isaiah. "Sup Zay?"

They hugged and some of the tension Isaiah felt left him.

Knowing one other person in the room made him feel a lot more comfortable.

"Man, it's good to see you," Tony said. "Your mother told us about the big decision you made. Now you here. Couldn't be more proud."

"Well, thank you. You know my head's been spinnin' like crazy but I've been learning a lot."

"Yeah, well, you're about to learn a whole lot more."

Isaiah saw one of the men he'd worked with at the food distribution center on Saturday, but he couldn't remember his name. Dale? John? He needed Joshua's memory secret.

Before the meal, Joshua called them together in a circle in the middle of the room. "Well, gentlemen, this is a good day. I want to introduce you to Isaiah Wright, who started working at Moore Fitness just recently." He put a hand on Isaiah's shoulder as he spoke. "And as of a few days ago, he is your brother in Christ."

The men warmly applauded and Isaiah couldn't help smiling. Joshua asked each older man to introduce themselves and their younger guests.

"Well, I'm his uncle so he already knows me. But Isaiah, this is Trey and Deon. And the gentleman standing next to them is Benjamin, but we just call him Coach B. We coach these guys on the football field and we keep up with them at the youth group in church."

"Isaiah," Coach B said. "Nice to meet you, man. Welcome!"

"Isaiah, I'm Jonathan. I'm on staff at New Hope Community Church and I've got my little bro, Levi, here with me. He's one of our college students."

"Nice to meet you, man," Levi said.

"Isaiah, I'm Vaughn, financial advisor, and here I have with me my son, Jerry."

"Nice to meet you, bro," Jerry said.

"Yo, that's the money guy, now," Jonathan said. "So if you need anything . . . that's where you go."

"You gotta know him," Joshua said.

Next up was the only white adult. "Hey, welcome. My name's Bobby and I'm a family counselor. This is Ethan and about two weeks ago he asked Jesus into his heart."

Ethan smiled as the other men applauded.

"And I'm James," the last man said.

James. That's it. Why didn't I remember that?

"Retired military and now I do a little bit of real estate. But this is my son, KJ. And I want to tell you, man, thank you for helping with the food distribution last Saturday. Brothers, this dude was working hard. He was puttin' it down. So, we appreciate you, man." James gave Isaiah a fist bump.

"Good stuff," Joshua said. "Isaiah, we are a growing group. Each man here has strengths he invests in other men. We eat together, we pray together, encourage one another, and we keep each other accountable as we follow Jesus."

Joshua paused dramatically. "Isaiah, welcome to The Forge." As the other men clapped, Joshua reached out a hand and Isaiah took it and firmly shook it and looked him in the eyes.

Joshua asked Tony to pray for their evening and the meal ahead. As soon as he'd said, "Amen," a server was ready to take their orders. It was no surprise to Isaiah that Joshua knew her name as well. There was talk at the table among the men, but when the food arrived, things changed. At that point, anyone who spoke had the attention of the entire group.

When he first saw the men, Isaiah wondered if he would be able to fit in and not feel nervous. But the more he listened to the conversations, the more he sensed the genuine care and concern around the table. It was as if he didn't have to pretend or try to be somebody he wasn't. He'd always felt like church was about putting on your best clothes and trying to appear like you were holy. But here, there was no pretending or wearing a mask. And he wasn't valued for being a good athlete or any other accomplishment. He was valued because he was a fellow believer. And the more the guys talked about their struggles and experiences, the more he let down his guard and a strange feeling came over him. It felt like he was coming home.

About halfway through the meal, Tony began to share a story about a money struggle he had been through recently. The way he opened up to the group, not hiding the fear inside but being fully vulnerable, made Isaiah want to do the same.

"I tried to work things out on my own, in my own power, but then I came to the end of myself, which is where I should have been all along."

"Amen to that," Vaughn said, chuckling.

"You know what I'm talking about," Tony said. "So I surrendered. I'm praying. I prayed all night, and I'm thinkin', man, why would God bring me this far, only to come to a financial gap that was impossible to cross? So I'm confused, but I kept seeking Him, seeking Him." He tapped his Bible. "That's when Hebrews 11:6 just jumped off the page and punched me in the face."

The men laughed as if they had experienced the same kind of thing Tony was talking about.

"This is where it says, 'Without faith, it is impossible to please God, because anyone who comes to him must believe that he exists and that he rewards those who earnestly seek him.' So I'm thinking about that and I'm like, man, I realize that sometimes God allows those gaps on purpose. Because if I could figure it out for myself, you know I'm taking the credit."

Again, the men laughed and agreed with Tony. It felt like the whole group was buoyed by his example.

"But when it looks impossible, and you put your faith and trust in Him, then He can provide a solution, but He'll do it in a way that only He gets the glory. Fellows, if you are earnestly seeking Him, then don't be afraid of the gaps."

Someone gave a whoop and others tapped the table in response. "That'll preach right there," Joshua said. "That's good stuff, good stuff!" He turned to his left and looked at the other side of the table. "All right, Bobby. What has God shown you lately?"

Bobby chuckled and pointed at Tony. "You're going to make me follow that?" He laughed, then began to share.

Isaiah turned to Tony. "How long have y'all been meeting like this?"

"Aw man, Joshua discipled each of the older guys in this room over the last fifteen years, including me several years ago. He spends about two years with each guy, teaching them how to walk with the Lord. But then he encourages us to invest in someone else to do the same thing. So all the guys you see in this room are discipling someone just like he did us. You know, just helping mold and shape their faith and character. That's why we call it The Forge. It's just a bunch of guys who come together, who grow together, who eat together. We share a meal every two weeks. It's one of the most important things I've ever done in my life."

Isaiah looked around the table at the younger men who were drinking in Bobby's words and story. There seemed to be a give and take—that this wasn't just older guys telling the younger ones how to measure up, but all of them were growing together.

"Glad you're here, man," Tony said, putting a hand on Isaiah's shoulder.

It was a feeling Isaiah had never experienced. It was like coming alive or opening his eyes for the first time. How had he missed this? He almost felt guilty enjoying the meal and the conversation so much. Then he smiled. That was the last thing God would want, for him to feel guilty about a gift freely given.

✦ ✦ ✦

On the drive home, Isaiah couldn't stop smiling. Joshua asked what he thought of The Forge.

"The food was fantastic, but being with the guys was pretty special. I can't thank you enough for inviting me."

"Everybody was glad you were there." Joshua reached in the back seat and handed Isaiah a gift-wrapped box. "There's one more thing before you go. Open it."

Inside the box was a leather-bound Bible with Isaiah's name engraved on the front. Each book was indexed along the side so he could find it easily.

"Man, I never thought I'd be this excited to get a Bible," Isaiah said.

"That's your sword of the Spirit. It's how we're forged. We use the Word of God and the fellowship with others to make us more like Jesus."

Isaiah ran a finger on his name.

"When you open it, you'll see some sticky notes I put in there for you," Joshua said. "Just some important verses and passages that have meant a lot to me."

"I can't believe this," Isaiah said. "How am I ever going to pay you back for all you're doing?"

Joshua smiled. "You don't pay back, you pay it to someone else down the road. And I would encourage you to begin praying for someone who needs to find the love and mercy of God like you have."

✦ ✦ ✦

Isaiah awoke early the next morning without the aid of his alarm. He sat up and held the Bible in front of him, looking at his name in gold on the front. He opened it and found a sticky note Joshua had left somewhere close to the middle of the leather-bound book. He was at Psalm 119. He'd always thought of the Psalms as short, just a few verses, but this one was pages long. He pulled the note away and read the verses underneath.

"How can a young person stay pure? By obeying your word. I have tried hard to find you—don't let me wander from your commands. I have hidden your word in my heart, that I might not sin against you."

He put his head back, noticing the light streaming through the window blinds, taking in the words on the page written so long ago. It was like they were written just for him.

"Lord, how can I put You first?" he said aloud, looking around his room. He had a lot of clothes. He had a lot of posters on the wall. Was God asking him to do something different in here?

"Is there anything I need to get out of the way?"

He glanced at his TV and saw a stack of video games and the controller. His heart sank. "Ahhh," he said, frustrated. He put the Bible on the bed beside him and stood, walking toward the TV, then turning away. He ran his hands over his hair and paced in front of his closet.

"No," he said, dejected. He looked at the game system again. "Aw, come on. Not that!"

His games had given him a break from life. They'd been there to help drown out some of the pain. It was his only escape, at times, a way to numb himself. Those games were like old friends who welcomed him anytime he needed them. Why would God want him to give up something good?

Then he remembered his father. Isaiah had wished his dad

would talk to him or throw a ball in the front yard, but he would always say, "Just need to finish this game."

That brought a pain in his gut. He didn't want to be like his father. He put his hands in the air and as an admission said, "I know. I'm addicted to it."

Just saying the words, acknowledging the truth to himself and to God felt like he was taking a step toward freedom, a step toward the truth. "Either You are Lord or You're not."

He let that sink into his heart. Isaiah could trust that God knew what He was doing. Or he could choose not to trust. Somehow, this felt like his first big test of walking by faith and believing God wanted the best for him.

"Either You're Lord or You're not," he said again.

The guys at The Forge had talked about surrendering to God and giving Him access to every part of their lives. Would Isaiah hold back or give God everything?

He took a deep breath. "And I say . . . You are Lord."

He grabbed his headset, then the stack of games and put them on his bed. Next came the system and controllers. He stacked them there and thought of the night his mother had tossed his dad's games in the trash.

He scanned the room again. "All right, what else?"

He went through his magazines and tossed most of them on the pile. He found T-shirts he hadn't worn in years, some with words or pictures he felt weren't him anymore. More on the pile. Then his books. Then the rest of his closet and dresser and desk. He was searching for anything that felt like clutter to his life.

"Distractions," he said, dropping more on the pile. He found water bottles he hadn't used and trash he didn't even know was there. It was as if he could really see again and the more he put on the pile, the freer he felt.

He picked up his phone. Here was a new battleground of

clutter and distraction. He deleted several apps that were no problem. Then he hovered over his main social media app, the one he turned to when he just wanted to scroll. It was a struggle, but he was beginning to feel real freedom.

"Yeah, you gotta go." He hit the delete button and felt a mix of sorrow and joy. Sad that he was leaving something behind but glad that he was taking weight off his shoulders. Another app for videos. "You definitely gotta go."

"How many I got?" he said, scrolling through his phone.

When he finished with the phone, he put all his clutter in a box on his bed, then tucked in the sheets and arranged the pillows and covers. He retrieved the vacuum from the laundry room. He had almost finished with the rug when he thought of his mother and what she might be thinking about him running the vacuum this early.

He checked the clock—he still had twenty minutes before he needed to hop in the shower. Then he remembered. This was a day off. He'd gotten up early thinking he was going to meet with Joshua.

He kept going, amazed at what was happening both in the room and in his heart. It was like someone had unhooked a chain from around him that he didn't know was there. He felt lighter.

His phone rang. It was Jamal.

"Dude, we ain't seen you in three weeks. We ballin' in ten. You comin'?"

"Yeah. I'm off today." He closed the closet door and realized it hadn't been closed since he was in high school. "I'm comin'."

"Oh, it's about time!"

CHAPTER 34

✦ ✦ ✦

Cynthia

The older I get, the harder it is to shock me. It's almost like you can't surprise me anymore, the way the world has changed and up is down and down is up and crooked is straight. I've learned to look at the headlines and shake my head but not be shocked.

Then God shows up and does something you don't expect, that you should have expected all along. He shows His power, and His timing is perfect.

But nothing could keep me from being shocked that Tuesday morning. I went to the cleaners early, picking up a few things I'd left with them the previous week. I've learned the hard way when I drop something off to write it on the calendar and pick it up when it's done or I'll forget.

When I returned to the house, Isaiah's bike was gone. He wasn't working, so my first thought was that he was playing basketball with his friends. I was excited about the changes in his life, but there was part of me that still had questions. Would

Isaiah be able to follow through with his faith? Would his heart be good soil?

A doubting heart will lead your mind all over the place, and mine went to Isaiah's work. He didn't talk much about what happened there. Were things okay? What had happened at the meeting he went to with Joshua? What if the man came on too strong with the spiritual things and Isaiah decided to quit his job and go somewhere else?

This is what a mind that is constantly swirling will do. You'll go from being at peace to thinking the worst at the drop of a prayer request.

I walked into the kitchen and immediately saw something strange on the counter. I hadn't put it there so the only candidate was Isaiah. The box was full to the brim and spilling over and I stopped in my tracks when I saw a sticky note that had three words written on it in Isaiah's block print.

To Pawn Shop.

What made me stop was the stack of video games in their blue boxes along with the game controllers right next to them. Underneath was his game console and it was all I could do to keep my jaw from bouncing on the kitchen floor. I put my purse down and picked up a controller. This was the system I'd bought for him for Christmas last year. Why was it going to the pawn shop?

I looked at his bedroom door, thinking there must be an answer in there. It was open—I don't make a habit of nosing around in my son's things unless there's a good reason. I walked back there and into the room and that's when I was shocked to my core.

His room was spotless, the bed made, the closet doors closed. His backpacks were hung on the hooks by his dresser. He'd even

216

folded the blanket that went over his beanbag chair. This was no longer ground zero.

I put a hand over my heart and did a little happy dance and whooped, "My son is growing up! Finally! Finally!"

I walked out, then had to walk back in and take one more look. It had been a while since I'd actually seen the floor in there. He'd actually hung up all his hats, too!

Now if Isaiah had been at home, I would have played it cool and not said anything, just waltzed in and out. But because I was all alone and feeling my oats, I did a little strut and said, "Oooh, you can't tell me nothing! I'm a good mother! Oh, I'm a good mother!"

I hung up my things and sat on my bed. I suppose any mom who sees changes in her son will wonder if he'll follow through with his commitments. The biggest question for me was whether he would become the spiritual man I wanted him to be. And then I looked at my own life and realized big changes often begin in small ways, small decisions that build on each other, like bricks in a well-built wall.

So, when he got home from basketball and jumped in the shower, I wondered what would happen with those dirty clothes. Would he toss them in the corner of the room and leave his wet towel on the floor in the bathroom?

He came into the kitchen while I was making dinner and I kid you not—he walked over to the trash can, took out the bag, put a new one inside, and walked out the back door.

You better believe I hurried to his room and looked inside. Sure enough, his dirty clothes were in his hamper and his wet towel was hanging by the shower.

I muttered, "What in the world have you done with my son?"

We sat down to dinner together and he told me about blowing off steam on the basketball court with Jamal. I played things cool and listened and *mm-hmm*ed and *uh-huh*ed. Then I brought up the elephant in the cardboard box.

"So, I saw you put your video games and the console in the pawn shop box."

"Yep."

"Is that it? Just *yep*?"

He smiled that big Isaiah smile, like he was waiting all day for me to ask and was wondering when I was going to get around to it. Then he put down his fork and his face said it all. Just as serious as could be.

"Mom, I've been doing a lot of thinking. The stuff I'm learning from Joshua and what I picked up at The Forge the other night—"

"The Forge? Is that the meeting you went to?"

"The guys get together every two weeks. They talk about life and their struggles. What God is teaching them. And they're honest. That's what I like most. They don't fake it. Uncle Tony shared about a financial struggle he's been having."

"Really?"

"Yeah. None of the guys pretend they have everything together. And as I was thinking about my own life . . . See, for a long time, I thought my goal was to be different than Dad. You know, more responsible, keep my promises. I wanted to be the anti-Dad. But then I realized there were ways that I was becoming him. I didn't see it."

"Like the video games?" I said that soft, not accusing or anything.

Isaiah nodded. "I got up this morning and was reading the Bible Joshua gave me. And I asked God to open my eyes and show me anything that was holding me back or cluttering up my life. I deleted some apps from my phone and got rid of a bunch of things in my room. But when I looked at the games and the console, I just don't need that filling my hours. I was addicted to it."

Water came to my eyes. God didn't need my help nagging my son. He was doing all the work on the inside. It was my job to trust He was up to the task.

"I want you to hear me say this," I said. "I am proud of you. A lot of men never get to the place where they're willing to look hard at their lives and make a change. I am proud of the way you are taking responsibility."

I kid you not, Isaiah sat there and with a straight face said to me, "I wish I could have seen your face when you saw my room."

We had us a good laugh at that one. Of course, I didn't tell him about my strutting around in there and taking credit for being a good mother.

"Since there's a pawn shop by your salon, would you mind dropping my stuff off and seeing what you can get for it?"

"I might be able to do that for a fee." I said it with a twinkle in my eyes. "You know, if I get a percentage."

"Whatever you get, it goes toward my rent this month," he said.

That was another shocker in a series of shocks. "Is that so?"

What I didn't tell him then, and what he wouldn't discover for quite some time was that I had a secret plan of my own. One that I hoped would shock Isaiah.

CHAPTER 35

✦ ✦ ✦

Isaiah had made his way around most of the stations on the factory floor, learning the importance of each in the overall scheme of teamwork at Moore Fitness. With each new slot he filled, he picked up tips on how to perform each job as quickly and efficiently as possible. He made mistakes, of course, but instead of seeing them as failures, he used the mistakes to learn how to do the job better.

Plus, he got to know the other workers on each team. It didn't take long at each station to notice those who were trusted by their coworkers and those who weren't.

As he passed Emmett Jones's office one day, he did a double take. Emmett was holding a black square, about the size of a base on a baseball diamond. He clicked something into place on the back of it and Isaiah couldn't quell his curiosity.

"Hey, Isaiah," Emmett said, as if inviting him inside.

"Hey, what's that?"

"This is a portable solar panel. One of our mission products."

Isaiah stepped into the office and got a better look at the

panel. On the wall were pictures of villages from other areas of the world and people holding the same water filters and lanterns as he saw in the office. One smiling child held a Bible.

"Mission products?"

"It's what we ship out every now and then along with the water filters, lanterns, tents, first aid kits," Emmett said.

Isaiah picked up a small lantern. "I didn't know this was part of the business."

"Well, that's not for profit. These are given away."

Isaiah gave him a look. "For real?"

Emmett turned his attention to Isaiah, as if noticing something he hadn't seen before. "Yeah. So Moore Fitness functions off of ninety percent of our income. The other ten percent is invested in products like these for missions and medical teams and ministry. That's why I respect Joshua so much. Even though it sometimes makes the budget numbers a little tighter than I'm used to."

Isaiah laughed and looked at the world map on the wall. There were red pins all over it—Latin America, South America, Africa, and countries Isaiah didn't even recognize.

Emmett continued. "But that's why we have to keep our top accounts healthy. They fund all this."

Isaiah pointed to the map. "This is where you send them to?"

"Forty-six countries so far. I mean he's helped teams dig wells, plant gardens, do flood recovery, and share the gospel. That is the mission account."

Emmett patted Isaiah's back and returned to the solar panel. Isaiah found a pegboard with notes and cards displayed. "This is a lot of thank-yous."

"That's just a sample," Emmett said. "We've gotten thousands."

Isaiah studied the faces in the pictures and the scrawled

handwriting. Some in different languages but all expressing gratitude for Moore Fitness and their work.

Isaiah thought of the verse Joshua had given him. "Whatever you do, work at it with your whole heart . . ." Joshua and his company had certainly done that with these projects. And Isaiah was beginning to see how it all fit together. He'd thought of companies as only being in business to make money and pay workers as little as possible while leaders did little and were paid millions. Now he was rethinking that idea, at least as it pertained to Moore Fitness.

The last station Isaiah learned was the loading dock. Todd led him to the back of the factory where there were two huge rolling doors. Trucks backed up to the loading dock and pallets filled with boxes were transferred onto them. Joshua Moore stood at an exit nearby with the door slightly open, watching for the next truck to arrive.

Todd held a clipboard as he explained the process.

"So your job is to confirm that the order is ready for pickup and let the driver sign off when his truck is loaded. Just follow the form."

It sounded so easy coming from Todd, but it felt complicated. Isaiah was a lot more comfortable with scanning barcodes and labeling boxes. Making sure all the products on the list were accounted for on the order and interacting with someone he didn't know made him nervous. Isaiah had a bunch of questions, but he took the clipboard and nodded, his stomach tight.

"You got this," Todd said, patting Isaiah on the shoulder.

"Okay, he's rolling up," Joshua said. He turned to Isaiah. "Remember, greet the driver. You want to go at a good pace, but sometimes they need encouragement, too."

"Be a fountain, not a drain," Isaiah said.

Joshua smiled and pointed to him like he'd passed the test. "Exactly." He paused and slowly repeated Todd's words, "You've got this. We're gonna let you run with it."

Joshua and Todd stepped away and Isaiah glanced at the stacked boxes behind him. Everything was in place—even snacks and a bottle of water for the driver if he wanted it. He took a deep breath and hit the button to open the bay. The large door rolled up, the motor surprisingly quiet for such a heavy door. Isaiah saw the driver's shoes as the door crept up and he glanced again at Todd and Joshua who were smiling like expectant parents.

Calm down. Stay focused.

When the bottom of the door reached Isaiah's chest, he saw the driver's dark-skinned hands and arms. When the door moved farther, Isaiah saw the man's face.

Something shot through him like a bolt of electricity.

He stared at the man, unable to speak, unable to think, unable to control what bubbled inside.

The man turned away for a moment. When he looked back at him, he spoke one word softly. "Isaiah."

Isaiah turned to Joshua and Todd, who clearly didn't understand what was happening on the loading dock. How could they? The rage building, he slammed the clipboard to the floor and walked away without saying a word.

Isaiah made it to an aisle of the warehouse before he ripped off his vest and threw it as far as he could. It fluttered to the ground harmlessly. Joshua followed him seconds later. Isaiah couldn't look at him, couldn't focus on anything, pacing like a caged animal.

"Isaiah," Joshua said, still moving toward him.

Isaiah pointed a finger and clenched his teeth. With venom in his voice he said, "That's my dad."

Joshua kept his voice even and controlled. "Let's just go to my office. Come on."

They walked side by side. Isaiah grabbed his head with both hands, the pain inside overwhelming. If he'd had time to prepare, if he'd known that after five years he would see his father on that loading dock, he might have had a different reaction. But he felt ambushed.

In the office, Isaiah couldn't sit. He paced beside the bookshelves wanting to throw something or kick something or punch someone—his father, of course.

Joshua stepped out for a moment but returned just as Isaiah let out a scream of pain. It was something he couldn't control and wasn't trying to. Isaiah saw him by the door and shook his head.

"Look, I'm sorry, man. I didn't mean to mess up the shipment."

"Todd's got it," Joshua said. "It's fine."

His voice was like quiet waters, bringing a little peace to the storm inside Isaiah. "Hey, come sit with me."

Isaiah sighed and plopped in the chair facing Joshua, exhausted from the emotions he had failed to control. He looked at his boss and felt the added weight of failing him. He shook his head and stared at the man's desk, unable to make eye contact. And right then he remembered his grandfather's prayer—what was it? Something about Isaiah being able to give his father a hug? Was that what Pop had said? God clearly hadn't answered that prayer because Isaiah felt like giving his dad a slug in the mouth.

Joshua sat, as if content to wait him out until he was ready to talk.

Finally, Isaiah felt in control enough to speak. "I told myself if I ever saw him again, I'd be cool, you know?"

Joshua listened without scolding or correcting. It was partly his response that caused something inside Isaiah to shatter. Seeing this man's face and saying the words released a torrent of emotion. Isaiah felt like he was losing all control, his face contorting, tears leaking. He hated this feeling. He hated feeling anything. He hated crying. It made him feel weak and like a child again.

When Joshua didn't speak, Isaiah felt the freedom to share more. "He made all these promises. Gonna stop drinkin'. Get a job. Fix the car. Pick me up from practice."

He locked eyes with Joshua and the pressure inside burst. "All lies!" he yelled, slamming his fist on the chair.

More tears. More emotion he couldn't control. And there sat Joshua, as if none of this was bothering him. As if he could handle it without pushing Isaiah away or locking him in some room to scream it out by himself. As if he was okay with Isaiah not being okay.

"I remember coming home from school and Mom's crying and I didn't know what happened. But after a few days I realized he left for good this time. He took all the money. I tried calling him. Left messages. Texted him." The memories flooded and the pain increased and he choked out, "He never responded."

Joshua remained silent, as if he was ready to hear anything Isaiah wanted to share.

"Then my mom finds out he cheated on her. And that hurt her. I wanted to bust him in the face!"

Isaiah made a fist and punched his open hand as the emotion rolled him like an ocean wave. He let the tears come, sobbing now. He'd never let himself feel all of this. He'd always turned to his games or his music or scrolled on his phone when he felt bad. Now, there was nothing to turn to but the friend who sat before him.

After a few moments, Isaiah shook his head and said, "I'm sorry, man."

Joshua watched the struggle in front of him and prayed for wisdom. He knew this place was holy ground. Not the office. There was nothing special about these chairs. What made it holy was the depth of pain Isaiah had experienced and was expressing.

Joshua had been given the gift he was now extending. A trusted friend had sat with him in a dirty garage, listening to Joshua's anger and hurt and deep grief. When the man with the greasy hands and black fingernails had listened all those years ago, Joshua had felt a release. And that's what he wanted to give Isaiah. The gift of presence. Not to push or prod him too quickly, but to gently lead his young friend through the rubble of his life like that mechanic had done for him long ago.

Joshua hadn't known the depth of Isaiah's pain, but he had sensed it. The young man had been so reserved, so in control, and now that control was spinning like a tornado. But Joshua also knew Isaiah wasn't alone anymore. He had God's Spirit to help him and friends who cared about him and a Savior who knew this kind of deep grief.

When Isaiah apologized the second time for his outburst, Joshua rubbed his hands on his pants and sat forward, elbows on his knees. He studied Isaiah's face and the tears that ran freely.

Lord, give me the words I need. Words from You.

"I know . . . what it's like to be angry. I wanted to get back at the man who killed my son."

Isaiah glanced at Joshua and something happened, some recognition. He'd touched a nerve inside—that was how deep Isaiah's anger was.

"I hated him," Joshua said. "I wanted him to rot in his cell."

A deep breath.

"But God sees everything."

"Hmm . . ." Isaiah said, as if dismissing the thought.

"He sees everything," Joshua repeated. "And He is a perfect judge. And He said 'Vengeance is mine, I will repay.'"

Isaiah wiped at his eyes and sighed, staring at a spot on the wall behind Joshua.

"I wouldn't let it go," Joshua said, images flashing through his mind. The rage he felt inside. The control he wanted over the man who had taken his son. "So I asked God to help me. And then I made the hardest decision that I've ever made. If your enemy is hungry, feed him. If he is thirsty, give him something to drink. For by doing so, you will heap burning coals on his head."

Joshua could tell Isaiah couldn't process what he was saying. Another verse came to mind. "'Do not be overcome by evil, but overcome evil with good.' I gave it to God, and I forgave . . . not because I felt like it. Feelings are not my driver. God has forgiven me of so much. Who was I to refuse to forgive? Who am I to ignore what Jesus did for me on the cross? When He says vengeance is His to take . . . I don't want to get in His way by trying to do it myself."

Isaiah struggled with those words and shook his head, the tears streaming, his eyes red. "So I'm just supposed to forgive? Huh?"

"If you hang onto it, it's going to poison you. Bitterness is like emotional cancer. When I chose to forgive and give it to God to handle, it was like a parking brake was taken off my life. And He started to replace all my pain with healing."

Isaiah set his jaw. "Look, I have no father."

Joshua gently, with great compassion, said, "Yes, you do. When you gave your life to Christ, you became right with God. And God is not like your daddy. God is the perfect Father. And God loves you, Isaiah. He loves you more than you know. You can trust Him. He loves you deeply."

Isaiah put a hand to his head. His face was wet with tears, but there was no shame, no holding back. He looked straight at Joshua and as if surrendering, giving up on the anger and rage, he said, "So, what am I supposed to do?"

"Ask God to help you give it to Him. Not out of feeling, out of choice. God is the judge."

Isaiah tried to gather himself, but he was still a mess. A wonderful, beautiful mess, Joshua thought. A masterpiece of God's design, struggling to become, struggling to awaken to real life.

Joshua stood and moved behind his desk and opened the top drawer. He took out a leather-bound book and held it in front of Isaiah.

"This is my first journal when I decided that I was going to be a disciple of Christ. It's got Scriptures in it that I used to help me want to forgive."

Isaiah opened it and read a few words. His voice was choked, nasal. He said, "But this is your journal."

"Yes, and it's full of Scriptures. In everything that God was showing me. Read it. I trust you."

Isaiah closed the journal and wiped his face with a hand.

"Let me get you some tissues," Joshua said.

"Man, I don't know if I can go back out on the floor today."

"Don't worry about that. I'll tell Todd. He'll be fine with you taking the rest of the day. Go home. Think about what we've talked about. Read the journal. And don't hold anything back from God. He can handle it. Tell Him everything you're thinking. Trust Him with all that pain. He wants to help you, Isaiah. He wants you to come to Him so that He can be the father you've never had."

"Yeah," Isaiah said.

CHAPTER 36

✦ ✦ ✦

Isaiah rode his bike home, but there were parts of the trip he didn't remember. He was deep in thought, recalling flashes of memories about his father. Isaiah waiting on the steps with a football. Waiting for his dad to toss it with him. That's the memory that hurt the most because he was so lonely as a kid, but he didn't have the words. He still had so much anger, he couldn't imagine getting to the point of forgiving his father.

Alone in the house, he opened Joshua's journal and wandered through the kitchen. As he read, he heard the gentle voice of Joshua Moore speaking through the pages. Inside the front cover he saw the words, *Devoted to Jesus.*

"Repay no one evil for evil, but give thought to do what is honorable in the sight of all. Do not say, I will repay evil. Wait for the Lord, and he will deliver you. But if you refuse to forgive others, your Father will not forgive your sins. The anger of man does not produce the righteousness of God."

Isaiah moved through the dining room, still processing the

words on the pages. It was as if Joshua had found words in the Bible that spoke directly to what he was going through—and the words were hitting Isaiah's heart and going deep.

"God opposes the proud but gives grace to the humble. So humble yourselves under the mighty power of God, and at the right time he will lift you up in honor. Give all your worries and cares to God, for he cares about you."

In the hallway now, Joshua moved toward his room, still reading.

"Stay alert. Watch out for your great enemy, the devil. He prowls around like a roaring lion, looking for someone to devour."

He walked into his room, the light muted here, but he was still able to see.

"In his kindness God called you to share in his eternal glory by means of Christ Jesus. So after you have suffered a little while, he will restore, support, and strengthen you, and he will place you on a firm foundation. All power to him forever. Amen."

Isaiah closed the journal. The face of his father flashed through his mind. Him standing at the loading dock. Him sitting on the couch playing his games. The drinking. The arguments with his mom. The tears. That little kid waiting on the steps. All of it pressed down on him.

He took a breath and dropped the journal on his bed. Then he paced the room, scratching his head as the struggle inside intensified.

"Okay, Lord," he said aloud, matter-of-factly. "Okay, Jesus. You've seen everything. You saw what he did. You saw what he took. You heard what he said!" He yelled the last part in anger, like a prizefighter digging deep for one big punch.

But Isaiah didn't feel like a prizefighter. He felt beaten and defeated. And the emotion came again, nearly doubling him over. Through tears he said, "Lord, I don't want to carry this anymore. I don't want to be bitter."

Sobbing, his body shaking, he tried to collect himself. "So Jesus . . . I give it to You. I choose . . ." He paced, the struggle making its way from deep inside all the way out, as if he were wrestling with someone way too heavy for his weight class. And then he realized he was wrestling with himself.

"I choose to forgive!" he yelled, his eyes looking toward the ceiling. And with each proclamation, the struggle continued. "I forgive my dad. I forgive him. But I ask that You show him where he stands with You. You meet him where he's at!"

It was a release, like Joshua had said. Even now, in the middle of his decision, he felt that parking brake on his life was finally disengaged so it no longer had control.

"But please, clean me out. Clean out my heart."

And then another image flashed in his mind. The woman who had been hurt by his father. The woman who had tried to be father and mother to him.

His voice softened and he said, "Lord, please bless my mother. Heal her. Comfort her. Strengthen her. Protect her. Walk with her! Because Jesus, You know I love her."

The weight of the guilt for how he had treated his mom pressed down, and then released as he remembered that he was forgiven. God had wiped his heart clean when he'd chosen to follow Jesus. So he continued to pray.

"Lord, You've seen what she's done for me. You've heard the prayers she's prayed for me. And You've seen what she's been through, Lord. So I ask that You bless her. And do what You want to do. And I thank You in advance. I praise you! And I worship You, Lord. Because You are my hope! You are my strength! And You, You are my father. Thank You, Jesus."

Undone, unable to stand, Isaiah fell by his bed and knelt, his hands over his head, his eyes buried in the covers and the tears still flowing.

"I give it to You, I give it to You," he sobbed and repeated over and over.

It felt like complete surrender. There was nothing left inside when he finished his prayer.

CHAPTER 37

✦ ✦ ✦

Cynthia

When I walked in the back door, I heard Isaiah shouting something like, "You heard what he said!" I thought he was in trouble and I was ready to run inside his room and see if he was on the phone with his boss. I thought maybe he'd lost his job. Or there was something going on between him and Jamal or another friend. My son is not the most expressive person on the planet, so I do a lot of guessing about what's happening in his life.

As it turned out, the person he was yelling at was in there with him, sticking closer than a brother. Glory! God shows up when you least expect Him but when you need Him the most. And right then, my son needed God's power to move in and through him like never before, but I didn't know that when I walked in.

I had the presence of mind to close the back door gently and then tiptoe to the dining room right next to his room. I put my purse on the table, then sat on a chair trying not to make a sound. There are some moments that are so holy, you know you just need to keep quiet and let the Spirit work.

And the Spirit was working overtime on Isaiah's heart. What had happened? Why was he so emotional? And what had caused him to cry out to God like this? I knew he had given his life to Jesus, but something else was happening now. Something so deep he couldn't hold back. I didn't know any of the answers to those questions or the five hundred other ones that came to me, and right then I did not *need* to know any answers. I *needed* to be still and know that God is God and that He was leading my son to a good place, even if it sounded awful.

That's one thing God has taught me the hard way. I want to know the *why* about everything in my life. I want the reason something bad happens so I can make sense of it in my head. But God seems disinterested in telling me the *why*, and I am beginning to believe it's because the greater need I have is the *who*. The struggles draw me closer to the *who* I need to trust.

Isaiah was crying out, telling God he didn't want to carry something and didn't want to be bitter. *About what?* I wondered. Hearing his anguish broke my heart. I wanted to make everything better, but right there in that chair by the dining room table, I knew that wasn't my job. Isaiah needed somebody bigger than me and more powerful to heal his heart.

"I forgive my dad. I forgive him."

Oh, when I heard those words it all made sense. He'd been holding the hurt inside for so long. I had done all I could to protect his heart, but there are some things a mother can't do. And there he was, forgiving his dad.

I was crying right along with him at that point, trying to keep my sobs from being heard. But what came next sent me over the edge. Isaiah was praying for God to bless *me*, strengthen *me*, protect *me*.

"Because Jesus, you know I love her."

With that I put my elbows on my knees and both hands over my face. It was too much for me to hear. I had prayed for Isaiah, all the ladies had joined me, but I never in my wildest dreams believed I'd hear what I was hearing coming from his room. It was like that verse in Ephesians that says God is able to do "exceedingly abundantly" more than we can ask or think. I've heard Miss Clara pray that, saying that she didn't want to pray a puny prayer, but an audacious one that showed God was truly at work.

Isaiah ended his prayer with sobs of praise and worship. Then his voice muffled and I imagined him face down on his bed, still crying out to God. And as my son surrendered, I kept one hand over my mouth and raised the other to receive this glimpse of glory, this abundant mercy God had allowed me to experience.

I don't know how long I sat there. Nothing felt as important as what I'd just heard and felt. If I'd had a box of tissues, I would have used each and every one of them sitting at that table. But I just let the tears flow and didn't try to stifle them.

I was still sitting there when he came around the corner and saw me. He wasn't upset that I was there, he smiled so big and gave me the biggest hug he'd ever given me. And by the look on his face, I knew that he knew I had heard his prayers. And I also knew he wasn't keeping anything from me at that point.

"I saw him today," Isaiah said, his voice small.

At first I didn't know who he was talking about, and then it dawned on me with his prayers about his father that he was talking about Darren.

"He was driving a truck to pick up a load at work. And when I saw his face, all the anger inside came out. Mom, I'm so sorry."

"Honey, you don't have anything to be sorry about."

"I feel like I let Pop down."

"What do you mean? Why would you say that?"

"Remember when we went to his house? Just before we left he said he was praying that when Dad showed up in my life, I would be able to forgive him. And I didn't do that. I ran away from him."

"Isaiah, don't you see? Pop's prayers were answered tonight. You did forgive him."

"Yeah, but Dad doesn't know that. He thinks I'm this angry kid who wants to punch him in the face."

"You are not a kid anymore, Isaiah. You are a man, and I love that heart of yours. And if God is good enough to do this work inside you, I have no doubt that at some point you'll have a chance to let your father know."

Isaiah went to his room and returned with Joshua's journal. "Reading this helped me. Joshua said he trusted me with it. Mom, I want to start a journal like this and copy verses and put down the things I'm feeling."

I smiled through my tears. "I think that's a great idea." And then I got up to go to the computer to order one right that minute, but Isaiah grabbed my arm and sat me down.

"I feel like everything is changing, from the inside out. And Joshua helped me see what I couldn't, you know?"

"I thank God for that man. He has been like a father to you, hasn't he?"

Isaiah put his head down on the table and the tears flowed again. All I could do was whisper, "Thank You, Jesus."

CHAPTER 38

✦ ✦ ✦

Joshua was finishing a phone call with Emmett, another tense exchange about Emmett's fears concerning sales and the encroachment of Slayer Sports. He wanted to chalk it up to Emmett being a worrywart, overly sensitive to the situation, but Joshua was just as concerned. Maybe more concerned than Emmett.

"Let's be ready to respond when the time's right," Joshua said. "And let this be an opportunity for both of us to trust God. He is using this to increase our dependency on Him."

"Or to show us how much we're depending on ourselves, right?"

"Exactly."

Janelle walked into the bedroom as Joshua hung up. "Emmett again?"

"Yeah. I'm trying to keep him calm. It's a full-time job."

"Especially when you have the same fears."

She gave him a knowing look and he shook his head. She knew him better than he knew himself.

Janelle picked up Joshua's Bible from the nightstand and

handed it to him, changing the subject. "Big night tonight. Does Isaiah have any idea?"

"Not a clue. But I did tell him to break out his blazer. Maybe he'll sense something's up." He tucked the Bible under his arm. "He's made so much progress."

"That journal of yours sounds like it helped."

"He returned it to me yesterday and showed me the one he started. You should see all the verses he copied. The ones that have meant so much to me and then others he's found on his own."

"I'll be praying that the breakthrough continues for him tonight. For all of you."

Joshua hugged her and drove to the Wrights' house. Isaiah walked out wearing a tan blazer and as he got in and buckled, Joshua said, "Lookin' pretty snazzy."

"Snazzy? Is that even a word?"

Joshua laughed. "It was when I was coming up."

"So, what's up with wearing a coat tonight?"

"It's something a little different we do. You'll see."

They were the last to arrive at the restaurant and all the men wore blazers and Joshua could tell they were prepared. They all stood in a circle and Joshua gave a nod to Bobby, who retrieved the claymore sword sheathed in its scabbard. He presented it to Joshua with both hands and a somber face, then took his place in the circle.

"Thank you, Bobby." Joshua looked at each man and paused dramatically. "The gentleman that took me through two years of discipleship showed me an example of my need for more brothers in Christ. I'd like to share that example with you. Isaiah, please step forward."

Isaiah, who stood by Bobby in the circle, looked like a deer in the headlights. Slowly he moved into the middle of the circle and Joshua met him and unsheathed the sword. The metal *zing* was unlike any other sound. Joshua held the sword aloft and locked eyes with Isaiah.

"Now this was shaped with intense heat and pressure in a forge. It weighs about ten pounds." Joshua rested the blade on his shoulder and extended the handle toward Isaiah. "Take the sword and hold it out straight."

Isaiah took it in his right hand and held it in front of him, straight as an arrow and pointing it toward the back wall.

"The more time we spend with the Word of God, in prayer, and following the Lord, the stronger we get. Ephesians 6 calls the Word of God our Sword of the Spirit. It's our primary weapon. Now, when you begin to learn it, at first, you may feel strong and ready, able to face any challenge that's in front of you."

Joshua glanced at Isaiah and noticed his arm begin to slightly bend. He noticed the beginnings of tremors in his arm.

"Now, it is true," Joshua continued, "that the more time we spend with the Lord, and with his Word, the stronger we become. But God wants us to love each other, encourage one another, keep each other accountable because the longer we try to walk it alone, the harder it gets."

The sword was moving now, with Isaiah trying to compensate for the muscle fatigue. Joshua looked at each person in the circle, recalling this moment they had shared in years past. Then he turned to Isaiah.

"Isaiah, how's that sword doing?"

With a chuckle, he answered, "It's gettin' heavy."

The men laughed and Joshua kept his gaze on Isaiah's face. "Yeah, it tends to do that. Such is life. Yet men will try to go as far as they can by themselves. But we need each other. God gives us strength when we stand together."

The sword bobbed and weaved as Isaiah's strength waned.

When he saw Isaiah was at the end of himself, Joshua gave another nod.

Bobby stepped forward first, then Ben. They put two fingers under the sword to steady it. Then Tony stepped forward and put his hand under Isaiah's and lifted it slightly. The sword stopped swaying and bobbing and pointed straight and true. Isaiah seemed to relax a little and take a breath. A serene look came over his face.

"Now there are times that you'll have to stand alone. But don't do it out of pride or stubbornness. If you need help, ask. When you see a brother in need, help him. Stand with him. Treat him like you want to be treated."

Joshua paused again and looked at the men before him. "Isaiah, how's that sword feel?"

"Way better."

Joshua thanked them and Isaiah lowered the sword. Joshua moved toward him holding the scabbard out in front of him. "Now Isaiah, this sword is yours. It's a gift from all of us. We encourage you to hang it up on your wall as a reminder that even though you can take a stand on your own, we need each other."

Isaiah felt overwhelmed by the gift. *Thank you* felt so inadequate, but he said it anyway.

During the meal, several men patted Isaiah on the back. James's son KJ leaned over and said, "Man, you held that thing up a lot longer than I did. I thought my arm was going to fall off."

Through the meal, Isaiah stared at the sword. He was grateful for the gift, but it gave him some anxiety. Ever since he was little he had to figure things out on his own without his dad. And when he looked at the sword, he wondered how he would hang it so that it didn't fall or make a big hole in the drywall.

After dinner, Bobby came up to him smiling. He handed him a wooden mount.

"Use that to hang it on the wall, Bud."

Just like that, the anxiety fell away. Why did he think his friends would give him something like this and not provide a way to hang it?

"Thanks, Bobby."

"You got a place picked out?"

"Oh yeah, it's going on the wall in my room."

"I did the same."

"How long have you known Joshua?"

Bobby paused in thought. "Um, we've been friends for over fifteen years. Yeah, he is one of my closest friends."

"How'd you guys meet?"

Bobby looked away. When he turned back there was something in his eyes. It felt almost like he was gauging what to tell Isaiah.

"Did he tell you about his son, Jalen?"

"Oh, Miss Janelle told me. That he was killed by a drunk driver."

Bobby nodded, his eyes misty. "Yeah." He looked at the floor, his eyes darting. Quietly he said, "I was that driver."

Isaiah's mouth dropped. He couldn't breathe. He stared at Bobby, unable to speak.

"Yeah, that's how we met. About a year after the trial he came to visit me with a man who was discipling him. And then, that guy," meaning Joshua, "he just kept on coming. You know how he is."

Isaiah's eyes clouded as he studied Bobby's face. "Yeah."

"Eventually, he led me to Jesus. Changed my life. I was the first one he discipled."

Isaiah couldn't believe what he was hearing. He glanced behind him and saw Joshua talking with Trey and Ethan. How did he get the strength to move toward Bobby? It was one thing to say you forgave someone, to work that out on the inside, but to move toward that other person, going behind prison walls to spend time with the man responsible for taking the life of your son?

An image flashed through Isaiah's mind. His father standing behind his truck at the loading dock. Joshua had talked about forgiveness being a choice, not a feeling. In fact, there was a section of Joshua's journal where he had mentioned someone with the initial *B* that he was meeting with and getting to know. Now Isaiah knew *B* was Bobby.

"I look at forgiveness as a release," Joshua had written. "It's a decision to not hold what *B* did against him. But it doesn't mean we're reconciled yet. *B* may not apologize or admit his guilt. But I am releasing him to God. So forgiveness is not about the reaction of the other person or the feeling I have inside. Forgiveness is simply trusting God with all of this. And when the bad feelings return, which I know they will, it's a chance to trust again and go deeper with the Lord."

Isaiah turned back to Bobby. "Can I ask you a question?"

"Go for it."

"I get that Joshua forgave you. That wasn't easy for him. But what about you?"

Bobby's eyes darted, as if he wasn't understanding.

"How did you forgive yourself for what happened?" Isaiah said. "For what you caused?"

A smile. A nod. "That was honestly the hardest part. It's still something I have to choose when the accusations come. But I don't see it as forgiving myself. I put it a different way. Joshua explained that when you become a believer in Jesus, you are in Christ, fully forgiven, an adopted son. So when I remember what I did, and what it cost Joshua and Janelle, I remind myself of the truth. I exercise my faith when the guilt overwhelms me. I am forgiven because Jesus paid the debt I owed. I choose to believe that. I'm not forgiving myself, I'm putting all my trust in what God did for me in Christ. So I'm choosing to believe what God thinks about me rather than how I feel at any given moment. I call that 'living forgiven'."

Isaiah took a deep breath. "I gotta write that down in my journal."

CHAPTER 39

✦ ✦ ✦

Cynthia

I got home late the night of The Forge meeting and my mind was awhirl. I was so wrapped up in what was going on in my head that I almost didn't see the clean kitchen counter and table. I say "almost" because how can you not notice something like that?

Isaiah walked in as I was putting a container of salon products on the counter and asked if I needed help.

"No, this is it," I said. "Just testing out some new products for the salon. Did you mow the lawn?"

He smiled like it was nothing. "Oh, yeah. I had some time before our meeting tonight."

"Well, thank you. Looks great. How was The Forge?"

"It was good. Uh, they gave me a sword."

"A sword?" I tried to watch my tone, but I'm not sure how well I did.

"Yeah. It's hanging up on my wall."

I must have furrowed my brow because he quickly explained it.

"It's a reminder to stay in the Word, but that we also need others in the body of Christ. Plus, you know, if somebody tries to break in, in the middle of the night, they won't expect me to have a sword."

He made this swinging motion and I could see him as a three-year-old with his Superman cape, jumping from the couch to the recliner. They always told me that time would go fast with him, and boy were they right.

"And if you need anything chopped up, lettuce, watermelon, *schwaaap!*"

He swung his arm forward as if chopping a head of cabbage and I had to laugh again.

"I got you, Mom."

"Okay, I'll keep that in mind, son."

I started lining up the products on the counter, figuring Isaiah would head back to his room. But he didn't. He lingered. What was happening with him? Cleaning the kitchen. Mowing the lawn. What he said next floored me.

"But um, did you get what I sent you?"

I looked at my phone and shook my head. Then I found a notification from the bank. What in the world?

"So I opened an account and I paid my tithes first, but I wanted to send you my first rent payment."

I saw the amount transferred and said, "Isaiah, this is more than it needs to be."

"No, it's what I wanted to do. And I also wanted to ask you if I can take you to dinner?"

A light breeze would have knocked me over right then. I studied his face and he looked so proud and confident, but also beaming with love. So I had to push back a little bit.

"Okay, wait a minute." I shook my finger at him and chuckled. "Hold on, my son is helping me around the house, he's paying me rent, *and* you want to take me on a Mama date?"

"Yes, ma'am. But I do need to use your car, if that's cool. But I'm saving up for my own."

My heart was swelling up so big I could hardly contain myself. "You know what? I would claim you as my son to anybody, anytime, anyplace."

"All right, I'll remember that," Isaiah said, beaming. He turned and went back to his room.

Alone in that kitchen, I just shook my head, wondering what in the world was happening in my house. And at the same time, thanking God for the changes.

Now I don't want to give the impression that my son became perfect. Let's be honest, a nineteen-year-old who's learning what it means to be a man still has some rough edges and can forget to take the wet laundry out of the washer and move it to the dryer. But here's what happened in me. I started seeing that as Isaiah took more responsibility, I got pickier with him. (Don't judge me just yet.)

I was glad he'd cleaned up his room, but I had a way of making the bed that showed no wrinkles or crinkles in the sheets. I looked at the sword he'd hung on the wall and wondered why he didn't hang it a little higher or even on the wall over his desk. Little things like that. And I began to see how perfectionistic I can be and what this must have done to his heart growing up.

I brought this up at the salon, being vulnerable and all, and Keisha and Tammy had a field day. They couldn't stop telling me all the ways I did the same thing with them. Persnickety is the word Tammy used. But I had to admit they were right. It's hard to see yourself and all the ways you fall short.

See, all this time I was praying for Isaiah, I was trying to get

God to change him and help him wake up to the truth. And when that happened, it's as if God woke me up and showed me things I never saw about myself. It just kind of spilled over on me and I realized God doesn't want to just change one heart at a time, but multiple hearts simultaneously.

In my head, I can hear Miss Clara say, "Hallelujah!"

I do have to say that I held back when Isaiah drove me to the restaurant. There was a better way to go, but to my credit I held my tongue and just let him choose the route.

"I don't want you looking at the prices and ordering the cheapest thing," Isaiah said when he parked. "Don't even look at the prices. Okay?"

I agreed, but it was hard for me because I knew how many hours he had to work to afford that meal. And then I looked at his face and how proud he was to be doing something for me and I decided I was not going to steal that from him.

There were white tablecloths and fine silver on the tables. There were mostly couples in the room and I figured they were on romantic dates. Isaiah had on his tan jacket and looked so grown-up. I had on the dress I'd worn to my engagement dinner. I had almost given that away because of the bad memories associated with it, but it was such a pretty dress and wearing it to Isaiah's Mama date made me feel like I was crossing some bridge to the other side of my heart. I don't know how to explain it.

The server came and we ordered. She brought our soft drinks and Isaiah leaned forward. "Can I ask you something?"

"Ask away."

"Does it get easier? You know, what happened with Dad?"

I took a long drink of soda and felt the bubbles tickle my throat. "The pain is still there. But it doesn't paralyze me like it used to. I'll actually go through a day and at the end think,

I didn't have any bad thoughts about Darren today. That means I'm making progress. How about you?"

"I have these imaginary conversations with him. You know, like he's at the loading dock again and I see him and I don't run away but just stand there and ask him how he's doing. Offer him a bottle of water or some chips."

"You don't want to punch his face?"

He smiled and it felt like something was happening at that table that had nothing to do with our dinner and everything to do with our hearts.

Our food came and it was a twelve on a scale of one to ten. Delicious squared. And it was so pretty on the plate I had a hard time disturbing it—until I took one bite and then I had no trouble. I asked about Isaiah's rib eye, his favorite.

He smiled. "It's good. I see why they charge sixty-five dollars for it, but I gotta get a raise before coming back here."

And right then I saw my son. I don't mean that I hadn't seen him before, but when I looked at him that night, I began to see him through different eyes. I wasn't happy with him for paying for dinner and taking more responsibility. I was just pleased that he was my son and that I had an opportunity to love him well tonight and receive love from him, too.

With a gentle voice that almost choked me up, I said, "Thank you for dinner, son. My goodness, I haven't been out like this in a long time. Long as I can remember. I'm so grateful."

"You deserve it," he said. "You know, I've been thinking about how you . . ."

"What?" When he didn't finish his sentence, I said, "Isaiah, you can say anything you need to say. What is it?"

"You know, I'm just realizing . . . I owe you a thousand thank-yous."

The way that he said it, what it did to my heart hearing those words, was more than I could take. I had told him he could say anything he needed to say, but so much emotion was bubbling that I had to put my hands up.

"Stop." I waved a hand at him, but I was really talking to myself. "Okay, stop. No, no. You're not gonna mess up my makeup and my whole situation I got going on today. Not today."

Isaiah was smiling now. I could tell he knew I had heard his heart.

"Talk about anything else. Talk about your steak, your potatoes, your carrots, whatever you want to talk about. Mmm, mmm."

"Yes, ma'am," Isaiah said, chuckling.

I was not going to get emotional here. I was not going to lose it in this nice restaurant. Then, Isaiah asked one more question that brought me to my knees.

"Mom, what happened to Randall?"

Part 4

THE CONFESSION

CHAPTER 40

✦ ✦ ✦

Cynthia

I had not been totally honest with my son, and to be truthful, I don't know that I had been honest with myself about the question he asked at the end of our dinner. Instead of giving the short version, which is what I gave Isaiah that night, I need to detail a few things here that deserve to be said, uncovered, and brought into the light.

Seeing Isaiah struggle to forgive his father made me look at my own heart toward Darren. Hearing what Isaiah prayed gave me permission to at least stick my toe in the water of forgiveness. (It was just the end of my pinkie toe, not the whole thing.) That means forgiveness is a decision, but it's also a process I am committed to over the long haul.

I could go more into that, but my confession is not about Darren. It's something else that has bugged, nagged, and haunted me.

Randall.

Buckle up, this is not going to be easy.

Isaiah had talked about Randall on our way home from Pop's funeral. He expressed some concerns about him and I wondered if Isaiah was just being protective. I've said that I pushed Darren and Randall to the back of my mind and tried not to think about either one of them.

That's not actually the whole story, which is why I told you to buckle up. Randall again reached out to me a week or two after Pop's funeral. I gave him my phone number and email because it seemed like a good idea. He texted and sent messages every few days. I don't know how he did it, but he figured out my love language and began to say the most encouraging words.

"You are such a light in this world, Cynthia. I hope you know that!"

You get that kind of *ding* on your phone before you even open your eyes in the morning and it will change your day. I looked forward to his little texts at breakfast, lunch, and dinner. He was pursuing me and I liked the emotional jolt he gave to my heart.

The problem was, I was still married to Darren. Of course, I knew he had run off with another woman and abandoned Isaiah and me. I was moving slowly toward divorce, but I hadn't gone through with it.

Looking back, there was a telltale sign that I knew I needed to slam the brakes on Randall. I didn't tell Isaiah about these conversations. I kept it to myself. I had opportunities to talk with Liz about him and ask her advice. I didn't say a word.

At church, I felt encouraged by the teaching and the songs we sang, but I also felt lonely. There were friends who would sit by me and invite me to lunch, but seeing all those couples together, smiling at each other when the pastor talked about marriage, sent my heart into the wilderness. I'm not blaming,

I'm explaining where I was when I put Randall under a bushel basket, so to speak.

He started calling late at night, just before I went to bed. And we'd get in these long conversations. I liked the sound of his voice, and for someone to pay that much attention to me after what I'd been through felt good. I thought I had finally found someone who saw me, who cared, and who wanted the best for me.

And when I'd hang up after those conversations, I imagined us going to church together. I imagined myself in his arms. I imagined our first kiss.

What I didn't imagine was getting so entangled that I couldn't see straight. I'd be at my station working on a customer's hair and a text would come and I would excuse myself and go to the office to read it. Then I'd text him back and that would go on a few minutes. It was like I was in middle school again, all the feelings swirling.

I realized later that I had created Randall in my mind to be a knight in shining armor who would rescue me and put my Humpty-Dumpty heart back together. And the more I kept this to myself, the harder it was to see the truth. His communication, his clandestine calls, took me into his confidence and created a cocoon. Our relationship grew inside the cocoon, in the darkness.

He was great at asking questions. He was great at listening to my answers. He was great at remembering my answer a week or a month after I had shared something from my heart. He paid attention.

When I shared spiritual things with him, something the Lord was showing me from His Word, he asked questions and seemed really interested. But when I'd ask him about what he had been learning or what he thought about what I'd said, he'd take the conversation in another direction. I chalked it up to the fact that some people are not as comfortable talking about spiritual things as others.

And then one day something told me to ask him straight up. So I did. "Randall, tell me about your relationship with the Lord."

Silence on the other end. Finally, he cleared his throat. "Well, that's complicated. I deeply respect your faith, Cynthia, and how you live it. You're not one who talks the talk, you walk it. I was just thinking the other day, when you said—

"Hang on," I said. "Finish the thought. You deeply respect my faith, but what about you?"

Silence again. A muffled sound of the phone moving. "Well, I'm not quite where you are yet."

"Okay. Then where are you?"

He laughed, I suppose at my bluntness. All this time I thought we were on the same page. From his tone, it sounded like we were in different chapters. Or maybe even in a different book.

"Well, I do believe there's a God. But I'm not as sure about the Christian thing as you are. That Jesus is the only way. That there's an afterlife where we'll either be with God or burn."

I was stunned because all along I thought he and I were arm in arm with Jesus. So I collected myself and asked him a few more questions about *why* he was where he was.

You would have thought with my commitment to the Lord that I would end the romance right there. Or I would at least call a time-out until he figured out where he stood. But I did a little theological two-step at that point. I kept thinking that God had brought us together. It sure seemed that way. And if God had done that, maybe I was the one who could lead Randall to the Lord. And I looked for any sliver of hope that he was opening his heart.

Now, what's the first thing you do if you care about someone coming to Jesus? You ask people to pray, right? Is that what I did?

Nope. I didn't give one prayer request to my sister, Miss Clara, Tammy, or Keisha or anybody in my Sunday school class. I didn't even put up an unspoken request. And that should have told me something. When you can't share what's on your heart with the people who care the most about you, something is off-kilter.

Somewhere deep inside, I knew I was on the wrong path, but it felt so good walking down that road. The flowers smelled fresh, the birds were singing, and there was a breeze in my hair. It was like I was walking a yellow brick road with all the compliments and affirmation he gave.

One night we were talking about the low moments of our lives, the valleys we'd been through. And I slipped in Psalm 23 because even if you haven't been in church all your life, you know about Psalm 23. Randall was all over that. He said, "I felt like I was in the valley of the shadow of death with my first marriage."

I sat up in bed and nearly knocked myself out on the headboard. "I didn't know you'd been married before. Why haven't you told me that?"

"It just hasn't come up, I guess."

Hadn't come up? Did I need to ask that specifically for it to come up? How many wives have you had? Do you have children? Are you a serial killer? There was a whole list of possibilities. How could you get so close to someone and not tell them that little tidbit of information?

Shake your head all you want, but even that wasn't enough to cause me to say goodbye to Randall. And you know why? Let me count the ways. He gave me attention. He said things that made me feel like he could be the one to deliver me from all the heartache. Night was my most vulnerable time of day, and he calmed me down and gave me hope that I might find something different than Darren.

One day Miss Clara asked if she could pray for anything

in my life other than Isaiah. I kind of hemmed and hawed and then said something about the salon and our finances, but what popped into my mind was Randall.

She got quiet on the line. "Cynthia, there's something else going on and I don't know what it is and you don't have to tell me. But I'm sensing you're holding something back."

She'd caught me. I don't know how she knew. It was like she had some kind of spiritual metal detector.

"Let me ask again, is there anything I can pray about for you?"

I paused and then told her I had a friend who was not a believer and I really needed her to pray for "this person's salvation."

"Mm-hmm. All right. Let me get my pen so I can write this down." I heard her shuffle some papers. "Okay, go ahead. What's the name of your friend?"

I took a breath. "It's Randall."

"Randall, did you say?"

"That's right."

"And how did you and Randall meet?"

Once I started it was like pulling a loose thread in a wool sweater. The whole story came tumbling out. And before I knew it I was crying. But I didn't know why.

Miss Clara listened, like she always does, with her spiritual antenna up. And then she gently pointed out some of the red flags she heard about Randall.

"Are you ready to hear some hard truth, Cynthia?"

She didn't call me "Sweet Cynthia," so I braced myself. "I'm not, but I know I need to. Go ahead."

"You've known all along about him, but you've disregarded your judgment because you're enjoying the feelings he gives you. Now, feelings are part of life, but you don't want feelings to get in the car and sit behind the steering wheel. Your actions and decisions have to be led by wisdom, which comes from following the Lord and reading His Word. Your feelings will drive you into a ditch. Which you already know."

"But Randall is not like Darren." I surprised myself with how quickly and forcefully I pushed back.

"No, he's not. You're right. He's different. The problem is not with Randall or Darren."

"You're saying I'm the problem?"

"Sweet Cynthia, your heart is the problem. It's been broken and dragged through the mud by your husband, so when Randall says things that charm you, that make you feel alive again, of course you're going to respond to that. But when you found out he's not a believer, and you kept going with him romantically, that's a sign that you're not guarding your heart."

I heard the rustle of onionskin over the phone line and I could see in my mind that old Bible of hers, so underlined and worn.

"Ultimately," she continued, "this is about trusting your heavenly Father. Do you believe He is for you?"

"Yes." I sounded like a mouse, but I meant it.

"Do you believe He loves you and wants the best for you?"

"Yes."

"Do you trust His heart, even though you feel alone?"

"I do."

"That's what Randall is teaching you, Sister. Randall has shown you that there's part of you that doesn't trust God to give you what you truly need. And what you truly need is more of Him."

I gave a heavy sigh into the phone. It was all I could do right then because I knew she was right, but I also knew there was a valley between God and my heart.

"I was reading Psalm 46 this morning. Sometimes I write out a verse in my own words, to try and get it to seep deeper into my soul. And you know how it says, 'Be still, and know that I am God.'"

"I've heard that verse a thousand times."

"Here's what I'm going to pray for you today. Lord Jesus, still the heart of Sweet Cynthia. Quiet her heart and take her to a new level of dependence on You because of this situation. Show her Your heart toward her, Your goodness and mercy. Show her that You have a plan for her life. Help her trust fully in You. Help her hear Your whispers of love You give us in Your Word. You know the feelings she has inside, the hurt and the ache and the questions. Still her heart. Help her see that the One who is in control of the nations, in control of the whole world, knows her loneliness and struggle and cares for her. Thank You that we can cast all our anxieties on You because You care for us. And that You are the one she needs and that she can run to when the struggle gets hard. Protect her heart, Lord. In Jesus' name, Amen."

I had felt guilty for not telling anybody about Randall before that phone call. I felt ashamed that I hid it from the people who cared the most about me. But that conversation with Miss Clara gave me the courage I needed to break open that cocoon. I reached out to Liz and described what had happened with Randall. She didn't condemn me. She did ask me what I was going to do. I told her I was going to call Randall because I didn't want to just send a text or an email. She agreed with me and asked when I was going to do it and she said she would be praying.

That's the power of opening the cocoon or turning over the bushel basket and letting the light shine. It's painful, it's hard, but in the end, you're not so alone.

That call with Randall was difficult, I won't lie. There were tears on the other end of the line and on my end, too. Sometimes doing the right thing will feel awful. Sometimes trusting God will tear your heart out. But when I hung up with Randall, I felt a sense of freedom I hadn't felt in a long while. And it felt good to let God be the driver of my love life again.

Part 5

GROWING

CHAPTER 41

✦ ✦ ✦

Over the next few months, Isaiah got into a new life rhythm.
Before, his identity revolved around basketball, gaming, and
hanging with his friends. Now, he had responsibilities at work
and the privilege of being part of The Forge. He plugged in at
his mother's church and was baptized, with Joshua and even
a few coworkers from Moore Fitness in attendance. He began
attending a college and career Sunday school class that was good,
but it didn't give him the same connection he had with the men
in The Forge.

A pastor asked if he would consider teaching a children's
Sunday school class. One of the teachers had taken a job in
another town and they were short one fourth-grade teacher.

"I'm not sure I'm ready to teach anybody," Isaiah said.

"Here's the thing," the pastor said. "You are going to learn
more than the kids because you'll be preparing every week. You'll
read stories in the Bible you've never heard and find nuggets of
truth to share. Don't worry about not knowing enough—God
will help you."

Isaiah couldn't believe how right the man was. Each week he encountered some biblical story and the lessons from it. It was actually one of the most rewarding things he did each week because the kids in class picked up on his enthusiasm.

Joshua still met with Isaiah, but he was also letting some of the other men spend time with him and Isaiah was learning a lot about finances and life lessons his father had never taught him.

Isaiah sent a text to Joshua one evening that said **Can you meet tomorrow morning? I'll bring breakfast.**

Joshua texted a smiling emoji and said **I'll be there.**

When Joshua arrived, Isaiah had two orders in Styrofoam boxes ready. "I figured you already got your coffee on the way in."

Joshua sat, smiling from ear to ear. "What's this for?"

"You've done so much for me, I wanted to buy breakfast for you this time. I took my mom out to eat not long ago and told her how much she means to me. I want you to know . . ."

An unexpected catch in his throat. He looked away, then back at Joshua. "I don't know what you saw when I showed up here looking for a job. You could've just kicked me out. But you didn't. And I want to be like that—not judging people by what's on the outside."

Joshua's eyes twinkled as he listened. "I lived a long time chasing success and putting people in boxes. And I asked God to open my eyes and help me see what He sees."

"That's what I want," Isaiah said.

"Now I've got something to ask you. You've been part-time with us and learning the floor. Todd said you know every station now and he can plug you in wherever he needs. You ready to move up to full-time?"

Isaiah smiled. "That was the other thing I was going to ask you. See, I've been saving up for a car. I talked with Jerry about getting a loan and he said I'd be better off buying a good used car. Maybe I can sell the old Mustang my grandfather gave me."

Joshua lifted his eyebrows but didn't say anything.

"Anyway, Jerry said if I get in over my head with monthly payments . . . Well, you know Jerry."

Joshua laughed. "Oh, I do. He's a smart man. It's good that you're listening to him."

"I don't know if I'm ready for full-time. But I was wondering if I could get some more hours. Maybe move up to thirty per week? I'd be excited about that."

"I think that's a good plan. I'll talk with Todd. Have you thought anymore about college?" Joshua said. "There are a lot of ways to get a degree."

"Diego mentioned he's taking a couple of classes at the community college. I might look into it."

✦   ✦   ✦

The men of The Forge spent more time with Isaiah over the next few weeks. He took notes of these meetings and wrote them in his journal.

"Uncle Tony said people today are focused on being whoever they want to be. But it's not about what I want to be. When I became a believer, my focus changed from what I want to be to discovering who God designed me to be.

"And that made me realize again that God has a purpose and a plan for me. And I want to follow that. Which is why Tony said that the key is obeying God and doing God's will and not my own. He quoted Matthew 7:21 where Jesus says only those who do the will of the Father will enter His kingdom. So nothing is more important than pursuing my God-given purpose above everything else.

"But what is my God-given purpose? And how do I find it?"

A few pages later, Isaiah wrote some notes from a conversation with Bobby. There was something about the man that was so genuine, as if he didn't need to hide anything, that he could tell God the truth about all that was in his heart.

"Bobby said something last night that stuck with me. Life is short and eternity is long. Then he mentioned a question Jesus asked His followers. It was something like, what does it profit a man to gain the whole world yet forfeit his soul? That hit me hard. Chasing after money or fame or influence—what the world says is important—is empty.

"Bobby said to not foolishly choose short-term pleasure because it might have long-term consequences. Make decisions with the bigger picture in mind. And the bigger picture is what God wants for me, which comes back to who He designed me to be."

Coach Ben took Isaiah to lunch one Saturday. There was something about hearing a man who had achieved success at different levels of sports talking about spiritual things that thrilled Isaiah.

"Ben told me to seek wisdom while I'm young and he quoted the book of James. If you need wisdom and want wisdom, we can ask God and He'll give it to us but only if we put our faith in Him alone. Don't trust the world to give you wisdom. If you do, you'll find yourself on a confusing roller-coaster ride."

Isaiah kept track of the money he had saved for a used car. He looked online and got discouraged every time he saw a car with low miles. The difference between what he had and what he needed seemed so great, even though he was working more hours.

Jerry, from The Forge, invited him to his office. In a conference room with a great view of the city, Jerry encouraged Isaiah to get on a budget and immediately put part of his paycheck in savings as soon as he deposited it in the bank.

"That money is not yours to spend," Jerry said. "Squirrel it away at the start and let it grow. You'll be surprised how fast it will build.

"Here's the truth. Money is a great servant, but it's a horrible master. If your heart is right, it can help you. If you get greedy, it's gonna destroy you. Do your best to stay out of debt. Honor God, work hard, and one day, your money could be working for you."

"That makes me think about Joshua," Isaiah said. "His company supports a lot of mission products that help people."

"Exactly. His business is not just employing people and making good products, he's using some of the profits to do what God created him to do."

There it was again, Isaiah thought. God's design. His purpose. But it had taken Joshua a long time to find that. How long would it take Isaiah?

Jonathan invited Isaiah to his church and long before the service began, the sunlight streaming through the windows behind the stage, Isaiah asked about how to know God's will, how to find the one purpose he was designed for.

"I mean, what about marriage? I want to find the right person, but how do I do that?"

"Don't focus on *finding* the right person as much as you work at *becoming* the right person," Jonathan said. "Find who God wants you to be and work on yourself, deal with the struggles inside, and you'll become a man who knows who he is rather than a man who needs a woman to make him happy. A woman wants to marry a man, not a boy who needs another mother."

"Ooooh," Isaiah said. "That's cruel."

"It is. But it's also true. You were talking about how to find your purpose and know God's will. Listen, Isaiah, in the verse that I've taken to heart, that I live by, Jesus makes it clear when he says, 'I am the vine; you are the branches. Those who remain in me, and I in them, will produce much fruit.' He says, 'Apart from me, you can do nothing.'

"There's so many people who are begging for first place while simultaneously putting God in last place. You can't have it both ways. You gotta seek Him daily, keep Him first, and make Him the priority of your life. When you stay connected to Him, I know from experience, trust me, watch what He does."

Another member of The Forge, James, invited Isaiah to his real estate office. Isaiah remembered that he was retired military. When Isaiah asked where he'd been and what he'd seen, he got quiet.

"I've been in a lot of tough situations and experienced some hard stuff," James said. "But the military showed me that when you're united in an effort, you're much stronger than when you're divided. And that goes for the church. We're stronger when every part of the body is working as it should because we're all connected.

"So each member of the body has to be as connected to God as they can be so they can be connected with each other. Luke 11:34 says your eye is like a lamp that provides light to your whole body. When your eye is healthy, your whole body is filled with light. When your eye is unhealthy, it's filled with darkness.

"This lets me know that I can't look at immoral or junky entertainment. You help guard your heart by guarding your eyes."

Isaiah thought about his decision to get rid of his video games. He'd cut out a lot of things that had tripped him up. He'd deleted apps on his phone. But near Christmas, Jamal called and asked him to see a movie that had just released and he found himself watching with different eyes. The language and some of the scenes made him want to get up and walk out. Then he wondered what he would say to Jamal. So he stayed and watched and talked about the movie afterward.

"I don't know, man," Isaiah said. "It was well-made, they put a lot of money in the special effects, but I didn't like the message."

"The message?" Jamal said. "Man, what's gotten into you? You used to love flicks like that. And you used to game with us all the time."

"I told you, I got rid of my system."

"I know, but you never told me why."

Isaiah wanted to explain it, but how could Jamal understand? Isaiah wanted to tell him that he'd become a follower of Jesus and that the men of The Forge were making a difference in his life. He wanted to tell Jamal about how he could find forgiveness and new life in Christ.

Instead, he shrugged. "I don't know. I just don't want to game anymore."

He felt like a failure. That night as he read through his journal he found a verse he had copied from Joshua's journal. It was from 1 Peter and it said, "And if someone asks about your hope as a believer, always be ready to explain it."

"God, I feel like I blew it with Jamal. I got scared. I was thinking about how he'd respond. Would You give me another chance with him? Give me the words to say. And forgive me for not being bold like I want to be."

CHAPTER 42

✦ ✦ ✦

Cynthia

If I heard it once, I heard it a thousand times. After Isaiah was born, women would take that little bundle from me and look into his round little face and then turn to me and say, "It goes fast."

And I believed them. But I was in the middle of diapers and dishes and working at a failing marriage and working at the salon, and suddenly I looked up and realized Isaiah was turning twenty years old. And "it goes fast" hit me like a pallet of hair gel.

As a surprise, I contacted Joshua to tell him my idea of a party. He showed how smart he was by getting Janelle to plan everything. It was a Saturday and I asked Isaiah if he'd run some errands with me, and as we drove past the restaurant where they have their meetings, I pulled in and said I'd never seen the place and wanted to take a peek inside.

He didn't have a clue! And when those men yelled, "Surprise!" Isaiah was just one big smile walking around the rest of the day.

"You didn't have errands," he said to me later.

"I got you good, didn't I?"

He just shook his head. Then, that night, as I was getting ready to go to bed, he came into the kitchen and sat. And I have learned when Isaiah sits down late at night, he's ready to say something important. So I tried to get all my yawns out and I sat across from him.

He was holding a legal pad and the pages had his telltale scribble all over it.

"I've been working on this for a week," Isaiah said. "Well, longer than that. I've been thinking about it ever since I saw Dad at Moore Fitness."

"You're writing him a letter?"

"Yeah. Trying to. But every time I think I have what I want to say, I say too much, or I say too little, so I rip it up and start all over again."

"And you don't want to call him? See him?"

He stared at the pad. "I like being able to put it down the way I want. If I talk with him, I'll get all tongue-tied. Or angry. This way, I can put the words down I really want to say the way I want to say it."

He tore out a page and handed it to me. "This is the closest I've come so far. Would you take a look? Tell me what you think?"

I looked from his face to the page and then back again. That he was trusting me with reading his words felt like a holy moment.

Dear Dad,

> *When I saw you at the loading dock, I was so angry I had to run. I was afraid I'd yell at you or something worse and they'd fire me. I guess I'm still mad about how you treated Mom and me. Sad that we weren't important enough for you*

to stay or just take the time to explain. But as I've thought about seeing your face that day, I wonder if you have regrets. Maybe you'd handle it differently now than you did back then.

Something happened to me not long ago that has made a big difference in my life. My boss is a Christian and he started sharing the changes God has made in his life. And one day I realized I was carrying around a lot of the anger I had about you and it was like a thousand pounds on my shoulders. And I couldn't do it anymore.

So I asked God to forgive me and change me. I received His forgiveness for all the wrong things I've done. And it was like somebody turned on a light in a dark room. I saw things I'd never seen. I began to see what Mom has done for me. I can't explain it, but if you're still reading this, I hope you find that kind of freedom from any weight you feel.

You see, one of the things I learned was, if God forgives you, He wants to give you that same power to forgive others. Instead of hanging on to the bitterness and the anger, you release that other person and let them know they're forgiven.

Like I said, I still have these feelings inside about what happened a few years ago. But I can honestly say I forgive you. I don't hold that against you any longer. I'm sorry I ran from you. I wish I'd had the courage to stand and talk with you, but like Joshua says (that's my boss who's a Christian), this whole thing is a process. God is working on my heart and I'm trying to do what He tells me to do.

I don't know if you'll get this letter. But if you do, I want you to know that I pray for you every day. I want good things to happen in your life, not bad things. I want you to know the forgiveness that I've found.

Your son,
Isaiah

I looked up from the letter. Isaiah was watching me the whole time I was reading it. I just shook my head and tried to keep my lower lip from trembling, but I wasn't doing a very good job.

"I wouldn't change a thing, Isaiah."

CHAPTER 43

✦ ✦ ✦

Joshua Moore awoke to the sound of his phone buzzing on the nightstand. It was still dark outside and Janelle rolled over as he held up the phone and saw it was Emmett.

"This better be important," Joshua said with as much of a smile as he could muster.

"Sorry, sir. I wanted you to know this before you got in today. I didn't want to text it or—"

"Just tell me, Emmett."

"Okay. My contact says Slayer Sports is really ramping up their production. And that makes me think they're after another account. I'm hoping it's not GymFit or HighStride. If it is, we're in real trouble. But there's a smaller account—actually two, that I haven't heard back from—"

"Emmett, we're going to make it, okay? We're going to do what we need to do. Come by my office later this morning when you know more. Okay?"

"All right, sir. And I'm sorry to wake you, I just . . ."

"I understand. I appreciate you letting me know."

He hung up and knew there was no getting back to sleep. He made coffee and got ready for work. When Janelle came down she asked about the call.

"Have you thought about what you're going to do if Emmett's fears are real?" she said.

He gave a big sigh. "It might mean some travel."

"If it does, both of us are going. You hear me? You're not doing this alone."

Joshua smiled, kissed her forehead, and drove to the office.

Midmorning, Isaiah stepped into his office holding a piece of paper. He ambled to the desk and said, "Mind giving me a ride to The Forge tonight?"

"Pick you up at six fifteen. What's on the page?"

Isaiah dropped the paper on the laptop in front of him. At the top it said, "College Freshman Application." Joshua looked it over and his eyes were drawn to the line that said, "Possible Career Plans." Isaiah had written, "Manager or Business owner."

"So," Isaiah said, sitting across from Joshua, "I can take three classes a semester and still keep my hours here."

Joshua studied a line at the bottom. "Bachelor's degree in business."

"Yeah. What do you think?"

A knowing smile. "I like it. And the cost?"

"I'm eligible for one grant, but I can get a partial scholarship if I keep my grades up. I can cover the rest, but I'm ready to get a car."

Joshua had watched Isaiah from his office window, riding that small bike to work. If he could get there on time every day on a bike, imagine where that kind of commitment could take him.

"I'm actually gettin' excited about it," Isaiah added. "But I know it's gonna be hard."

He was talking about the car, but Joshua was thinking about his life. "Don't be afraid of doing hard things, as long as they're worth doin'. Honor the Lord. See what He does."

"Speaking of hard things, I've been praying for my dad. And I decided to write him a letter. I mailed it off to the company he was driving for, so I hope he gets it. But I said everything I needed to say."

"And if he doesn't respond?"

"I mean, I've already given it to the Lord. I'm becoming more settled with the fact that God is the Father I need most. But I thought I would give it a try, you know?"

"You've done well, Isaiah. No matter what happens, I know the Lord is going to bless you."

A knock on the door. Joshua saw Emmett with an iPad in front of him. The look on his face told him something bad had happened.

"Sorry to interrupt, sir," Emmett said, "but they now have both."

"Slayer Sports got both accounts?"

"Yes, sir. Again, it's two of our smaller accounts, but they are moving fast. We can keep the mission products going for now. But we can't lose another account. I think they're gonna go after GymFit or HighStride."

Joshua took in the information and couldn't help seeing the dominoes falling, no, crashing into each other. There was no question now what he needed to do.

"See if you can get a meeting with our top three accounts. I'll fly out and talk to them."

A bit of relief showed on Emmett's face. "I'll do it."

Emmett left quickly and Joshua felt Isaiah's gaze. He had tried to keep his fears from the employees. They didn't need to know the day-to-day rumors and machinations of management. But he was beginning to wonder how long he could keep this news to himself.

Isaiah stood, then sat again. "How can you be so calm right now? Man, I'd be freaking out if I'd heard that news."

"I am concerned. No question, the wheels are spinning in my head. But I have chosen not to freak out."

"It's as simple as that? You just choose?"

Joshua grabbed his Bible. "I read Psalm 33 today. Listen to this. 'But the Lord watches over those who fear him, those who rely on his unfailing love.' And then, verse 20. 'We put our hope in the Lord. He is our help and our shield.'

"When you let God's Word wash over you each day, when news like this comes, you have a settled heart. You know that God already knew this was coming. So I give it back to Him and ask for wisdom in how to respond. Even when another company is trying to undercut us or even put us out of business, this is an opportunity to trust God."

"But you're not just sitting back and chillin'. You're thinking about meeting with those other companies."

"Absolutely. Trusting God sometimes means you wait. You don't want to rush ahead of Him and do things in your own strength or out of fear. Meeting with those companies is a wise course. I've been through things like this a few times. And the key to this business is the relationship we've built with our clients. They trust us. They know we take care of them. They know what we're about. So while I'm stirred up over this Slayer thing, I believe we'll find a way through with God's help."

"It's like that verse you had in your journal. The one about taking your anxiety to God."

"Exactly. 'Give all your worries and cares to God, for he cares about you.' 1 Peter 5:7."

Isaiah stood. "I assume you want me to keep this Slayer thing on the down-low?"

"If you wouldn't mind."

When Isaiah left, Joshua closed his eyes and whispered a prayer. "Lord, help me believe what I just said."

The rest of the day was a flurry of activity for Joshua, going back and forth with Emmett about meeting times. Janelle was coordinating with them, working on possible flights. When the evening rolled around, he was ready for a mental break and the young men of The Forge provided it in the form of a memory verse. Trey, Ethan, and KJ teamed up to recite Psalm 119:1-3.

"Joyful are people of integrity, who follow the instructions of the Lord. Joyful are those who obey his laws and search for him with all their hearts. They do not compromise with evil, and they walk only in his paths."

Joshua's heart was full when the boys finished and he stood in the circle of men. As they applauded what they'd heard, the problems and stress of the day didn't disappear, but a settled peace came over him.

"Well done!" Joshua said. " I tell you what, gentlemen. As we spend time with the Word of God and hide it in our heart, the Holy Spirit will remind us of it when we need it most. The more I treasure it in my own life, the more it ministers to me." He looked at the three young men who had just spoken. "Thank you for sharing that with us."

Joshua took a breath and raised his voice. "I want to do something tonight that the older men and I have been talking about for a few weeks now. You younger men have been walking through discipleship so well, and we want to affirm you, each and every one of you, every step of the way in your journey.

"Tonight, I want to start. So Isaiah, go ahead and step forward."

The men clapped and said Isaiah's name to encourage him.

Joshua locked eyes with him, and as he spoke, he gripped his Bible tightly.

"I have some things I want to say to you. I have known you now for a year, and I have watched you grow and mature in so many ways. You have grown in character, in responsibility, in your faith, even in the way you carry yourself."

As he spoke, Isaiah seemed to grow taller, the words lifting and buoying him.

"In fact, gentlemen, if I may be blunt, a man is standing in front of me."

"Yes, sir!" someone said, and there was more clapping. Isaiah's eyes misted.

"Isaiah has embraced Jesus Christ as his Lord and Savior. He has worked hard to learn and to apply biblical principles to his life. He has fought to forgive past hurts and surrender them to the Lord. And he has done it. I have watched him walk as a man. A godly man."

Isaiah wiped a tear from his eye and stood straight. With each sentence Joshua spoke, he took a step into the circle and moved closer to Isaiah.

"So Isaiah, I want to bless you in the name of the Lord. I bless you with respect, love, and friendship as a brother in Christ. And I call you a strong, faith-filled man of wisdom, with a bold future. From today forward, may God's hand of goodness rest upon your life. May you experience His love, His forgiveness, His power, and His provision."

Tears streamed down Isaiah's face and he didn't try to hold them back. With each blessing, Joshua moved closer and lowered his voice almost to a whisper.

"May His blessings cover you because you put your faith in Him. And may you now walk in victory and never in defeat. I love you, and I am proud of you . . ."

Joshua reached out a hand and placed it on Isaiah's chest and kept it there. ". . . and I bless you in the name of Jesus, our Lord and Savior."

Joshua looked deeply into Isaiah's eyes and saw his own reflection. He smiled and raised his voice. "Men of The Forge, join me. Let's pray over him."

The circle collapsed on Isaiah as the older men placed hands on him and began to pray with Joshua. And with every word the men responded with their affirmations of his prayer.

"Father God, may You bless Isaiah, our brother in Christ. I ask You to lead him, to guard him, mold him, teach him. Fill him with wisdom, discernment as he walks with You. Place Your hand upon his life and his heart. Father, I ask You to strengthen him with insight. Strengthen him with grace. Strengthen him with favor and place yourself all over him. Bless him when he comes in, and bless him when he goes out. Father, bless everything he puts his hand to. I ask you to protect him from anything that would pull him away from You, fill him with knowledge and understanding. Put him on the path that You have chosen for him. Give him the wife that You have chosen for him. And may he be a blessing to others all the days of his life. Father, I don't ask that You make him one in a million. But that You make him one *of* a million. And I ask this and receive it in the name of our Lord and Savior, Jesus Christ. Amen."

The older men patted Isaiah and the younger men clapped. Joshua pulled Isaiah into an embrace and for a moment, it took him back to another embrace he experienced years earlier. The final embrace of his son.

CHAPTER 44

✦ ✦ ✦

Isaiah paced the kitchen in front of his mother, trying to explain the evening and the feelings that stirred.

"It was like, they were giving me something that I'd never had before. Calling me a man. Joshua said he loved me. And I could tell it was true. He really does."

Cynthia put a hand over her mouth, then waved a hand in front of her face to stop the tears.

"I've never felt like this," he said.

"So it was a good day, huh?"

Isaiah laughed like it was the understatement of the year. "Yeah, it was."

"Well, son, the day is not over."

She said it like she knew something he didn't. She said it like there was a better feeling around the corner, but he couldn't imagine what it was.

"What do you mean?"

She smiled at him with such a knowing look that it unnerved him. "Come on, Mom. What's up?"

"Follow me," she said.

When she opened the back door, he said, "You didn't get a new trash can, did you?"

She led him to the driveway and the closed garage.

"Okay, what is this?"

"I just got something to show you. Can you lift up the garage door, please?"

Isaiah already knew what was behind there. It felt a little like the story in one of the Gospels where Jesus tells Peter to let down the net and he does, even though he doesn't think anything good would come from it.

He turned the handle and lifted the heavy door and it rolled up with a clacking sound. He peered inside at the dusty old Mustang that was a symbol of his father's neglect. All he didn't have was sitting in that garage rusting out.

Except there was no dusty Mustang inside.

Instead, he saw a gleaming, sky-blue 1966 Ford. Speechless, he walked past the shining fender to the passenger side. The leather interior looked brand new.

"This . . . this is not my car," Isaiah said.

He turned to his mother and she had that look on her face, like she was enjoying seeing him amazed.

"This is your car," she said.

He leaned down and looked at the dashboard. The old radio. The steering wheel. The gear shift in the floor. Everything was in pristine condition. No way this was the old Mustang.

"How'd you do this?"

A tear ran down his mother's cheek as she watched him. "Um, Joshua. He knows a man who does this. And," she said, drawing him in with each word, "and, there's another young man I know who's been paying me rent for a little while now. So you know, I've had some extra income and I've been saving it."

Isaiah put his hands on the roof of the car, the emotion overwhelming him. Earlier, Joshua had looked at him and had said the words he longed to hear from his own father, "I love you." And now his mother was saying the same thing, only with her actions and her plan she had put in place months earlier.

He felt her hands on his back. And then her voice, filled with emotion. "Thank you, Lord, for my son. I thank You Father because I see what You're doing in his life."

She hugged him and thanked God again. And the two of them wept together.

Finally, Isaiah turned and wiped his eyes. With a straight face he said, "Now is the day over? Because I don't think I can handle one more good thing happening."

She laughed and they hugged.

CHAPTER 45

✦ ✦ ✦

Isaiah drove with the window down, his arm out, sunglasses on, and a song he liked on the radio. No more pedaling to work or the basketball court. He felt like a king with the sun on his face and the wind in his hair on this picture-perfect day.

When he pulled up and parked by the basketball courts, Jamal was the first to see him. His mouth dropped and his eyes grew wide.

"Is that your car?" Jamal raised his voice. "Let's go, Zay!" He clapped. "Let's go, Zay!"

Isaiah hugged him, but Jamal was transfixed by the car. He couldn't stop looking at it.

Andre and Keenan walked toward the car, stunned at what they saw. Round and round they went, not believing this was the same car that had been in Isaiah's garage.

"How in the world did you do this?" Keenan said.

"I didn't do it," Isaiah said. "My boss knows a guy who restores old cars. And my mom took it to him."

"Is she rich?" Andre said. "This must have cost thousands."

"I been paying rent. She saved it and spent it on this."

"Man, I can't even get my mom to make a ham sandwich," Jamal said.

Isaiah laughed. "Better not let your mom hear you say that."

Keenan couldn't stop walking round and round the car, kicking the tires and running a hand over the leather seats. He even opened the trunk and looked inside.

"Are you for real, Isaiah?" Keenan said. "This is the same car you showed me in your garage? That ratty old dusty, rusty pile of junk?"

"Not a pile of junk anymore, is it?" Isaiah said.

"You got that right. This is a sweet ride."

Andre leaned over the hood and put a hand to his forehead. "Man, I can see my reflection in this thing. Shiny as a mirror."

"So, no more riding your bike to work?" Jamal said.

Isaiah chuckled. "You kiddin' me?"

Jamal turned serious. "Okay, so shoot straight with us. How come you don't hang with us anymore? I know you got a job and everything, but it's part-time. You're a ghost around here."

"Yeah, a ghost," Andre said.

Isaiah thought a moment, remembering his conversation with Jamal after the movie. "You really want to know? Because I'll tell you."

Andre's eyes grew wide. "Ooh, sounds scary."

"Yeah, tell us," Jamal said.

Isaiah's heart beat faster. He took a deep breath and prayed a quick prayer for wisdom. *Lord, give me the words to say.* And then he began to tell them what had happened to him. The three of them listened, for the most part. Andre was the first to disengage. He grabbed the basketball from Keenan and started dribbling. When Isaiah got to the part where he read the Romans Road pamphlet, Jamal shook his head.

"Man, I get this Jesus stuff from my mom all the time. I didn't expect to get it from you, Zay."

"Yeah," Andre said, bouncing the ball onto the court. "Let's play some ball!"

Keenan was the only one left. Isaiah stood by him, facing the car.

"My life was like that car you saw in the garage. Flat tires. Bad engine. No transmission. God did something on the inside when I asked Him to come in and change me."

Keenan stared at the Mustang. Then he looked at Isaiah. "That religion thing did all that for you?"

"It's not the religion thing. I met Somebody who knew all the bad things I'd done in my life. And He loved me anyway. He's given me a purpose in life. He even helped me forgive my dad."

Keenan glared at him. "He came back and asked you to forgive him?"

"No. I just saw him one day and—"

"Hey, you two going to talk or play?" Jamal yelled.

Keenan waved Jamal off and lowered his voice. "You know what happened with my dad, right?"

Isaiah shook his head. "I don't know the whole story."

"Well, my dad makes your dad look like an angel. I can't imagine forgiving him for all the stuff he pulled."

Isaiah stayed silent. Keenan walked toward the court and turned. "So you're too good for us now? Is that it? You find God and stay away from us because we're sinners?"

"It's not like that, man."

Keenan waved him away. "Go on and enjoy your new car and your new life, Isaiah."

Isaiah hung his head. He had tried to give an answer to his friends. But he felt like he had failed.

Part 6

THE CHALLENGE

CHAPTER 46

✦ ✦ ✦

Joshua made sure he had everything he needed on his laptop, including some new spreadsheets Emmett had made just for the trip to Dallas. He stored the computer and headed for the door, then turned and gave the office one more look.

"I think I'm going to need you, too," he said as he walked back to his desk and picked up his Bible.

He slipped it in his computer bag and hurried into the hallway just as Janelle was giving last-minute instructions to a newer employee. The sight of his wife in her blue jacket and white shirt, with her favorite jewelry, made his heart flutter just like it had when he saw her the first time thirty-six years ago.

He'd been invited to a party at a friend's house and he'd seen her across the room. Everything and everyone else in the room faded because he couldn't stop staring at the face of this angelic being. He'd gotten the courage to walk across the room and speak to her. One smile from her and he was smitten.

Though they were both getting older, she had a glowing

beauty that seemed to flow from her gorgeous smile. Everyone at the company loved working with her because she had a way of bringing out the best in others.

He needed to tell her about the heart flutter thing—it was something he often felt but rarely communicated. Maybe he'd tell her on the way to the airport.

"Hey babe, you ready?" he said, walking up to her.

"I was just about to come get you," Janelle said. "Our flight leaves in ninety minutes for Dallas."

Joshua heard someone rush into the hall behind him. Then he heard Emmett's voice. He sounded upset.

"Joshua and Janelle, I know you're on your way to meet with HighStride. I just need a minute. I just learned that Grayson Lance, the new president of GymFit, is having a meeting with Slayer Sports this morning. They're trying to lure him over."

Joshua could hear the fear in Emmett's voice, and a little whine. Joshua had to admit he was feeling the fear as well.

"Is he not responding to us?" Janelle said.

"We've reached out several times, but without a relationship with us, he's just seeing what's out there."

Joshua took a breath and calmed himself. How should they prioritize the situation? Finally he said, "Okay, we'll fly to GymFit after we meet with HighStride. I don't wanna seem desperate, but we need to talk face-to-face."

"I was hoping you'd say that," Emmett said, pumping a fist. "I will let him know you're coming." And with that he was off down the hallway.

"Thanks again, Emmett," Joshua called after him.

Joshua and Janelle picked up their pace and walked stride for stride. Janelle glanced at him and said, "We'd better pray all the way there."

CHAPTER 47

✦ ✦ ✦

Not far from Moore Fitness, Isaiah parked his car by the curb and matched the address on the front of the business with the one on the box in his passenger seat. Moore Fitness delivered equipment across the country, but this business was owned by one of Joshua's friends and Isaiah offered to deliver it personally.

He wore his Moore Fitness polo shirt and khaki pants, making sure he looked professional when he made the delivery. He got out and closed the door, still not believing he was driving the car his grandfather had given him, the car that had impressed his friends at the basketball court. They had basically shut down any communication about spiritual things and that made Isaiah think he'd said something wrong. Then he remembered how he'd treated his own mother—he had done the same to her. How many times had she tried to have a conversation about spiritual things?

A man was waiting at the door and took the box from Isaiah and thanked him. Isaiah shook his hand firmly, just like Joshua had taught him, and turned to leave.

Back at his car he opened his door and glanced across the street and saw the Cornerstone Coffee shop. He immediately felt a flash of pain at the memory of that shop. He'd had an argument with the owner. He tried to shake the memory, thinking he would just get in and drive away, but something kept him there.

James, the real estate agent who was a member of The Forge, had talked with Isaiah about regrets in relationships. Isaiah had talked about mistakes he had made as a teenager and how ashamed he was when he thought about them.

James had said that those regrets could become breakthroughs. When Isaiah pressed him to explain, James said, "Instead of letting the mistakes you've made hold you back, let them propel you. When you think of something that you're ashamed you did, use that as an opportunity to thank God for His forgiveness and reach out to the person you offended and apologize."

"What if they don't forgive me?"

James smiled. "You don't control how they react. You just humble yourself. Most people will appreciate you being thoughtful like that."

Standing next to his car, he felt he couldn't let the opportunity pass. He closed his door and walked across the street, pausing at the door and whispering a quick prayer.

Inside, he saw the owner's daughter at the counter, the girl he'd been enamored with when he saw her through the window. *Abigail,* he thought. He walked to the counter and she smiled and said hello.

"Hey, how are you?" Isaiah said.

"I'm fine, thank you. Is there something I can help you with?"

She didn't recognize him. That was a good thing.

"Uh, by chance is your father here?"

She looked a little puzzled by the question. "He is. Um, do you need to speak with him?"

"Yes, please, if it's not an inconvenience, of course."

"Okay, sure. Just be a second."

As she stepped toward the back, Isaiah thanked her. His mouth felt as dry as cotton. What was he going to say? *Hello, sir. I'm the guy who acted like a jerk in your store last year and I wanted to apologize.*

He glanced at the customers at tables around the restaurant. All women. All in conversations. What had he gotten himself into?

The owner came from the back and walked up to Isaiah. "Hello, sir," he said.

"Hi, I'm Isaiah Wright." He extended his hand and the man shook it.

"Tim Watson. Pleasure to meet you. What can I do for you?"

The man didn't scowl or push him out the door. He didn't recognize him either. He could easily make up something about Moore Fitness and their equipment, but he decided to be honest.

"Well, uh, I wanted to speak to you a moment because I believe I owe you an apology, sir."

Mr. Watson looked a little confused. "An apology?"

"Yes, sir. I was very disrespectful to you and your daughter, and I'm very, very sorry."

Mr. Watson glanced at his daughter, then turned back to Isaiah. He laughed. "I'm sorry, son. I don't believe we've ever met."

"We have," Isaiah said with a smile. "About a year ago I came here, but not to buy coffee. And you asked me to leave, and you know, I said some things that I shouldn't have. And I apologize, to you both. I just hope you can find it in your heart to forgive me."

Mr. Watson looked closer at Isaiah, as if he was finally

connecting the dots. He studied Isaiah's face and with a serious tone said, "You are not the same young man."

Isaiah laughed, thinking of the drastic changes he'd been through in the last year. "No, sir, I'm definitely not."

"I can respect the fact that you've come here to do this, Isaiah. And yes, I can forgive you."

A feeling of relief washed over him and he smiled. "Thank you, sir. That means a lot."

Mr. Watson held out a hand and they shook again.

"I appreciate you taking the time to talk with me," Isaiah said.

"You're certainly welcome."

Isaiah waved at Abigail. "Take care."

He walked out of the shop feeling like he'd had another weight lifted from him. He saw his car gleaming in the sunlight and waited on the sidewalk for traffic to slow so he could cross.

"Isaiah," someone said behind him. It was Mr. Watson. When he reached him, he said, "What happened to you?"

It was the same question Jamal and Andre and Keenan had asked. He thought a moment, then said, "Well, I became a follower of Jesus Christ. And, I'm learning what it means to walk with Him. I've got a lot to learn, but I'm grateful."

Mr. Watson nodded and chuckled, as if he knew exactly what Isaiah was talking about. "Well, I'd say keep going. And if you're ever in the area again, why don't you drop on in and say hello."

"Sounds good," Isaiah said.

"Take care."

"You, too."

When Isaiah drove away, Abigail was looking out the drive-thru window. She smiled and gave a little wave.

His heart fluttered.

CHAPTER 48

✦ ✦ ✦

The flight to Dallas was only two and a half hours, but there was a delay in Charlotte, then a gate problem at DFW. Joshua sat stewing on the plane, going over what he would say in the meeting with HighStride. When the pilot came on the intercom and told them of another holdup, Janelle patted his hand and said, "More time for us to pray, right?"

What was God doing here? Joshua had told the men he had discipled, including Isaiah, that circumstances don't dictate the peace inside a believer. Trusting God fully enables a Christian to live differently. But there were so many questions and frankly, so many fears, he was struggling with finding peace.

By the time they got to their hotel, they were both exhausted. As they were getting off the elevator, Joshua took a call from Emmett.

"Sir, there's been a development. We are definitely in a fight with Slayer over GymFit."

"Janelle and I are headed there after we meet—"

"I know. But now there's no reason to meet with GymFit."

"Are you sure?"

Janelle gestured for Joshua to put the call on speakerphone as they walked into the room. Joshua caught Emmett's response mid-sentence.

". . . and he's opening the door to get the account based on who can fill the order. Apparently, Slayer Sports is saying they can have it ready by noon tomorrow."

"Are their products even the same quality?"

"Grayson Lance says they consider them equal. Slayer has matched our prices and is saying they can deliver them faster. So Mr. Lance has asked for these three thousand units as a demonstration of who can provide them first."

Joshua put his computer bag on the desk in the spacious room. Janelle looked pensive as she listened.

"Send me his number. I've gotta talk to this guy."

"Please. Losing GymFit means closing the mission account or cutting a third of our crew. You don't wanna have to pick your poison. I'm sending his number."

"Thanks, Emmett," Joshua said. He ended the call and felt untethered. Everything seemed out of control.

"Could we even fill an order that fast?" Janelle said.

"Our crew just worked an eight-hour shift. They'd have to work another sixteen hours or more."

His phone dinged with the contact info for Grayson Lance. Joshua sighed and whispered a prayer. "Oh God, show me what to do."

CHAPTER 49

✦ ✦ ✦

Isaiah was spent after a grueling Friday shift at Moore Fitness. Like his basketball days, he'd left everything on the floor, meaning he had worked as hard as possible. He and the other two dozen employees were getting ready for the weekend. He pulled out his phone to text Jamal and see if he wanted to go to a movie, but heard a commotion in the break room. Wyatt was yelling something, which was not out of the ordinary. Wyatt always seemed to be louder than everybody else.

He put his phone away without sending the text as he heard Wyatt yell, "Hey, if you haven't gotten your tickets yet, eight more! We're carpooling to the game. Come on guys, how often do you get to see an NBA game for twenty bucks?"

Wyatt sounded like a carnival barker, encouraging people to "Step right up!"

"All right, we're leaving in five minutes!"

Isaiah walked into the break room and saw Wyatt by one of the tables.

"Curtis, you in?" Wyatt said.

Curtis, clearly exhausted from the day, was slumped in his chair. "Nah, maybe next time."

Wyatt turned and walked out, looking for a few more takers for his tickets. "All right, we're headin' out! See you on Monday!" His voice reverberated in the room.

Isaiah stood by Curtis. "How'd he get twenty-dollar NBA tickets?"

"I do not know."

Diego was taking off his vest and turned to Isaiah. "Wyatt said a company called and gave them to him."

"What company?" Isaiah said. "And if they gave them to Wyatt, why was he charging twenty bucks?"

Curtis chuckled. "The question is, why didn't he charge thirty?"

Isaiah got his backpack and clocked out. He was looking forward to driving home, his windows rolled down. He joined a group walking toward the parking lot that included Diego, Carlos, Curtis, and Wanda.

There was another commotion ahead, but this time Wyatt wasn't involved. They heard raised voices, which wasn't normal, especially coming from Emmett. He was in a heated discussion with Todd.

"Are you kidding me?" Todd said. "Why do they have to have it tomorrow?"

"It's not that they have to have it tomorrow. They're opening the door to whoever can demonstrate that they can get the job done on short notice."

Isaiah and the others in the group stopped. Emmett was usually calm and collected, but his tone was different now. Almost desperate.

"So what are we supposed to do?" Todd said. "I mean, they're notifying us as we're shutting down for the weekend."

Isaiah took the lead and moved toward the two men and the others followed.

"I'm just sayin' that that is a strategic move. That is a 4.5-million-dollar account."

Isaiah stood by Emmett now, his backpack on his shoulder. "What's up?"

"We got a wolf in the chicken coop, that's what's up."

Emmett turned to Isaiah. "Our top account, GymFit. They have a new president and our five-year agreement with them is up this month. Now, another company is saying that they can give them comparable fitness products, and faster. So, GymFit's president is requesting a three-thousand-unit order to whoever can meet it, as a test."

"Who's the other company?" Isaiah said.

"Slayer Sports," Emmett said.

There was an audible groan in the group.

"Wait a minute," Diego said. "Isn't that who sent the NBA tickets?"

"Exactly," Emmett said. "And I just found that out. They want our account and they told GymFit that they could have the order ready by noon tomorrow. Slayer sent those tickets knowing our employees couldn't be called in to help. And when I think about it, we're also farther away. So if we wanted to beat them, we would have to have the order ready over two hours earlier. Man, it was a slick move!"

"Yeah, that's real slick," Todd said. "And now there's no way, man."

Isaiah felt something rising up inside. There was injustice here. What Slayer had done wasn't illegal, as far as he knew, but it was like cheating—and they had home-court advantage because they were closer to GymFit. Something sparked that reminded him of his high school games. The coach who had always been negative, always criticizing, couldn't lead them because he was so afraid of losing. What they needed in the locker room they needed now. Someone to believe. Someone to lead.

"No, no, wait," Isaiah said. "Do we have the products they want?"

"Yes, but that's not the problem," Todd said. "It would take twenty-four people two days to fill that order."

"If they work normal shifts," Isaiah said, looking at the group.

Curtis was the first to speak up, and his voice was tired. "Bro, we just got off an eight-hour shift."

Isaiah cut him off. "But if we lose that much income, it's gonna impact all of us. And it could shut down the mission account, right?"

Emmett's face fell. "Yes."

"So listen," Isaiah said, suddenly energized. "If Slayer wants to make that move, we outplay 'em. We go all night if we have to and have the orders ready by morning."

"Whoa, whoa, whoa, Isaiah, all night?" Todd said. "We've only got six of us. Seven including Emmett."

Wanda shook her head. "Wait, you're not asking me to work another sixteen hours, are you?"

Isaiah held her gaze. No looking down or away. "I'm saying I'm willing to go the second mile. We can't just walk out and do nothing."

"But there's no guarantee that we could fill that order by morning. And if Slayer beats us, we will have stayed up all night long, nearly killed ourselves, for nothing."

Isaiah remembered the pass to him beyond the three-point line. The shot he didn't take. He stood tall and said, "Look, then let me lead. I'll take the blame. And you can tell Mr. Moore it was all my idea."

An uncomfortable silence followed. Todd looked dumbstruck. Emmett closed his eyes, like they didn't have a prayer of getting that order completed. The others weighed Isaiah's words and remained unmoved.

Finally, Carlos stepped forward. "I'm in."

Isaiah could've hugged him right there, but he didn't.

Curtis turned to Carlos and said, "Dude, are you serious?"

"Joshua Moore is the best boss I've ever had," Carlos said. "He's helped too many people for me to walk away."

"I agree," Diego said. "I'll do it, too."

Curtis turned to Isaiah, as if he didn't have a choice about what to do. "Okay. Well if we're all in, I won't be the one to walk out. But if we goin' for that knockout punch, we better connect."

Isaiah looked at the last member of the group. "Wanda?"

"You're really doing this? Can it even be done?"

With confidence, Isaiah said, "Hey, not without Wanda Woman."

She gave a laugh but didn't seem convinced.

"Hey Wanda, we need you. This can't happen without you."

She glanced at Diego and Carlos and with a confident smile said, "I'm in."

Todd spoke next. "Isaiah, if this doesn't work out then what are you—"

"It's on me," Isaiah said, cutting him off. "Listen, it's all on me."

"All right, man," Todd said. "It's all you."

Emmett turned to Isaiah. "What do you need?"

"I need the detailed product order. Then we're gonna need some food and a lot of caffeine."

Emmett hurried off and the crew donned their vests again.

Isaiah watched the crew spring into action. Todd took over the floor robots and began moving products. In the warehouse, Wanda shifted boxes into a robot cart from a storage bin. As Diego and Carlos attacked a different aisle, Isaiah looked up at the unused robots overhead, then hurried to Todd.

"Hey Todd, we also need storage robots on the second floor."

"I can't control those," Todd said, alarmed. "I can only program the floor carts. We need an engineer for those."

"Okay, Isaiah, think," he said to himself. He ran toward the packing area where Curtis was making boxes.

"Hey Curtis, we gotta get the products ourselves. We'll do a hundred at a time. Come help me."

Curtis dropped the tape dispenser and ran with Isaiah.

CHAPTER 50

✦ ✦ ✦

Cynthia

For me, Friday night is my down evening. I order some takeout, watch a movie or read a book. Sometimes I run a bath and just soak my troubles away. Or I call Liz and check in with her. Or I'll go to bed early and not think a thing about how boring my life might seem to others. That's one way I've matured, I'm beginning to care less about what others think. You wind up living somebody else's worries when you care too much about what they think of you.

Isaiah wasn't home from work and I wondered if he had gone to a movie with Jamal or Keenan. I kept waiting to see his car lights on the kitchen wall. And it made me think of the look on his face when he first drove away in that car.

My phone rang. It was Isaiah.

"Let me guess—you went to the movies and you're leaving your mother—"

"Mom, I can't talk long. I'm still at work."

I heard it in his voice. Stress and worry. He sounded like he was playing basketball, he was so out of breath.

"Still at work? You were supposed to get off at—"

"Mom, I need you to do something for me. I need you to pray."

That stopped me short. "What for? What happened?"

He quickly explained about needing to get an order done overnight, that a few of them had stayed behind and would probably work all night.

"Wait, wait, wait, when do you have to have this done?"

"By morning. We gotta beat another company to save our top account, and the mission account. But we gotta figure a way to get our storage bots working. Just pray for us. I gotta go. I love you."

I wasn't even able to say goodbye he hung up so fast. And I wasn't sure I understood anything about that call other than the prayer part. I flipped through my contacts, hit call, and waited.

"Sweet Cynthia, now what would you be calling me about on this Friday night?"

"Miss Clara, I just talked with Isaiah and he asked me to pray about a situation at Moore Fitness. For some reason they have to work all night to get an order out and he asked me to pray. So I'm wondering if you would do the same."

"I would be honored to do that, but I'm not sure what to pray for other than strength to stay awake."

"He mentioned something about storage bots, which I think are robots that move products from one place to another."

"Is that so? Well, I can't say that I've ever prayed for robots before. Although last week I did pray about my dishwasher."

"Your dishwasher?"

"Uh-huh."

"And what happened?"

"Oh, it's workin'."

I laughed. "Well, Isaiah is real concerned about doing this for Moore Fitness. It sounds like they have to get this job done or they'll lose a big account."

"Oooooo, I see," Miss Clara said. "Looks like it's going to be a long night for all of us."

"I can't thank you enough for doing this. Wait. He just texted me. He said to pray they will get the three thousand orders done before the deadline."

"Three thousand? That sounds like an awful big prayer. Let me lead us right now."

She took a breath and I closed my eyes.

"Heavenly Father, first I want to thank You for Isaiah's heart for this company. And the way the owner uses the profits for kingdom work. You know what they need right now, Father. They need these robots or whatever they are to start working. I don't understand it, Lord, but You do. And I pray You would wake up somebody who knows how to work those machines and get them down there. You calmed the storm on the sea of Galilee, You parted the waters of the Red Sea, and I know You can take care of these robots if it's Your will, and I pray You'll do it miraculously.

"Give Isaiah and the others with him supernatural strength to do what You've called them to do. Some trust in chariots and horses, some trust in robots, but we are going to trust in the name of the Lord. Do something that can only be explained by Your intervention here. I pray this in the mighty name of Jesus. Amen."

"Amen. Thank you, Miss Clara."

"Now you keep praying, girl," Miss Clara said. "And you let me know any robot update you get. You hear?"

"I will call you as soon as I hear anything."

CHAPTER 51

✦ ✦ ✦

Joshua paced by the hotel room window as he waited for Grayson Lance to pick up. It was the old keep-them-waiting routine to show them who was boss. Joshua knew it well because he had used it early in his career. Now he saw it for what it was— a power play. He could tell by the look on Janelle's face that she felt the same way. She was setting up the laptop to connect with the server at Moore Fitness.

Finally, the man picked up. "Mr. Moore, what can I do for you?"

"Well, I've heard some distressing news and I wanted to hear it from you. We've had a long relationship with GymFit and I feel like we've served your company well."

"That's what I'm told. And we've honored our contract with you. But as the new leader here, I'm looking for ways to make this company better. And Slayer Sports is prepared to prove they're a cut above. You're not suggesting we shouldn't negotiate with another company, are you?"

"Mr. Lance, you certainly have the right to talk to anybody you'd like. But this timeline, it's a surprise to me."

"This is a real-world situation, Joshua."

Joshua winced at hearing his first name used by the younger man.

"But tomorrow morning is an unusual request."

"And that's the request I'm making if you want us to continue with your company. You deliver sports equipment. Surely you're not afraid of a little competition to earn my business?"

"Yes, I understand."

"Good, so let me know your decision. You have my number."

"I'll call you soon."

Joshua gave a sigh of frustration and closed his eyes. How could the man be so obtuse?

"He's just trying to establish himself as a leader willing to make risky changes," Janelle said.

She always had his back. When he was wrong about something, she wasn't afraid to call him on it. But when she sensed others were being unfair, she could be a fierce supporter.

Joshua held out his hands. "I can't shut down the mission account. I can't do it. I don't want to lay off anybody either. That's just too many hours to ask our crew to work. I need to call Emmett."

As he pulled up Emmett's contact, Janelle hit a few keys on the computer. "Uh, Joshua. I just pulled up the security cameras to take a look at the storage area. You need to come see this."

Joshua couldn't tell by the look on her face if this was good news or bad. He walked behind the desk and saw movement on the screen. Workers in vests were pulling product from the shelves by hand.

"Isaiah?" Joshua said, staring in amazement.

"You do have a crew," Janelle said, flipping to another

camera. There were at least six people working as a team. "And it looks like they're trying to fill this order."

Joshua's mind raced as he studied the screen. "To do three thousand, they're gonna need the storage bots. See if you can reach out to Cody. We may have to do this remotely."

"I'm on it, babe," Janelle said, opening a second computer. She kept the phone on speaker and Cody picked up on the second ring. She apologized for calling late.

"Can you control the storage robots from where you are?"

A noise that sounded like a bag of chips on the line. "Uh, the storage? Yes. Yes, I can."

"Wonderful. Would it be possible to get your help? One of our competitors is trying to take away our largest account, and we have a team at the factory trying to stop them. But we need those robots."

Joshua heard clicking in the background. "Well, they're undergoing a firmware update currently, and I don't have the order information, so I don't know how I would do that."

"I can tell you the number of products and where they're stored," Janelle said. "But we need to move quickly."

"Okay, I can pull the program up now but I'm gonna have to access the robots one at a time."

"We'll take it," Joshua said. "And we need to run them at full speed."

A pause on the line. Cody said, "Sorry, um, we've never done that before."

"Oh, we're doing that tonight," Joshua said.

CHAPTER 52

✦ ✦ ✦

Isaiah and Curtis worked quickly to push carts full of products to the boxing station. Wanda, Diego, and Carlos followed with their own carts. They were working as fast as humanly possible, and Isaiah wondered if they kept it up all night if it would be enough.

Todd walked toward him with a grim look. As he shook his head, he said, "Isaiah, without those robots we're only going to be able to do fourteen hundred units at best."

Isaiah stared at him, then looked toward the second floor, darkened and inactive. They could work all night and not get halfway done with the shipment.

Instead of despairing, Isaiah threw up a prayer. "God, I need those."

A moment passed. Suddenly, lights tripped. The second floor came alive with brilliant light and machines powered and whirred to life.

"Todd!" Isaiah yelled.

"Who turned those on?" Todd said.

"I don't care," Isaiah said. "Keep working!"

"You've got the first portion, I'm pulling up the second," Joshua said to Janelle.

"Okay, Cody, we gotta move fast," Janelle said. "You ready?"

"Yes, ma'am," Cody said.

Janelle leaned forward to confirm the numbers on her screen. "Bot 21 to Port 15 for twenty units. Bots 23 and 24 to port 35 for thirty units each."

"Got it," Cody said. "Sending them now."

Isaiah heard the glorious, wonderful sound of bots moving overhead. They glided together like a technological orchestra, and the human members of the team worked in tandem, running from station to station, each doing the work of two or three.

Isaiah ran to a bin where newly arrived products came down the chute and settled. He picked up two packages and scanned them with his iPad, hoping these were the items on the order list. The blip of the scanner confirmed his hope.

"This is it!" he yelled. "This is what we need."

The others stared at the bots, amazed at the speed they were moving, and doing so with no engineer upstairs at master control.

"Uh, Curtis, we need boxes!" Isaiah said, trying to anticipate their next moves. "Diego, Carlos, run the conveyor at full speed. Todd, we gotta start packing."

"How is this happening?" Todd yelled, incredulous.

Wanda ran to the floor carts and Isaiah glanced overhead. Was this because of his mother's prayers?

"Keep praying, Mom," he said as he ran.

"Bot 45 to port 19 for eight units," Janelle said to Cody. She muted the phone. "Joshua, how is it looking?"

He showed her his calculations. "At this pace, we'll be short of three thousand."

Janelle gathered herself and unmuted the phone. "Cody, can we go faster?"

"Uh, yes, I'm willing to try."

"You let me know when you need a break, but we gotta keep movin'. Are you ready?"

"Go for it, Mrs. Moore."

Emmett had never been in the building this late. It was a little spooky being in the break room alone. But the hum of activity in the factory almost sounded like the middle of the day.

He was loading a cart with food, water bottles, and iced coffee drinks when his phone rang. It was Joshua.

"Emmett, was this your idea?"

"You're not going to believe it, Joshua. It was Isaiah. He got us all believing we might do this."

"I'm seeing the cameras. So it's you two, Diego, Carlos, Wanda, and Curtis?"

"Yes, it's just those six and me. I'm getting food and drinks for them right now. I think it's gonna be a long night!"

"Thank you, Emmett," Joshua said. "Give them whatever they need. We'll help Cody to keep those robots working."

Isaiah had run sprints in basketball practice that had him switching directions and running up and back on the court until he was dizzy and drenched in sweat. But he had never done anything so taxing or so rewarding as what he was doing now. He kept thinking of the faces of those children in far-off countries who needed the help Moore Fitness provided. That drove him as he put more orders in containers and put them on the conveyor.

"Man, if only everybody else hadn't gone to the NBA game," Todd yelled over the noise.

"Hey, focus on who's here, not on who's not here," Isaiah said with a wink.

"Here we go fellows, I've got drinks on deck!" Emmett yelled as he rolled a cart into the area. He handed Todd a coffee, tossed a bottle of water to Wanda, then one to Curtis. Isaiah ran past and grabbed a drink and an energy bar and flew back to work.

✦　✦　✦

Cody had been playing a computer game earlier in the evening. His mother had looked over his shoulder at the animated robots on the screen. Now, feverishly typing on his computer, lasered in on the bots he controlled, his mother approached in her robe.

"Are you still playing that robot game?"

"These are real robots now, Mom. Everything is real! It's all real."

Cody had tried to explain what he did at Moore Fitness, but she had never seen the computerized, motorized, wheeled robots that he talked about moving above the factory floor. She leaned closer to the screen, watching the squares moving from right to left, trying to make sense of the numbers he typed.

"How is it real?"

"It's for work, Mom. There's a crew working overnight. Now, I need to concentrate, okay?"

✦　✦　✦

As darkness settled on the Dallas skyline, fatigue set in for Joshua. He felt it mostly in his shoulders as he leaned over the desk and watched the orders fly. His calculations about where they might be by morning were changing every few minutes.

Janelle was still at his side, calling out instructions to Cody on the phone. "Bots 58 and 59 to port 5 for twelve units each."

Joshua held up his phone and studied the numbers. "At this pace, we'll land at 2,780." With resignation in his voice he said, "I'm making the call."

Janelle glanced at him, then held up her phone. "Cody, let's take a three minute break and come right back."

"Will do," Cody said.

Joshua dialed a number and Janelle muted her phone.

"Are you sure?" she said.

Grayson Lance answered as if expecting him. "Mr. Moore."

"Mr. Lance, you said whoever can have this order ready first will get this account. I understand that you already have an offer of noon on the table."

"We do, and they're closer. They're working on it right now. So to beat that, you'd have to make it around nine thirty a.m. your time."

Joshua spoke with renewed vigor now. "I believe I can have this order ready at nine. And we're interested in keeping this account for years to come."

Janelle gave Joshua a look. When he said he was going to call it, she thought he meant they couldn't hit the goal.

"Are you telling me that you'll have all three thousand units ready for pickup?" Lance said.

Joshua glanced at the security cameras on his screen and saw Isaiah and the others moving at lightning speed. "Mr. Lance, send your trucks."

✦ ✦ ✦

Isaiah and Diego pulled two handcarts filled with orders to the first delivery door. Two full rows of pallets were ready.

"Hey!" Todd called as they approached. He smiled and pumped a fist in the air. "That's a thousand. We beat Wyatt's record."

"The record will be three thousand when we're done," Isaiah said confidently.

"And I cannot wait to see Wyatt's face when he finds out," Carlos said, transferring boxes from the cart to a pallet.

"Yeah, but three thousand is a long shot," Todd said. "You guys know that, right?"

"That's what's so motivating," Diego said, transferring a heavy box to a pallet. "We do the impossible!"

"Aren't you guys tired?" Todd said.

Diego kept lifting. "Yes, very!"

Todd shook his head, then placed his iPad on a stack of boxes and joined them.

"Lord, You know how tired I feel right now," Cynthia prayed. She was sitting up in bed with her hands clasped. "I can only imagine how tired Isaiah and the others are. I pray You would give them strength to meet this goal. Preserve the company for the workers, for Joshua, and for those who need to know about You in other lands. Don't let the enemy discourage them, but give them momentum to complete each task well."

Miss Clara was in her war room with her Bible open. She was rocking back and forth in her chair, as if gaining some kind of heavenly prayer momentum.

"Jesus, You said You are the vine and we are the branches.

And Isaiah is one of those branches. Help him draw his strength from You tonight and help him be a light to those around him.

"Lord, You know there are people working there who probably don't know You. Would You use this test of their abilities to show them they need to trust in You for salvation, for it's only in the name of Jesus that we are saved. Give Isaiah boldness, Lord. Raise him up and build him up in You. Make him flourish like a tree planted by a holy stream of water. Use this crucible to make him shine and show those around him that he is a leader, strong and filled with grace and truth. Be a stronghold to him in this time of trouble and deliver him because he takes refuge in You.

"And I pray the Holy Spirit will empower him right now. Give all of these workers unity, Lord, and no discord, no contention. Help them work together and not argue or complain.

"And Father, I ask that those robots will do what they were programmed to do, and give them even more speed in that factory than ever before. Amaze the workers with what can be done. Amaze the company that is asking them to do this hard thing. And give them victory."

Wanda tried not to look at the factory clock. There was something about seeing the numbers that reminded her of how tired she was and how long she had been there. And that it was now Saturday. At one forty five a.m. she glanced up, saw the time, then quickened her pace.

A floor bot hummed through an aisle and Wanda caught up with it and ran past it carrying an armful of boxes. "Too slow, Robot! I'm Wanda Woman!"

Then she screamed it again, at the top of her lungs and heard Isaiah laugh a few rows away.

She met the guys near the bay doors and the four of them worked together transferring boxes to pallets, the larger ones on the bottom and smaller ones at the top for easier loading. Wanda was impressed with the ways the team was working without a lot of direction. It was as if they all knew what to do next and just ran to get it done. Or maybe it was exhaustion that kept them from talking. No sense wasting energy on words, when it could be used for moving boxes.

Joshua had worked side by side with Janelle to start Moore Fitness, but he had never worked this closely or through the night. That they were doing this from such a distance from their home made it even more special.

Janelle gave him a look. "I need to go wash my face and stretch my legs."

"Go, I'll take over with Cody."

She gave him a peck on the cheek and he called out more directions.

Joshua had a hard time not watching the cameras at the loading docks. There were rows of full pallets lining the floor and the team's movement was mesmerizing.

"Bot 75 to port 7 for fifteen units," Joshua said. He looked at the counter and double-checked his calculations. "Cody, that's two thousand."

Joshua heard a muffled whoop on the phone line, then Janelle returned. "All right, I'm good. I can keep going."

"Are you sure?"

Janelle laughed as she sat next to Joshua. "I'm in the groove, so we gotta move."

Joshua kissed her on the cheek and thought of his "fluttering heart" when he had seen her in the hallway before their flight. He still hadn't told her about that.

"You are amazing," he said.

She smiled, then went back to her phone. "Cody, you still good?"

"Yes." It sounded like he slapped his hands together. "Sorry. My fingers are running a marathon, but I wanna cross the finish line!"

✦ ✦ ✦

Isaiah felt part coach, part player, and part cheerleader. He was proud of the crew and how tirelessly they worked, even though he knew they all wanted to go to the break room and sleep for a week. Several times as they passed each other there were high fives and fist bumps.

"You guys are crushing it," Isaiah said.

He finished unloading a cart and was returning it to the packing area, when his iPad gave him a notification. His heart swelled and he held it up.

"Hey, that's two thousand!"

Wanda gave a weak, "Wooo."

"Feels like ten thousand," Todd said, out of breath and sweaty.

"Let's stop for just a minute," Isaiah said, circling a hand for the team to huddle. "Let's bring it in."

He could see the exhaustion setting in. But they were still working, still struggling to make boxes, pack them, and get them on the pallets.

"Hey, we're doing it," Isaiah said. "We've worked faster than anyone, and we're almost at the finish line. So, let's stay in it. And remember, it's not just business we're keeping. It's every missionary and ministry team that uses the water filters, solar panels, and lanterns that this company provides. We have to keep that available. All right? If Mr. Moore could see us, he'd be so proud."

"He can see you," Emmett said, walking up next to Isaiah and smiling bigger than Isaiah had ever seen him smile. "He's been watching you for the past ten hours from Dallas over the security cameras."

Isaiah glanced up at one of the cameras and smiled. Then he looked at his coworkers and couldn't contain his joy.

"And, they've been working with Cody this whole time to keep the storage robots running," Emmett said.

Curtis pointed to the second floor. "So that's how they been doing that?"

"They can see us?" Wanda said.

"He texted me earlier." Emmett read, "'I have never been so proud of this crew. They've gone above and beyond anything I could have asked, and I will never forget it. They're not sleeping, so we're not sleeping. We're watching, working, and praying for them. We love them so much!'"

Isaiah drank in the words that gave him even more resolve to finish well. "We gotta punch this thing in the end zone, all right? We're not stopping."

"Hey, Mr. Isaiah," Diego said. "My body is *cansado*. But my heart is ready."

Carlos took a deep breath. "Give me caffeine and I am with you."

"Wanda, what do you need?" Isaiah said.

"Oh, I got enough caffeine in me to go until next Tuesday." The others laughed.

"Todd?"

"Oh, this is beyond crazy. Why are we gonna stop now, huh?"

"Curtis?"

Curtis had his hands around his vest like he was too tired to let go. "Oh, I'm gonna sleep for about two days after this. But until then . . ." He clapped his hands. "Let's roll!"

✦ ✦ ✦

Cynthia's phone rang and it startled her. Not because she was asleep but because she wasn't expecting anyone to call at four thirty a.m. The screen said *Clara*.

"Have you heard any update from Isaiah?"

"Miss Clara, are you still up praying?"

"Honey, I haven't stopped since we talked before. I'm believing God for some kind of robot miracle. The boxing of the three thousand!"

Cynthia shook with laughter. "You are something else, you know that?"

"I'm going to have me a good nap later this morning. But I'm on pins and needles. What has Isaiah said so far about their progress?"

"I'm sorry I didn't call you. I didn't want to wake you, in case you'd fallen asleep."

"There is no sleep for me when there's a battle to be fought in prayer."

"He sent me a text a couple of hours ago. He said they had passed two thousand units—"

"Glory!"

"—and they are all still working to meet the deadline."

"Praise the Lord!"

"You keep praying, Miss Clara."

"And you do the same, Sweet Cynthia."

✦ ✦ ✦

The sound of tape unrolling and boxes being placed on the floor filled the area as the crew continued stacking. Isaiah heard a notification on someone's phone and turned as Emmett yelled, "Hey Isaiah, the trucks will be here in thirty minutes!"

Isaiah felt the energy from his toes to his head. He jumped as he yelled, "Okay, we got thirty minutes! Finish strong! Finish strong!"

✦ ✦ ✦

Janelle saw orange on the Dallas skyline that turned yellow and gave way to blue sky overhead. She had gone through every order and was down to the last line.

"And bot 8 to port 12 for seven units," she said. "And that's it."

"The last sixty orders are on the conveyer belt," Joshua said. "They have to seal, label, and stack them."

"Cody, it's up to them now," Janelle said.

Cody's voice showed his exhaustion, but his resolve came through. "I can't go to bed until I know we made it."

Joshua stood and stretched and walked to the other side of the room. He turned back to Janelle.

"Those trucks have to be close," he said.

Janelle leaned close to the screen, watching the last pallet being filled. "I can't wait to see the look on those drivers' faces when Todd opens those doors."

Joshua got a funny look on his face. He dialed a contact and held the phone up.

"Yes, sir?" Emmett said on the speakerphone.

"Emmett, get a blazer from the staff closet. Give it to Isaiah. Let him greet the drivers."

"You got it," Emmett said.

✦ ✦ ✦

Isaiah ran to the boxing area and scanned the codes of twenty boxes Wanda and Carlos had just placed there. He did all twenty in four seconds and Todd's mouth dropped.

"How'd you do that so fast?"

"Too many video games," Isaiah said.

Emmett rushed to him, out of breath. "Isaiah, the trucks are almost here. Joshua wants you to greet the drivers. I have a jacket in my office whenever you're ready."

Isaiah glanced at Todd. He was the one who should be at the loading door.

Todd shook off any resentment. "Isaiah, go! We got this!"

Isaiah sprinted for the break room with Emmett close behind. He grabbed a paper towel and wiped his face, then threw the blue blazer on. A low rumble sounded and Isaiah glanced at Emmett.

"They're pulling in," Emmett said.

Isaiah sprinted back to the loading area. "Is that it?" he said.

"That's it!" Todd said. "We're done!"

At the door, Isaiah glanced at the clock. "It's 8:58. We got two minutes to spare! Let's go!"

✦ ✦ ✦

Joshua watched the loading dock camera and couldn't contain his joy as Curtis and Isaiah slapped hands in victory. Diego and Wanda and Carlos and Todd joined them, celebrating.

"Look at 'em, Janelle. Look at our team. Oh, thank You, Jesus!"

Janelle was near tears and overwhelmed. She leaned toward her phone. "Cody, we made it! It's done!"

Joshua couldn't make out the words, but it sounded like Cody was doing a bot dance in celebration.

His phone rang. It was Emmett.

"Joshua, the order is ready and the trucks are here."

✦ ✦ ✦

With the doors still closed, Isaiah turned to the team. Todd moved closer and looked him in the eyes.

"You impressed me, brother," Todd said. "I didn't think this was possible."

"Hey," Isaiah said. "You helped me. We got it done."

Todd gave a whoop of victory and Isaiah glanced at the clock. 8:59.

"Isaiah," Emmett said. He stood looking through a partially opened side door. "Isaiah, Grayson Lance is here."

"What?" someone on the phone said. Isaiah recognized Joshua's voice.

"Joshua, you want to talk to him?" Emmett said.

Silence. Isaiah looked at the clock. The numbers flipped to 9:00.

"No," Joshua said. "Isaiah's got this."

Isaiah stared at Emmett, taking in his boss's words. And instead of backing down or arguing or passing the ball to someone else, Isaiah walked to the door and took a deep breath.

"God, please give me favor."

He hit the green button to open the door and stepped back. As it slowly moved up, Isaiah remembered the time he'd hit the same button and seen the face of his father on the other side. Instead of that being a wound that incapacitated him, he thanked God that he'd had the chance to see his dad and that he'd been able to reach out to him.

Grayson Lance stood about six feet tall, white, and he wore a gray blazer with no tie, gray slacks, and trendy shoes. He looked to be in his thirties with perfect hair, perfectly cropped beard, perfect physique. He could have passed for some Hollywood type, exuding confidence, swagger, and power. Behind him stood three men in matching shorts and shirts—Isaiah assumed these were the drivers for GymFit.

"Mr. Lance," Isaiah said, stepping toward him and extending a hand. He shook firmly and looked the man in the eyes. "Good morning. Isaiah Wright. Welcome to Moore Fitness."

"Good morning to you," Lance said.

Isaiah turned and led him inside the loading dock. His coworkers stood watching and Isaiah remembered that Joshua and Janelle would be able to see through the cameras and could probably hear his conversation via Emmett's phone.

"You had an early start," Isaiah said.

"Five a.m. When Mr. Moore said you'd be ready at nine, I wanted to come see for myself."

"I'm glad you did. We'd love to show you the company."

"Mind if my drivers check the order?"

"Absolutely, be our guest." Isaiah swept his hand behind him at the line of boxes on pallets. "We have three thousand and one units ready to load."

The man turned and gave a slight nod and the three men dutifully moved to inspect the shipment. Isaiah tried to think of something to say, some kind of small talk that would fill in the space, but Grayson Lance spoke first.

"You know, I just learned that your competitor sent your employees NBA tickets for a game last night."

"They did."

"Now I understand the timing of their offer. Clever move. So how in the world could you have this order ready?"

"Mr. Lance, your account means a great deal to us. We value our partnership with GymFit and we're willing to go the extra mile to keep that. We had a small group that stayed up all night until the order was done. You won't find a better team any-where."

Isaiah motioned to his five exhausted coworkers who looked on with pride. Then he turned back to Grayson Lance.

"And you won't find a better partner in business than Joshua Moore. And as you can see, it is our privilege to help you win and keep this partnership going."

Grayson glanced at the others, then locked eyes with Isaiah. "That's pretty bold. I like that."

Isaiah knew that the last contract had been for five years and was now up. A win would be for another five-year contract.

"Listen, I'm a competitive person, but I also want to trust my partners. Slayer Sports tried to slow you down, yet they're still working on their order. So, I'm willing to go another five years with you guys."

Isaiah felt the energy of his coworkers' excitement and he imagined Joshua and Janelle's reaction from Dallas. But he kept his face controlled. Serious.

"Mr. Lance, you've seen what we're capable of, with a partial crew. So, why not be bold and keep a good thing going? Let's do seven years."

Lance stared at Isaiah, then glanced at the crew to the side. He looked behind Isaiah and one of the drivers must have given him a thumbs-up to confirm the order.

Lance extended a hand. "Done."

Isaiah shook his hand firmly and smiled. "Again, we value your business." He turned and made a circling motion with a hand. "All right, let's load it up!"

CHAPTER 53

✦ ✦ ✦

On Monday morning, Joshua and Janelle drove to the office with a new sense of excitement. What had been a stressful trip to Dallas, filled with questions and foreboding, had become a victory for the company.

Janelle worked with the accounting department to cut bonus checks for the team that had worked all night. As soon as the checks were in hand, Joshua had Emmett gather the group in the conference room.

Joshua hugged Isaiah and beamed with pride.

"You heard the whole interaction with Lance, didn't you?" Isaiah said.

"You'd better believe it," Janelle said. "And you should have seen his face when you asked him for seven years."

"I thought I was going to die!" Joshua said.

"It was all I could do to keep from saying, 'No!'" Emmett said.

"But I'll give him this—Grayson Lance, as young as he is, saw what had happened," Janelle said. "And he honored our integrity. So we're moving forward with someone I think we can trust."

Joshua turned to Isaiah. "When you shook his hand and looked him in the eyes, I couldn't hold back from thanking God for you. I was as proud as any father could be of a son. And I felt the same way for each of you who stepped up. You didn't complain. You didn't make excuses. You just got to work. Thank you."

Cody jumped in with a story about Janelle calling him and interrupting an online game he was playing that turned into an all-night event. "I thought Mr. and Mrs. Moore would fall asleep before I did, but when they kept going, I kept going."

"I told Joshua I was going to turn into a zombie if I didn't get some sleep Saturday morning," Janelle said.

"Best sleep I've had in years," Joshua said.

Janelle handed him a stack of envelopes.

"And as a token of appreciation for your work that went above and beyond, I want each of you to have a little bonus to honor your faithfulness and dedication to doing the impossible."

Joshua handed checks to each person. There were raised eyebrows and gasps when they saw the amount of the bonus. When Wanda opened hers, she waved the check in the air and yelled, "Wanda Woman!" Then she covered her mouth with a hand and said, "Sorry, Mr. Moore."

"No apology needed, Wanda Woman."

CHAPTER 54

✦ ✦ ✦

Isaiah felt like he was walking on air all day Monday. The weekend's events had created a bond between him and his coworkers. Those who had gone to the game slowly heard about what had happened. Most were congratulatory and grateful for the team beating the deadline.

However, Isaiah couldn't wait to see Wyatt's reaction. That came in the break room at lunch on Monday. Wyatt swaggered in and began to talk about the great seats they had at the game and how much fun it was. "I'm sure we're going to get more tickets soon, so anybody who missed out, don't let that happen again."

Clearly, Wyatt hadn't heard about the events at work Friday night. That is, until he looked at the corkboard and saw that his twenty-four-hour box record had an *X* through it. Beside it was a new certificate that said the new record was 3,001 units and the record holder was Isaiah Wright.

"What?" Wyatt yelled. His face had flashed red when he

turned back to the table. "There's no way it's real. That's a joke, right? You can't do three thousand units that fast. This is impossible!"

Isaiah sat with Curtis, Carlos, Diego, and Wanda. All five of them tried to contain themselves.

"With just six workers on the floor, you can't do it! You can't. Don't do this, guys. I'm supposed to be the leader here. Just tell me the truth! Come on, man, tell me."

The veins on Wyatt's neck bulged. He turned to Isaiah's group. "No? You, Curtis?"

Curtis got up and extended his arms and walked toward Wyatt.

"No, I don't want a hug. I want the truth, bro." He backed away, then pointed at the corkboard. "Just take it down. Guys, we know it's not real. Guys, I'm not joking!"

He avoided Curtis and quickly moved toward the door. He paused before he left. "Take it down!" His parting shot was a cross between a yell and a whine.

"That was almost as good as getting the check," Diego said.

"Almost," Carlos said.

After work, Isaiah deposited his bonus check and drove home. His mother had texted him to say she had a surprise waiting. When he got there he found his mother and Miss Clara sitting at their kitchen table. His mom had told him Saturday evening, after he had collapsed in his bed and slept all day, that she and Miss Clara had prayed all night.

"So this is the young man I've heard so much about," Miss Clara said when he walked in.

"I'm so glad to see you," Isaiah said, giving her a hug.

The three of them sat at the kitchen table and Miss Clara was the first to speak. "So, I understand that you stayed up all night long with an army of robots to save the world," she said.

Isaiah laughed. "Well, not the world, but, you know, it turned out to be a good thing. And I understand that you stayed up several hours praying for us. So, I just wanted to say thank you."

"Your mother's been telling me about how you've been chasing after the Lord, becoming a disciple of Jesus Christ."

"Yes, ma'am. I'm learning."

"Well, don't you stop. Never stop. And you keep your eyes on the Lord more than yourself, and your heart on heaven more than this world. And don't you keep taking one step forward and then one step backwards with your faith. 'Cause baby, that ain't nothing but the cha-cha."

Isaiah and Cynthia both laughed at the humor of the old woman and also the warmth they felt from her.

"No, you devote your heart to following the Lord, no matter what the cost. 'Cause He's worth it."

"Yeah, He is worth it," Isaiah said. He thought a moment and something came to mind. Why not enlist this woman who could awaken robots to help him in something even more important?

"Can I be selfish and ask for prayer?"

Miss Clara smiled and glanced at Cynthia and they had a moment together just taking those words in.

"So, you know, I want to go after my friends. And I really want them to know and experience the Lord for themselves. I don't know where to start, but I know I want to help disciple them."

Miss Clara studied him as if she were looking at a priceless painting or sculpture. "Well, I will be praying, that your friends would open up their hearts to the truth, and when you open up your mouth to speak, that the Lord will give you the words."

As she spoke, she touched his arm with a hand and emphasized each word.

"And I'll tell you this, Isaiah. We need more young men and women just like you chasing after the Lord!"

She said it with such conviction that her head shook and she made a fist as if in defiance of any enemy that would come against Him.

"Unashamed of following Him," she continued. "So I will be praying. Praying that the Lord will raise up a million more just like you. We need to be the salt and the light now more than ever before, because the days are getting darker."

She paused, as if reaching some difficult moment in her charge to Isaiah. "And the church." She shook her head as she said, "The church, the church." Then she raised her hands and whispered. "The church has to wake up. And step up." She pounded the table and shouted now. "Because the time is short! There's no time to waste."

Miss Clara leaned close, her voice quiet again. "We need devoted followers of Jesus. Because you see, Jesus, Jesus, Jesus is the hope that this world needs."

CHAPTER 55

✦ ✦ ✦

Cynthia

Seeing Isaiah and Miss Clara together at our table was such an encouragement to me. I couldn't stop smiling. My heart was overwhelmed with gratitude.

Before she left, she asked Isaiah what happened when they got all the products ready for shipment on time.

"That's the crazy thing, ma'am. The owner of the other company showed up and I got to tell him how hard we worked to get the order ready. He said he wanted to stay with Moore Fitness for five more years."

"Is that so?" she said.

"But I suggested he extend that to a seven-year contract. And he agreed right then and there."

Miss Clara raised her hands and bobbled her head back and forth. "Now that's what I'm talking about. That is the definition of boldness. I'll bet your boss down there at that factory was jumping for joy."

"Pretty much," Isaiah said. "We all were."

"Mmm, mmm, mmm," she said, looking at him with misty eyes. She gave both of us a hug before she left and my heart was full.

Then it overflowed the next day when Isaiah asked me to go with him for a drive. I got in and resisted the urge to tell him which lane to get in, but only because he didn't tell me where we were going. When he drove by the community college campus, he slowed, gave his signal, and pulled into a parking lot.

"Why are we stopping here?" I said.

"I thought you'd like to see my new school."

My mouth dropped open. "When did you decide this?"

"I've been talking with Uncle Tony and Joshua and some of the other guys at The Forge. They thought this would be a good next step for me. So I'm going part-time so I can keep working. You know, I still have to pay the rent."

I just shook my head. If you had asked me a year ago what my top prayer requests were, they would have been Isaiah, Isaiah, and Isaiah. I wanted God to do something to shake him up and get him on the right path.

But here's what I have learned along this path. God wants to change hearts and He started with mine. I was so focused on God doing something to Isaiah. That's all I could think about. But God wanted to do something in me and He used Isaiah's struggles in my own life. And I learned that the greatest 'mission' in my life is *sub*mission to His will. I learned the greatest 'ender' in life is *surr*ender.

Now, don't get me wrong. I say this to everybody who asks me to pray about something in their life. I do *not* promise that if you do *x*, *y*, and *z* and 1, 2, and 3, you'll get all your prayers answered positively. I prayed a long time for Darren and look how that turned out. But I *do* promise this. If you give God your life and commit your way to Him and trust in Him, He will change *you*. And that's a gift you can give the world every single day.

So if you are facing trouble in your life, hunkered down waiting for the next bad thing to hit you over the head, worrying and fretting and thinking the worst, take a good look at my son. God did something in his life that I can only explain by His mighty power.

Trust in Him. Period. Give it all to Him.

And find a prayer partner, because it's easier to carry a burden with two people and it's a lot more fun celebrating when the changes begin to happen.

CHAPTER 56

✦ ✦ ✦

Isaiah walked across the community college campus with his back-pack on his shoulder. He wore his crisp new jeans, sneakers, and a stylish shirt. He felt a little out of place being at school again, like a fish out of water. Everybody seemed to know where they were going and what to do once they got there. He was just trying to find a building with the name "Mitchell" on it.

He glanced at the campus map on his phone as he passed a group of students. He looked up just in time to see someone right in front of him. He tried to stop, but he bumped into her.

"Oh, excuse me," he said.

"I'm so sorry," she said quickly.

He looked at her. The curly hair and dazzling smile. Isaiah did a double take and she seemed to recognize him, as well.

"Hey, it's Abigail, right?"

An easy smile. "And you're Isaiah."

"Yeah. Good memory."

"You go to school here?" she said.

"Yeah, I just started. But I'm still learning my way around campus. You a junior?"

"Sophomore. Interior design."

"Nice."

"You?"

"Business. I hope."

Abigail laughed and Isaiah thought that was the best sound in the world.

Abigail shifted her books on her arm. "Hey, just so you know, you made an impact on my dad."

"Oh yeah?"

"Oh yeah. He's brought you up a few times now."

Isaiah nodded, unsure what to say. "You know, I appreciate him for taking the time to talk to me. I might have to drop by and say hello sometime."

"But not to get coffee," she said with a smile.

Isaiah couldn't believe she remembered that. "I mean, I just, I don't know. I never got into it. I mainly drink energy drinks."

"It's cool. I get it. But coffee is better for you. And there's actually a really good shop here on campus."

"Oh well, I might have to try that out. But I may need some suggestions. Just sayin'."

"Okay," Abigail said. "Well, where are you headed now?"

"Glad you asked." He pulled out his phone. "I'm looking for . . . here it is. Mitchell building?"

"I can show you."

"That'd be great. And hey, coffee on me."

"Sounds good," she said.

Isaiah felt a flutter in his heart. Nothing earth-shattering. No lightning bolt. Just a warm feeling that someone had seen him and had taken an interest. Someone whose father he'd made an impression on.

He had a feeling he was going to like community college. And he had a sudden desire to try a cup of coffee as soon as his classes were finished for the day.

✦　✦　✦

Working and going to school kept Isaiah busy, but not too busy to check in on his friends. Though he didn't game with them, he still played ball every chance he got. Of course with work and homework, that wasn't every day, but he got to the court at least once a week.

They had just finished a best three out of five contest that went all five games and it came down to the last shot, which Keenan hit. Isaiah gave him a fist bump, congratulating him.

"We'll get you next time," Isaiah said.

He sat beside the court and loosened his shoelaces. One by one the others left, but Keenan stayed behind.

"You need a ride?"

"Nah, I got my car," Keenan said.

"Okay. You guys playing next Saturday?"

"Maybe. We'll call you."

Isaiah got up to leave. He was almost to his car when Keenan called after him. "Zay, hold up."

Keenan walked slowly toward him. "Last time, you said something."

"About what?"

"About your car. How it was kind of like your life. All dusty and rusty and whatnot."

Isaiah wracked his brain. When had he . . . Then he remembered. "Oh, yeah. That. What about it?"

"I don't know, I just . . ." Keenan left it there and stood beside Isaiah, not looking him in the eyes. "What you've got going on. You know, it's like, things seem to be lining up."

"Yeah, man. I'm on a lot better path than I was on before. And there's just one big difference."

Keenan crossed his arms. "This where you talk about Jesus and God and all that?"

"You want to hear what made the difference or not?"

Keenan bit his cheek. He looked away, toward the basketball court. After a long silence, he finally shrugged. "I haven't left yet, have I?"

Isaiah smiled and said a silent prayer. And he wondered if somewhere there was an old woman on her knees praying for them.

CHAPTER 57

✦ ✦ ✦

Cynthia

It's easy to move from one thing to the next and forget God's goodness and faithfulness. I suppose we're like children in that way. We ask for candy and when we finally get it, we want more or something else because we forget the ache that causes us to want it in the first place.

I had an ache in my soul for Isaiah to follow Jesus. And now that he is, it's easy for me to take that for granted and not remember what things were like when I was at the end of my rope with him. But now I see God used the end of that rope to draw me closer to Himself.

I wanted Isaiah to be the anti-Darren of my life. I did not want him to wind up like his father. So I can see now that I was guided by my fears. I was so scared of that happening and I felt so out of control because I was. And it was when I surrendered my son that I was able to believe God was working whether I could see it or not.

Isaiah has not become the anti-Darren. I see now that was
the wrong request. Isaiah has become himself. He is more himself now than he's ever been because of a work I could not do in
his heart. And for that I give thanks.

Now the issue of Darren.

I guess I've come a long way to even be able to mention his
name. I heard he was driving a truck from Isaiah and the scuttle-
butt I heard at the salon. I also know that Isaiah wrote him
that letter and that Isaiah has not heard a word in response. Of
course, that upsets me more than I can say.

When I think of Darren, I still have hurt and anger. I don't
deny it. God knows it, and it doesn't do Him or me any good
for me to paint over the wound with platitudes. But I decided to
move toward forgiveness. And now, I'll think about Darren in an
unguarded moment—something good will come to mind. How
he pursued me when we were dating and the tingly feeling I got
when he paid attention to me. Because that's the truth—there
were moments that were genuinely happy for us.

I found a picture the other day of the three of us, when Isaiah
was just learning to walk. I don't know who took it—maybe Liz?
I'm not the kind of person who rips people's faces from pictures.
I understand the sentiment, but ripping Darren's face from every
picture feels like giving him way too much power in my life.

Anyway, I was looking at that photo, at the smile on my face
and at the look on Darren's face as he watched Isaiah. Darren
had his hands out, as if he was ready to catch his son if he fell.
And that photo made me think, *That's the real Darren. That's
the Darren that could have been but wasn't. That's the Darren who
got off track for whatever reason. That's the Darren who could not
become who God wanted him to be.*

And I realized as I studied it, that something else had happened inside. The pain and anger and rage and desire for revenge

against my ex-husband, and the regret for not seeing what I felt I should have seen, had turned into something else. I don't know what to call it. Maybe it's pity. Maybe it's sadness that he is missing out on the man Isaiah has become.

Miss Clara talks about trying to see other people the way God sees them. When Jesus looked at the people He met—the lepers, the blind, the lame, the needy—He looked at them like they were sheep who needed a shepherd. He looked on them with compassion.

Miss Clara asked me one day how I thought God looked at me. I tried to give her a biblical answer, something I thought she wanted to hear. And she just stared at me with those glasses working their way down her nose. Didn't say a word. Then I got honest.

"I know what the Bible says, that He loves me and sees me as his daughter. But I can't help thinking I'm a big disappointment to Him."

"So if you are good and obedient, He likes you. If you mess up, He takes His love away. Is that what you're saying?"

I gave a big sigh. "Yeah, I kind of made Him in my own image, didn't I?"

"Now we're getting somewhere," Miss Clara said. "Now you're telling what's really inside. And that's exactly what your Father in heaven wants. Be who you are with Him. Let Him meet you right in the middle of your misconceptions. And let Him pour out His love and compassion for you and show you that He doesn't love you because you perform well. He loves you because you are His beloved daughter. And when you see yourself the way He sees you, you begin to live from the love He gives. And you obey Him not because He's going to be angry if you don't. You obey because you know He has your best interest at heart. He wants to make you more and more like His beloved Son. And He is doing that, Sweet Cynthia. I can see it."

I drank in her words, but I still felt this queasy feeling about Darren, and I told her that. She took a sip of tea and swished it around.

"The other thing that happens, when you see yourself as God sees you, is that you are able to look at others the way He sees them. Now, if somebody cuts you off in traffic, you can shake your head and think they're probably having a really bad day and you can say, 'God bless that crazy driver,' and go on your way. But when somebody hurts you deeply, when they wound you all the way to the heart, it takes a supernatural work of God to reach into that deep place. It takes time, of course. But eventually you come to see that other person as the lamb who has wandered away and is in need of the grace and mercy of God, just like you are in need of it."

She put a hand on my hand and looked at me with that Miss Clara grin. And she didn't say anything more. She just let me think about it.

And I've been thinking about that ever since. And I've been wondering when I will get to the place where I can do what Isaiah did. Forgive and release Darren from all the hurt in my heart.

CHAPTER 58

✦ ✦ ✦

In the parking lot of the restaurant where The Forge met, Isaiah pulled in and saw Joshua waiting by his car.

"How's the business major doing?" Joshua said.

"Business major just got a C on a pop quiz. Man, I've never done this much reading in my life."

"You'll get the hang of it," Joshua said, giving him a hug. "Hey, I wanted you to know I'm going to give you a chance to say something at the end of the meeting. You okay with that?"

"Oh, I got a lot I can share."

"Good." Joshua lingered at the car. "I wanted to ask if you've heard anything from your dad."

"Nothing but crickets," Isaiah said.

"How do you feel about that?"

"I don't know. I kind of expected it, given his track record. But part of me was hoping that . . ." His voice trailed.

"You know, there's a chance he never got the letter. Might have moved on from that company."

"You telling me something you know or something you're just guessing?"

"I don't know anything about your dad. I'm just sorry he didn't respond. That's gotta be hard."

"Yeah. Even if he called and said he ripped up the letter and never wanted to hear from me, that would at least be a response. You know?"

Joshua nodded. "I do." He glanced at the pavement and when he looked at Isaiah, there was water in his eyes. "You know, when we lost Jalen, it was so sudden and final. If he'd have survived the accident and had been in the hospital, it would have given us time to hope. Time to process. But he was just gone.

"And for a long time I held God responsible. He could have prevented it. He could have had Bobby take a different road that night. I wanted God to change things or at least explain. But He didn't."

Joshua took a deep breath. "I went by the cemetery on the way over here tonight. I go to Jalen's grave every now and then to make sure it's cared for. I know he's not there, but I still find comfort in visiting that place where we said goodbye to him. I cry a little. And then I thank God for the time we had with my son.

"Today, I realized God still hasn't given me the answer to my *why* question. But he has shown me the *what*."

"I don't understand," Isaiah said. "The what?"

"He's shown me a little of what He wanted to do in my life after Jalen's death. He's made me more compassionate to people who are struggling."

"Like me?"

Joshua smiled. "When I saw you in the lobby that first day, with your attitude and that baseball cap turned backwards, I could have just opened the door and sent you on your way. But God had done enough in my heart to help me see beneath the surface."

"You looked past my attitude and saw my heart."

"Exactly. Only God can do that inside work. And I give thanks to Him today for helping me and doing the same for you."

✦ ✦ ✦

The meal was good, as usual, and Isaiah felt the verses given and the teaching were exactly what he needed to hear, especially after his discussion with Keenan. God had opened a door for Isaiah to share, but Keenan was pushing back hard.

At the end of the evening, Joshua called them into a circle and gave some closing words. Every meeting he held his Bible and emphasized what he said by waving it, like it was a double-edged sword.

"Before we close our time together," Joshua said, "I wanted to give Isaiah a moment to share with you."

Isaiah cleared his throat and looked at the faces of the men he had done life with. He felt the same gratitude that Joshua had talked about in the parking lot.

"I've been a part of this group for a little over a year now, and I just want to say thank you. It's hard to put into words what this group means to me. And I've lost count of the times . . ."

Emotion caught him off guard.

"I've been blessed just to be here and walk this thing out with you. I needed this. I needed godly men to challenge me, to keep me accountable, to study the Word, pray for me and with me. And now I want to do this for someone else."

There was a deep response from each man around the circle, a low, resonant agreement with Isaiah. That sound propelled him forward.

"I'm asking God to show me who, but it feels good to say I'm ready to help someone else get to know and follow Jesus Christ. So, again, thank you."

Isaiah stepped to the side and Joshua moved into his place. He tapped his Bible on a hand and said, "Whoo," overwhelmed with Isaiah's words. He collected himself and looked around the circle.

"Gentlemen, The Forge needs to expand. But not by addition. It must be by multiplication. Groups like this must spring up everywhere. Most churches are trying to win converts, but not enough are effectively discipling them. We've got to go serve them. The world doesn't need more lukewarm churchgoers.

"Jesus said, in the Great Commission, go out into all the world and make disciples. We need more believers who are wholeheartedly following Jesus. That's what the world needs to see. We have to go after them, because whoever wants the next generation the most will get them. This culture is aggressively chasing after their hearts and their minds with views on morality, purpose, and truth that's continually redefined."

Joshua held his Bible high. "But God has given us the truth. His Word is the anchor to hold on to. So just like I have prayed for Isaiah, I pray for you. That you not be one *in* a million, but one *of* a million.

"So I say, let's go where they are. In the schools, in the marketplaces, the ball fields—wherever they hang out, let's do what Jesus did. Let's love them enough to take the truth to them. Sometimes it'll be a battle. But our Savior is worth it."

Isaiah felt as if they were all being called into something bigger than The Forge, something that might change the world.

"Let's take them Jesus," Joshua said. "Who's with me?"

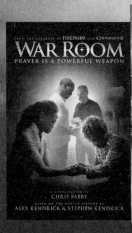  

DISCUSSION QUESTIONS

1. Isaiah promises himself that he will never make the same mistakes his father made. Are there ways that you want to be like your parents? Are there ways that you don't want to be like your parents?

2. Miss Clara has a closet she calls her "war room," where she likes to pray. Do you have a particular place where you like to pray? In what ways can this practice be helpful?

3. Are you sometimes like Cynthia, afraid that your problems are a "great big bother" to God? How do you remind yourself of the truth, that He wants us to cast our cares on Him?

4. When they first meet, Joshua poses these three questions to Isaiah: *In what ways do you want to grow in the next year? What kind of man do you want to be? And what do you want people to think when they see you coming?* How would you answer these questions?

5. Have you ever had someone interact with you the way Joshua Moore did with Isaiah, making you feel like they had all the

time in the world to spend with you? Have you been able to give that gift to others in your life? Why is it often hard to do?

6. Joshua says God asked him to give up golf. Why was golf an issue for Joshua, even though it might not have been for someone else? Has God ever asked you to give up something unusual?

7. Joshua encourages Isaiah to forgive his father, telling him, "Bitterness is like emotional cancer." What does that mean? Have you ever made the choice to forgive someone, even if they haven't asked for your forgiveness—and maybe don't even deserve it?

8. Isaiah has a hard time telling his friend Jamal about his new faith in Christ. How do you feel when someone asks about your faith? Do you feel bold and confident? Or do you feel hesitant and unsure? Have you ever tried to tell someone about Jesus, but they did not respond the way you hoped they would?

9. After the coffee shop owner accepts Isaiah's apology and forgives him, Isaiah feels like a weight has been lifted. Have you ever asked for and received forgiveness from someone? What was that like?

10. Miss Clara and Cynthia pray through the night for Isaiah and his team. Have you ever prayed long and hard without stopping as you asked God for a miracle? Have you ever seen God answer a prayer in a way that was so miraculous there was no question that it was God?

ABOUT THE AUTHORS

Chris Fabry is an award-winning author and radio personality who hosts the daily program *Chris Fabry Live* on Moody Radio. He is also heard on *Love Worth Finding* and *Building Relationships with Dr. Gary Chapman.* A 1982 graduate of the W. Page Pitt School of Journalism at Marshall University and a native of West Virginia, Chris and his wife, Andrea, now live in Arizona and are the parents of nine children.

Chris's novels, which include *A Piece of the Moon, Dogwood, June Bug,* and *Almost Heaven,* have won five Christy Awards, an ECPA Christian Book Award, a Carol Award, and two Awards of Merit from *Christianity Today.* He was inducted into the Christy Award Hall of Fame in 2018. His most recent novel, *Saving Grayson,* is a love story about a man with Alzheimer's trying to solve the mystery of his life. Chris's books include movie novelizations, like the bestseller *War Room*; nonfiction; and novels for children and young adults. He coauthored the Left Behind: The Kids series with Jerry B. Jenkins and Tim LaHaye, as well as the Red Rock Mysteries and the Wormling series with Jerry B. Jenkins. Visit his website at chrisfabry.com.

Alex Kendrick is an award-winning author gifted at telling stories of hope and redemption. He is best known as an actor, writer, and director of the films *Overcomer, War Room, Courageous, Fireproof,* and *Facing the Giants* and coauthor of the *New York Times* bestselling books *The Love Dare, The Resolution for Men,* and *The Battle Plan for Prayer.* Alex has received more than thirty awards for his work, including best screenplay, best production, and best feature film. Alex has spoken to churches, universities, and conferences all across America and in other countries. He has been featured on FOX News, CNN, *ABC World News Tonight, CBS Evening News, Time* magazine, and many other media outlets. He is a graduate of Kennesaw State University and attended seminary before being ordained into ministry. Alex and his wife, Christina, live in Albany, Georgia, with their six children. They are active members of Sherwood Church.

Stephen Kendrick is a speaker, film producer, and author with a ministry passion for prayer and discipleship. He is a cowriter and producer of the movies *Overcomer, War Room, Courageous, Fireproof,* and *Facing the Giants* and cowriter of the *New York Times* bestsellers *The Battle Plan for Prayer, The Resolution for Men,* and *The Love Dare.* Stephen has spoken at churches, conferences, and seminars around the nation and has been interviewed by *Fox & Friends,* CNN, *ABC World News Tonight,* and the *Washington Post,* among others. He is a cofounder and board member of the Fatherhood Commission. He graduated from Kennesaw State University and attended seminary before being ordained into ministry. Stephen and his wife, Jill, live in Albany, Georgia, with their six children. They are active members of Sherwood Church in Albany.

kendrickbrothers.com

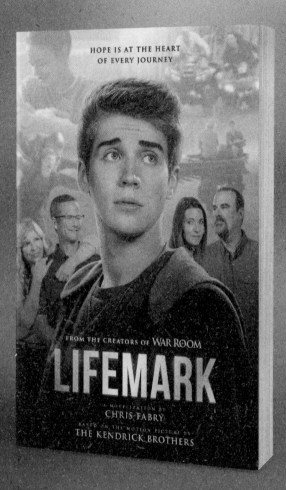